Pirates of the Siren's Sea

A Magic of Solendrea Novel

Book 1 of the Second Swordmage Trilogy

by

Martin F. Hengst

Martin F. Hengst
PO Box 86
Windsor, PA 17366
www.martinfhengst.com

Ordering Information & Quantity Sales: Special discounts are available on quantity purchases by corporations, associations, and others. For details, contact the author at the address above.

Printed in the United States of America

ISBN: 978-0692344187

First Edition

14 15 16 17 18 / 10 9 8 7 6 5 4 3 2 1

TABLE OF CONTENTS

PROLOGUE

The world of Solendrea, a world where science, magic, and technology exist in an uneasy accord. Quintessentialists, called mages or wizards by some, control the arcane forces of the Quintessential Sphere, the Ethereal Realm from which all living memory flows and from which the forces of magic are channeled.

Such great power comes at a price. Iron and steel, the most common of metals, are deadly when wielded by a mage. A Quintessentialist who takes up a sword in defense of home and honor will be dead in minutes or hours. They will fall to a burning in the blood that will consume their very essence, leaving nothing more than a withered husk.

There are tales, rare enough to be considered legend, of a unique few who surpass these limits. They are Swordmages, capable of wielding the full power of the Quintessential Sphere in one hand and a steel blade in the other. They exist in secret, hiding their abilities from a society that would brand them as rogue mages or freaks, monsters to be put down.

Tiadaria is one such Swordmage, and these are her continued adventures.

CHAPTER ONE

The table where Tiadaria sat bore the score marks made by hundreds of knives over an uncountable number of years. A strange softness had been imbued upon it by the caress of a hundred thousand hands. It had an odd texture, as well. Almost slippery to the touch.

So it has come to this, she thought to herself with no small amount of bitterness. *I'm so bored that I'm fascinated by wood.*

As if to save Tiadaria from herself, a serving wench in a simple, sky blue dress and a grease-stained apron stopped by the edge of the table. The wench gave the wood surface a perfunctory swipe with the tatty dishtowel she kept draped over the front pocket of her apron and deposited a wooden tray in front of Tiadaria.

"Thank you," Tiadaria said, but the serving wench had already gone on to the next table.

For noon on a workday, the Bawdy Bard was doing a fair amount of trade. There were merchants taking a break from hawking their wares, a few farmhands in from the fields just beyond the city, and a number of soldiers from the Imperium military. The soldiers were huddled around a table near the back, playing dice. Tiadaria wondered if Torus knew they were here. Perhaps she'd mention it to him the next time she saw the burly Captain of the Grand Army of the Imperium. Then again, perhaps not. She wasn't a squealer.

Slicing into the roast breast of fowl on the metal plate, Tiadaria pondered while she chewed.

A general feeling of unease permeated the Imperium these days. Near constant attacks by the Stavanshi elves had brought relations between the people of the Imperium and the enigmatic elves to a boiling point. There were also rumblings of sedition in the far south, with some of the larger baronies balking at recent edicts by the King. There was certainly enough conflict to go around.

Then there was that incident in Blackbeach last year when some students had let a summoning get out of hand, but the Quintessentialists had cleared that up on their own without any assistance required from the capital.

Through all of this, Tiadaria hadn't been called on to assist the realm. Though she'd been readily available to Torus and the King, she'd been all but ignored. Time and again, Torus had said that the time would come when the Imperium would once again call on her unique services, but that time had never materialized. There was good reason for her to be bored.

Tiadaria sighed. At least the food was good. The fowl was juicy and tender and the carrots were steamed to perfection. Just soft enough to be able to spear with a fork but not so soft as to be mushy.

If there was anything Tiadaria hated more than boredom, it was mushy carrots. Then there was the mead. Mead was the main reason anyone came to the Bawdy Bard. They made the finest honey-wine in Dragonfell, as far as Tiadaria was concerned. The long line of ribbons tacked to the shelf behind the bar told her she wasn't alone in her opinion. Not a single one among them was anything less than first place.

Floorboards creaked as the door to the street opened, admitting a new customer. Once rough-hewn, the floor had undergone a similar transformation as the tabletops, taking on a patina of age and warmth that had grown over a hundred years of spilled drinks, sloshed grease, and other messes that Tiadaria didn't really want to think about. The walls hadn't been given any such treatment. They'd been carved down by hand, large planks with scenes from tall tales and popular songs. The carvings seemed to be scattered across the wide common room, as if the artist hadn't been able to decide where to put them and then just settled on wherever his eye fell.

Tiadaria's eye, however, fell on the newcomer. He was a solid lad, hovering on that edge between boyish charm and manly haggardness. Not quite an adult, yet not a child either. He was teetering between two worlds. In a thick leather bag he wore over one shoulder, Tiadaria could see bunches of folded paper shoved inside all the way up to the brim. The tips of his fingers were black, and similar smudges adorned his otherwise pink nose and cheeks. A mop of curly black hair perched over pale blue eyes that were far too serious for his age.

"Oy!" he said to no one in particular, rather addressing the room at large. "Get yer paper 'ere. Finest news in Dragonfell and points beyond. Biggest press in three cities."

Tiadaria laughed, and with a sharp look from the paperboy, covered her mouth and turned it into a very weak cough. It was a source of great pride to the engineers of Dragonfell that they'd managed to build a printing press that put those the Quintessentialists had been working on to shame. The last few months had become something of a competition between the two cities, with Dragonfell's engineers working double and sometimes triple shifts to beat out the Quints in Blackbeach.

They'd done it, too. Dragonfell's press had been up and running for almost two months now. Blackbeach had just announced they'd finished theirs last week. If one were keeping score in the friendly rivalry between the largest cities in the Imperium, the capital would have earned a point by beating the Quints to the punch.

Once Dragonfell had their press up and running, it took all of about three weeks for an enterprising engineer to partner with a retired scholar and start printing up sheets of news. A week after that, there were boys in every bar, halfway house, and tavern hawking their newspapers for an eighth of a crown.

"What's the story today, scamp?" Bailey asked from behind his bar. The man was so short he had to stand on a stepstool to tend the bar. The wild tufts of white hair over his ears made him look like a wizened old owl. "More nonsense about Xarundi in the city sewers?"

This time, Tiadaria wasn't the only one who laughed. Some of the 'news' being printed was a hair's breadth away from being outright fabrications. Apparently the outrageous claims kept the gold crown coins coming in, and as long as that kept happening, stories with very little merit would continue to be printed.

"Naw, Bailey," the kid said and grinned at the barkeep. "Another ship disappeared off Blackbeach. Some say it were pirates, some say sirens. Either way, they're all dead. No bodies and not a trace of the ship left, either."

A murmur began at the back of the common room and raced its way across those in attendance. Nothing like a good bit of blood lust to get the pulse pounding. There was always a market for doom and despair. Tiadaria found her curiosity piqued. It seemed she wasn't immune to the subtle manipulation employed by the paperboy's masters.

She reached into her pocket and withdrew an eighth of a crown. The coin was small and thin, but had enough weight for her to be able to flick it to the boy after catching his eye. He took a folded paper from the top of his pouch and tossed it to her, then continued making sales to other patrons.

Tiadaria settled back into her seat, flipped open the fold, and scanned the text. The story was sensational, written to tease and tantalize, but there was a ring of truth to it that Tiadaria felt deep in her bones. A passenger ship from the southern land of Theid had been sailing toward Blackbeach when it was attacked by parties unknown. It had been seen by an Imperium warship in the area, and then it had vanished, as if into thin air. The ship was sunk and all souls were lost. No bodies were recovered. At the bottom of the story, almost as an afterthought, there was a note that this was the third passenger ship lost in as many weeks.

The third ship in as many weeks? How could Torus have let this happen? He was responsible for overseeing the safety of the realm. The Admiral of the Imperium Navy reported to Torus, and Torus reported to the King. Surely Greymalkin wasn't content to let these attacks continue unchecked.

Tiadaria glanced down at what was left of her food. She didn't feel very hungry anymore. Instead, she felt annoyed and anxious. Why had no one told her about the attacks? More importantly, why had no one done anything about it? She wanted answers. Something that would settle the gnawing worry in the pit of her stomach.

Sliding a five crown coin onto the tray beside her plate, Tiadaria squeezed past the news boy, who was still doing a considerable trade, and out in the streets of Dragonfell. The Bawdy Bard was just off to one side of the main market square, which meant that the street was packed with people. Though she had to navigate through a sea of many bodies, Market Square was still one of Tiadaria's favorite things about Dragonfell.

Stalls big and small lined the edges of the square, their banners fluttering in the lazy wind. A few larger carts were parked in the middle of the wide-open space, forcing those who came to do their shopping to wind their way through numerous temptations.

On one corner of the square, a harried-looking spinner was doing his best to service his customers. A dozen women were gathered about the stall and every one of them was clamoring for his attention. Not that it was any great wonder; the fabrics he had on display were beautiful. Rich yellow and orange silks, like the licking flames of the sun, were draped across the upper part of the stall. Spread across his work surface were bolts of fine blues and greens. Tiadaria's eyes landed on a length of shimmering gold silk that caught and reflected the light in a thousand tiny motes. She didn't consider herself to be in touch with what "normal" women her age were interested in, but there was a part of her that wished she had a fancy dress and an occasion to wear it. As it was, her armor and some very basic breeches and tunics were all the wardrobe she had to her name.

You're thinking about this now? she chided herself, with a shake of her head. Putting thoughts of dresses and fancy parties out of her head, she slipped between two women arguing over the price of roast at the nearby butcher's stall. It took a few minutes to weave through the throngs of people scattered around the street, but she soon found herself on the wide cobblestone path that led down toward the Dock District.

Tiadaria hoped Torus would be in his office. They needed to talk, and she wasn't going to take no for an answer this time.

~ ~ ~

Nestled in the southernmost inlet of Crystal Bay, Dragonfell's massive docks served as both a trade hub and the command center for the Imperium's navy. Though technically an autonomous unit, it was tradition that the Admiral of the Navy reported to the Captain of the Grand Army of the Imperium. The Captain would then take all military matters to the King and his council for their input and direction.

Tiadaria wasn't sure Torus had known what he was in for when he was promoted to the position vacated by her former mentor. Royce MacDungren had been the Captain of the Grand Army before his retirement and had left Torus with very large shoes to fill. Torus was at a distinct disadvantage. Royce had been a Swordmage, one who could wield a blade in one hand and the full force of the Quintessential Sphere in the other. Poor Torus had to do the job without the benefit of mystical powers. She often wondered if there wasn't some small amount of resentment toward Royce that was harbored deep in the heart of her oldest and dearest friend.

She shrugged that thought off as she walked. Torus was a pragmatist by nature. He'd do the job he was assigned with a dogged determination until it was done, or until he couldn't take it any further. She admired his tenacity. If he was dissatisfied that the responsibility of protecting the realm had fallen to him, he gave no indication of it. Torus was a soldier, through and through, and a brilliant tactician to boot. Tiadaria wasn't sure he'd thrive in any other position.

As she descended down the road, she caught sight of tall masts towering over the squat buildings of the Dock District. One of the big sailing ships must have just come in. Tiadaria made a quick decision that her questioning of

Torus could wait a few minutes. She wanted to see the ship.

Though Tiadaria had never been aboard a sailing vessel, they fascinated her. They had a certain majesty to their size that made her pulse quicken. The cobblestones gave way to wide wooden planks that made hollow thuds as she walked. A gentle breeze blew in from seaward, bringing with it the smell of brine and sea. It made her long blonde hair flutter behind her as she walked.

Tiadaria closed her eyes, relishing in the warm sun on her face. The large brass bell at the top of the dock watchtower began to toll, announcing the arrival of another ship. During work hours, it wasn't uncommon for the bell to toll three or four times an hour. Dragonfell's docks were almost always busy.

She heard a man shout at the same time she collided with something sturdy. Her sapphire blue eyes snapped open and she realized she'd run into someone coming up from the ship berths.

"Hey!" he snapped, his voice sharp. "Watch it!"

"I'm so sorry," Tiadaria answered, untangling herself from the man and stepping back. She put a hand out to smooth down his ivory robes and stopped. She peered at him. Tiadaria knew this man. His hair was a little grayer, his face a little more gaunt, but she knew him as well as she could know anyone.

"Faxon!" she cried, folding him into an aggressive hug and making him stumble backward. "I'm so glad to see you."

Faxon Indra dropped his travel case to the dock and braced himself against the railing with one hand to keep his balance. With his other hand, he gave Tiadaria an awkward one-armed hug.

"Oomph. Easy, Tia. I'm glad to see you, too." He chuckled and gave her a gentle shove. He pushed her back to arm's length and took her chin in his hand.

Her face tingled from the link-shock that danced between them—the subtle feedback caused by the power of the Quintessential Sphere jumping between two living vessels. Just when she thought the touch might make her eyes start to water, he released her.

"You're a sight for sore eyes, Tia, that's for certain. Torus keeping you busy?"

"Not really," Tiadaria replied with a sigh. She scuffed the dock with the toe of her boot and watched other passengers pass them by. A couple of them eyed Faxon's case with suspicious glances, and Tiadaria retrieved it from the middle of the walkway before she continued. "I'm not sure what's going on with him lately, Faxon. I used to report to him for duties all the time. I don't even bother anymore. He's stopped assigning anything to me. I haven't been out in a month or more. It's weird. And I don't like it."

Faxon narrowed his hazel eyes, scratching with one hand a beard that had gone mostly gray. "He nearly died, Tia. Give him a little while to get back on his feet."

Tiadaria's eyes widened. She had been on the training mission that ended with Torus's close brush with death at the hands of a rogue Xarundi pack, but it had been kept as quiet as possible. She didn't know that anyone else knew the whole story.

"How did you find out about that?"

Faxon chuckled, his hazel eyes dancing with laughter.

"I have my ways, Tiadaria. You, of all people, should know that by now." He paused, his eyes ranging over the low cement buildings clustered just off the Dock District. "Walk with me. I need to speak to Torus about the latest predations in the Siren's Sea."

"You mean the ship that just disappeared?"

Faxon frowned. "Yes. How do you know about that?"

"I have my ways, too," she said with an air of mystery, then sighed. "It's all over the papers. Pirates or sirens, the story said."

Faxon's frown deepened.

"I'm not sure how I feel about these papers. A little knowledge is a powerful thing. I think I might have preferred fewer people to know about this particular incident." He shook his head as if accepting the inevitable. "Anyway, I think in this case, they were doubly right. I think it was pirates *and* sirens."

Tiadaria narrowed her eyes at him. "How can you possibly know that?"

He held up a hand. "I don't *know* it, but I have a pretty strong hunch. Come on. Walk with me."

Tiadaria hefted his case and Faxon held out his hand. When she ignored him, he shrugged and started walking. They stayed close together so he could keep his voice low but still be heard.

"I told you I was just out of Overwatch. What I didn't tell you was that Tionne was there."

"WHAT?"

Tiadaria dropped the case to the plank-way with a resounding thud. She whirled to face Faxon, her eyes blazing.

"Are you kidding me?" she asked loudly.

"Keep your voice down, Tiadaria," he hissed, his eyes darting around them. People moving away from the dock had stopped and looked at them when Tiadaria shouted. With a smile and a nod, he encouraged them to move along. As they started to go on their way, he turned his gaze back to Tiadaria. "I don't want it to be common knowledge that she was in Overwatch, so please keep your voice down."

"Sorry," she mumbled, though she was in no way sorry. If Faxon had known Tionne was in Overwatch, he should have started the conversation there. "Go on."

"Anyhow, I think Tionne is in command of those pirate ships that have been plaguing the trade lanes. There have always been pirates on the Siren's Sea, at least as long as there has been trade, but they've never been this organized. It's been like they're looking for something."

"Like what?"

"Like a map."

Tiadaria ground her teeth. He was drawing this out on purpose. There were times when his sense of suspense made her want to grab him by the throat and shake him until he just spoke plain and proper.

"A map of what? Faxon, I'm losing my patience."

Faxon gave her a boyish grin and ducked his head. No matter how old Faxon got, Tiadaria thought, some things would never change. But if he thought that his charm was going to get him off the hook about Tionne, he had another thing coming.

"An ancient, indestructible weapon that could turn the entire world into an army of siren thralls."

Tiadaria peered at him. It was almost impossible to tell when Faxon was being serious. His sense of the ridiculous made him very difficult to read. He could either be pulling her leg or be completely serious, and she wouldn't be able to tell the difference.

"I'm not laughing, Faxon."

"I'm not joking, Tiadaria." He shrugged. "While I was in Overwatch, I got a tip from an IIS agent that there was a packet of information in the possession of a Baron that I would find very interesting. The Baron was implicated in the illegal, even by Overwatch's standards, trade of mystical artifacts. Gunther and I went to steal those papers and we did, but Tionne stole them from me before I could get them safely back to Dragonfell.

"Although I eventually managed to steal them back from her, I have no doubt that she got exactly what she was looking for out of the information before I was able to get them back. The name and travel route of a ship that was carrying a journal. A journal that tells the location of the Horn of Requiem."

Tiadaria's head was spinning. There was so much to take in, and the fact that Tionne was involved didn't make it any easier for her to accept. She held up a hand with a shake of her head.

"Wait a minute. You mean Tionne's a pirate now?"

"*That's* the part you're going to focus on?"

"Baby steps, Faxon."

"Okay. No, I don't think Tionne is a pirate. I think she's leading the pirates. I think they're methodically destroying every ship in the Siren's Sea until they find that journal."

"And where do the sirens come in?"

Faxon shook his head and folded his arms into the wide sleeves of his ivory robe.

"I haven't figured that out yet," he said with a sigh. "But if I had to guess, I'm betting that Tionne's piracy and the sirens are connected somehow. For one thing, if they weren't in cahoots, why wouldn't the sirens just kill Tionne and her crew? Something about this doesn't add up."

"Perhaps I can fill in some of the blanks," a low voice said from very close behind them.

Tiadaria whirled, cursing herself for not keeping a closer eye on the people around them. Her hand fell to her hip and then she realized that her sword belt was hanging on its peg in her room. With no duties to speak of, she had no reason to carry her weapons every day. That realization, coupled with being taken by surprise, put her in a waspish mood.

"And you are?" she asked with more heat than was necessary.

The girl didn't flinch. Her long brown hair was pulled back in a ponytail and her brown eyes jumped from Faxon to Tiadaria as if they were being cataloged. There was something about that regard that made the hairs on the back of Tiadaria's neck stand on end. The interloper was near enough Tiadaria's height that they could almost see eye to eye. She was dressed in a russet tunic and plain brown breeches. Her boots were leather but bore none of the hallmarks of the famous makers. It was as if her entire appearance was built, layer upon inconspicuous layer, to be completely forgettable.

"You're with the Imperium Information Service," Tiadaria blurted. It wasn't a question. It was a statement of fact.

"Indeed, Swordmage," the agent said, ignoring Tiadaria as she jerked back in surprise. "My name is Jena and I'm with the Service. We should talk somewhere less…open."

Tiadaria's eyes met Faxon's. This day was getting stranger by the second.

"What about Torus?" she asked the Quintessentialist. Faxon shrugged and tilted his head toward the IIS agent.

"You should probably hear what I have to say first, Lady Tiadaria." Jena's eyes scanned the area around them. Tiadaria noticed that she stopped, even if just for a moment, on every person who was nearby. "Then you can decide who else you trust with that information."

The agent started walking, and then looked over her shoulder and called to them.

"Come on, I know a place we can talk."

CHAPTER TWO

Jena led them to a small, out of the way pub just up the lane from the docks. It was dark, it was quiet, but most importantly, it was empty. Faxon stopped at the drink rail for a quick word with the barman. They spoke a few words. The man came from behind the bar, closed and locked the door, and then went up a creaky flight of stairs that led to what Tiadaria guessed was the living quarters upstairs. They could hear his heavy footfalls clomping against the ceiling and occasionally a fine sifting of dust would float down out of the joists.

Tiadaria and the agent were seated at a round table toward the back of the great room, and they were already deep in conversation when Faxon came to join them.

"So, Jena, you can't be much past your 14th nameday, if even that. How is it that you're an agent in the Service?"

Jena untied her ponytail and ran her hands through her hair, light brown tresses that fell to just below her shoulders. Even in the dim light of the empty pub, her eyes, almost the same color as her hair, danced with amusement. She pulled back her hair again and tied it into another ponytail before she answered. Tiadaria got the distinct impression that the girl was stalling, deciding how much to say.

"I grew up in the service," she said at length, arching her back and making her spine pop so loudly that Faxon winced. "Mom and Dad are both agents. Neither of them wanted to stop working when I was born, so I got taken along on the jobs that weren't too dangerous, and I stayed with other agents for the ones that were." Jena shrugged. "Now I can take care of myself. Petitioned the Service last year to take the Agent trials. There were no rules on age when I asked."

Jena smirked. "There are now. But I passed. So here I am."

"Have girls really changed so much since my youth?" Faxon said with a sigh of long suffering. "Whatever happened to playing with dolls?"

"I played with dolls," Jena said in a somber tone. "Of course, I was usually pretending to test poisons on them, but I played with them."

"That makes me feel so much better." Faxon brought his hands together and rubbed them, as if he were cold. "Now, tell us what you know about the ships being sunk in the Siren's Sea."

Jena's lively face clouded and she took a moment before she spoke, as if she needed to collect her thoughts. An abundance of patience wasn't something Tiadaria had been gifted with, but antagonizing the girl wasn't going to get things done any faster. Jena might be young, but if she'd passed the Service trials, then she was certainly fit for whatever duty they'd assigned to her. At least she had a job. That was more than Tiadaria could say for herself as of late.

"You were right to think that the pirates and the sirens are working together. When the pirates started stepping up their attacks on our merchant vessels, the Service was asked to put a few discreet agents in among the crews to see what we could find."

She paused and took a deep breath before continuing.

"We lost half a dozen good agents on those ships. The three ships you've heard about are ours. There have been others, too. Ships from Moramos headed to Solorest or Theid. The dwarves aren't happy that they're losing shipments to these pirates either.

"There was talk about an official complaint to Dragonfell, but I don't think we've gotten to that point yet. In fact, that's why I'm here. The Service sent me to warn the King about the dwarves and to see if there's anything we can offer them to smooth things over."

Tiadaria frowned. She wasn't at all interested in the political ramifications of what Tionne was doing. She wanted to know where the girl was so that she could be stopped. As far as Tiadaria was concerned, the Imperium wouldn't be safe until Tionne was in their custody. If she couldn't be reformed, she'd have to be censured, or killed. Otherwise, the Imperium would always be in danger. They couldn't leave Stryne's pawns to run around and muck up whatever they damn well pleased.

"You said something about the pirates and sirens working together," Tiadaria said, trying to steer the conversation back in the direction she was most interested in. "How do you know? If your men were lost, how could they tell the tale?"

Jena reached inside her tunic and took out a small glass vial. It was capped with a dull black metal, inset with a ring of silver. Inside the vial was a small piece of rolled up paper. Jena unscrewed the cap and upended the vial on the table, letting the paper fall free. She smoothed it out and produced a stylus from another hidden pocket. She scrawled a message onto the paper, and Tiadaria watched as strange, blood red symbols faded into view. It was unlike any language Tiadaria had ever seen, and judging by Faxon's furrowed brows, he was just as perplexed as she was.

The agent rolled the paper back up and dropped it into the tube. She screwed the cap back on and gave it a good shake. The rolled up paper bounced from end to end in the vial for a second, and then there was a bright flash. Jena stopped shaking the vial and held it out in her palm for Tiadaria and Faxon to examine. It was empty!

"May I?" Faxon asked, and without waiting for permission, he plucked the vial from Jena's palm. He turned it this way and that, even going so far as to unscrew the cap and sniff the air inside. He put it back together and returned it to her hand. "Clever piece of enchantment, that. So where does the displacement terminate?"

Jena's face sagged, a bit crestfallen at the Quintessentialist's blithe acceptance of a wondrous tool. For those not able to command the forces of the Ethereal Realm through their own mind-to-mind contact with the Quintessential Sphere, enchanted items were the closest to performing real magic they would ever come. Tiadaria kicked Faxon under the table and he yelped.

"*I* think it's amazing. Ignore him," Tiadaria said to the girl, who brightened at the appreciation. "But where does it go? So very curious!"

Jena glared at Faxon for a moment, as if challenging him to spoil her big reveal. The Quintessentialist made a show of zipping his lip and throwing away the key. Jena laughed. Faxon had a way of disarming people. Very few could stay angry with him for long. Jena leaned forward in a conspiratorial fashion.

"Any messages sent by Flashtube go back to the Service headquarters. They get read and shunted off to whatever tier will get the most use out of them."

"What tiers are there?" Tiadaria asked. The Imperium Information Service sounded like it was much more entertaining to work for than the Grand Army.

Jena shook her finger at Tiadaria, her eyes guarded. "Nope. Can't tell you that. Trade secret. I can tell you, though, that we got three different messages back from agents in the field. Every single one of them said that when their ships were boarded by pirates, there were sirens in the water, circling as if they were waiting for something."

Tiadaria shuddered. She'd grown up in the Frozen Frontier, where all water, even seawater, formed a sheet of ice several feet thick. She had never been on a boat and had never been out on the open water. The thought of such a great expanse of openness that could hide such a dangerous threat under the surface gave her the shakes.

Faxon scratched his chin, deep in thought.

"So what would Tionne want with sirens? Or perhaps the question is, what would the sirens…" He trailed off and slapped himself in the forehead. "Stupid, stupid, stupid. How can I be so brilliant and so thick at the same time?"

"What is it?" Tiadaria asked.

"They're after the Horn. That's why they're following Tionne around. She's looking for the journal and the sirens want her to find it."

"How would the sirens know about it?"

"They made it."

Tiadaria sat in stunned silence for a moment. She glanced at Jena, who didn't look nearly as disturbed as Tiadaria thought she should. Faxon was muttering to himself as he often did when he was putting together pieces of a puzzle that no one else could see, much less hope to understand.

"We need to speak to the King," he said, snapping out of his frenzied conversation with himself. "If the sirens get their hands on the Horn of Requiem, it could be the end of all of us."

"Isn't that a little dramatic?" Tiadaria asked, chiding the Quintessentialist. The look he turned on her withered her condescension on the vine.

"Not even a little, Tiadaria. When the Horn of Requiem sounds, it plays the same enthralling song that the sirens themselves do. It's difficult, almost impossible, to refuse its call. They could summon entire towns with a single blow of the Horn."

Tiadaria shrugged. "But how much damage could they really do? They can't come on land, right? They'll die. So we might need to fortify some of the villages closer to the sea."

"Oh no," Faxon said, shaking his head. "It's much worse than that. Imagine what would happen if you gave the Horn to a land dweller. Someone who could walk into the center of Dragonfell's Market Square and sound the call?"

"Tionne," Tiadaria said and a weight like lead settled in her stomach.

"Exactly."

"We need to speak to the King," Tiadaria said, getting to her feet so quickly that her chair toppled over backward. "Now."

~ ~ ~

"I'm sorry, Master Indra. No one is being admitted to see the King. Under any circumstances. That's the final answer you're going to get on the matter."

The King's steward was a mousy little man that Tiadaria wouldn't have credited with having much of a spine at all. His watery green eyes and bulbous red nose reminded her a bit of Cerrin, the slave trader who had taken her from her home in the Frozen Frontier and plunged her into the world of the Human Imperium. Perhaps that's why she'd taken an instant disliking to the little man who was now standing squarely in Faxon's way, preventing him from passing through the doorway beyond.

In fairness, Tiadaria thought, it might have been the two guards stationed behind the steward with their crossed steel spears blocking the doorway that kept Faxon from barging through, but she decided to give the steward this little victory in her mind. He looked as if he didn't get many victories to celebrate.

"We have to see *someone*," Jena whispered to Tiadaria as Faxon launched into yet another tirade against the steward and members of his family both living and long dead.

"I know, but we won't get Faxon to move until he's exhausted his rather extensive repertoire of insults."

Jena giggled and the steward's disapproving eyes flicked to her face. The agent bowed her head and found a reason to inspect the carpet for wear. Tiadaria rolled her eyes. Life would be much easier if Faxon could learn to take 'no' for an answer. Not bloody likely.

After another half-hearted harangue of the King's steward, Faxon tossed up his hands in frustration and stomped off. Tiadaria and Jena had to half-run to catch up with him.

"That's it?" Tiadaria asked, surprised. "We're just going to turn around and go home?"

"No, but if we can't go in the official way, we'll have to go in the unofficial way."

Tiadaria cast a critical eye on him, a tight knot of apprehension forming in her belly. Faxon could be downright devious when he wanted to be, and she wasn't sure this was the time or the place for his tomfoolery.

"Maybe we can try again tomorrow?" she asked, though she feared she already knew what his answer would be. It wasn't unexpected when he rounded on her and exploded.

"We don't have *time* to wait until tomorrow! Tionne's out there right now, and every second we waste, she could be getting closer to the Horn."

Tiadaria put her hands up and took a step back. "Easy, Faxon. I understand, but there's a time and place. We can't just go breaking in to the King's council room. I'm pretty sure they regard that as treason."

Faxon peered at her a moment, his head cocked to one side.

"You thought I…" He chuckled and gave a little shake of his head. "You give me far too much credit, Tia. But treason…now that's an idea."

"Faxon…"

"No, I think I know of someone who might listen to us, and we won't have to break down any doors to get there. Trust me. It'll be fine."

"I've heard that before," Tiadaria replied with a sigh. A flicker of something crossed his face. Amusement maybe. Or annoyance. Either way, she was right. If she had even half a crown for every time Faxon had told her to trust him just before things went sideways, she'd be a *very* rich woman.

"This time it's safe. I promise."

"Famous last words," Tiadaria said, her tone dire. She waved a hand, indicating that she would follow where he led. Jena had been watching their exchange, her head snapping back and forth as they traded verbal volleys. Tiadaria glanced at her. "Neck getting sore?"

Jena stiffened, as if she wasn't sure what to make of Tiadaria's remark. Then she laughed.

"No, I'm fine. Let's go."

Faxon led them down the long entrance corridor to a side hall that took them through the servants' chambers. Tiadaria had never been in this part of the palace before. While the upper levels were appointed with all manner of finery, there was a marked change in decor the further they went into the tunnels that ran deeper back in the cavern. The carpets were threadbare and worn, and the colors on the wall cracked and peeling in places.

As they walked, Tiadaria found herself wondering how the servants were treated here. In all her visits to the King's Palace, she hadn't ever been beyond the official spaces. The contrast surprised her. It was like having the curtain pulled back on an illusionist's trick. Tiadaria wasn't sure she wanted to see how the magic was made.

They passed through a vault-like kitchen with titanic stone ovens set into the outside walls. Huge beasts were set to roast, turning on spits as long as spears. Long tables were laid out with preparations for the evening meal. Vegetables of every color, shape, and size were arrayed on one. Another was dusted with flour, where a baker was busy making Dragonwings.

A second baker pulled a basket of Dragonwings from a large kettle of oil and began transferring them to the table, sprinkling the doughy treats with powdered sugar. Tiadaria's stomach rumbled loud enough for half the room to hear. Both Faxon and Jena burst into howls of laughter.

"Shut up, both of you. I haven't eaten since lunch."

Faxon grinned at her.

"Work first. Then we'll eat. I'll even buy. It's the least I can do for torturing you so."

"Shut up, or I'll show you real torture."

The Quintessentialist kept chuckling until they were beyond the kitchen and climbing up a narrow set of steps beyond. They wound their way upward for a very long time, and Tiadaria wondered if they would be level with the top of the tall statues that stood outside the palace cavern. At long last, they came to a simple mahogany door set into the stone. Faxon gave it a sharp rap and they waited.

And waited. And waited.

"We didn't come all this way for nothing, did we?" Tiadaria asked.

Faxon shook his head, lowering his chin to his chest. He closed his eyes and Tiadaria felt the air around her shift. It wasn't strong enough to be considered a breeze; it was just a movement of the air. Jena didn't even notice it, but the flames in the lanterns that were hung around the landing flickered a bit in response to the unseen forces. He raised his head and looked at Tiadaria. She raised an eyebrow, but he just shook his head.

Tiadaria heard movement inside the room. She shifted from one foot to the other. Whatever they were doing here, she wanted to be done with it. It felt as if the already small landing was growing smaller with every passing minute. It seemed like a very long time before someone opened the door. A soft click and a finger-width border of darkness were the only indication that the door had opened at all.

"Who's with you?" a voice asked from inside the darkened room.

"Agent Jena, of the Imperium Information Service, and Lady Tiadaria, Your Grace. May we come in?"

"Only if you promise to dispense with the 'Your Grace' nonsense, Faxon. You've known me since I was born."

"That doesn't change the station of your birth, Your Grace."

There was a bark of laughter and Tiadaria wondered how a voice so light could sound so bitter.

"As you will, magician."

Faxon's hiss told Tiadaria that the barb was well aimed. Calling a Quintessentialist a magician was one of the worst ways you could insult one. It was akin to calling a cleric or healer a charlatan.

Or a tradesman a swindler. It just wasn't polite. Magicians dealt in illusions, trickery meant to fool the viewer into believing they commanded forces far beyond their ken. Quintessentialists, on the other hand, controlled very real forces from the Ethereal Realm.

The door opened further and the voice spoke again.

"Let them enter, Primrose. See to Beauregard."

Faxon stepped through the door and Tiadaria followed, leaving Jena to bring up the rear. Tiadaria gasped as she entered the room. She had to step past a statuesque woman with long, dark hair and when she did so, she felt a wave of latent power wash over her. Tiadaria shook it off and kept walking. The woman's strange violet eyes followed Tiadaria, but she didn't speak.

Just as Tiadaria was wondering who, or what, Beauregard might be, she saw the abundant form of a mastiff lying near the doorway. Abundant wasn't the right word. If the canine had stood on his rear legs, he could have easily laid his forepaws on Tiadaria's shoulders and looked out over her head. A chill ran up her spine and gooseflesh spread down her arms. The features were just a little too close to Xarundi physiology to be comfortable.

The room was a good size with several windows set into the outside wall. Tiadaria guessed they must be on the upper tier of the King's Palace from the size and direction of the windows. However, no light from outside penetrated this sanctuary. Heavy shutters were closed tight against the window frames. Instead, the chamber was lit by a handful of oil lanterns hanging from hooks in the ceiling, and a large ornate lamp on wide oak desk spread with paper and parchment. Such clutter fell over the surface of the desk that Tiadaria was put to mind of Faxon's own desk, and she wondered if the owner might be a student of his.

"Tiadaria, Jena, this is Princess Felyn," Faxon said as he went to one knee.

Jena was quick on the uptake and followed Faxon's lead, leaving Tiadaria to fumble like an idiot as she finally matched Faxon's words to his actions. By the time she had taken a knee, her ears and cheeks were burning. Faxon was going to get a right good kicking at the end of this.

The princess stepped forward out of the darkness that shrouded the majority of the room. Tiadaria gasped, felt like a cretin, and then felt much better as Jena repeated her surprised aspiration. Princess Felyn was draped in white robes from head to toe. Quintessentialist's robes, if Tiadaria wasn't mistaken, but that wasn't the most shocking thing about her appearance. Her hands and face, where not hidden by the robes, were a shade so pale that Tiadaria could only call it white.

Even in the semi-dark, Tiadaria could see faint blue traces creeping from the girl's wrists up into the darkness of her sleeves.

Felyn pushed her hood back, letting it fall away behind her, revealing hair so white that Tiadaria would have thought it painted if she hadn't known better. It fell down the Princess's back in a straight line, brushed back from a dainty face. Tiadaria tried not to stare, but Felyn's eyes held her fast. There was something supernatural in that regard. Something that reached inside Tiadaria and looked past her body and into her soul. Felyn blinked, temporarily hiding her crimson eyes from view, and the feeling passed, as if a thread had snapped.

"I'm very pleased to meet you both," Felyn said, sweeping them with her curious red eyes. "Primrose is my constant companion and bodyguard. Where I go, she goes. Please, make yourselves comfortable." To Primrose, she said, "The door, please?"

Primrose nodded and slipped a long staff from a sleeve slung across the back of her leather tunic. The warrior glanced at Beauregard without as much as a single word. The massive canine stood up and fell in line with his mistress. Tiadaria felt a faint echo of the same power she'd felt when they had entered, and then the two of them slipped out of the room and closed the door behind them.

When the door was closed, the Princess waved a hand toward a small table near the desk where rested four goblets, a jug of wine, and a plate of sugar-powdered Dragonwings.

"I anticipated your arrival and prepared accordingly," Felyn said with a curve of her pale pink lips. "I trust we have much to discuss."

CHAPTER THREE

An acrid tang hung over the deck of the Direwake, though the smoke from the cannons had long cleared. The ship cut through the sea like a dagger, bringing them ever closer to the passenger ship that was adrift to port. A single volley from the guns was all it had taken to convince the Imperium captain that running meant dying. A smile twisted the corner of Tionne's mouth. She'd really wanted them to run. No matter. There would be time for play later.

Passengers were lined up on the deck of the Imperium ship. Many of them were citizens of the Imperium, but judging by the style and color of their dress, there were more than a few foreigners among them. Some of the women and children were crying. Men were wringing their hands, and a low murmur, like a hundred thousand locusts, buzzed around the ship. They had every right to be worried. They weren't going to make it out of this alive.

Tionne glanced above, looking through the swaying rigging and the billowing sails to see the black flag fluttering in the breeze. The Bloody Cross, the pirates called it, and rightly so. Dark as midnight and slashed from corner to corner with crimson streaks, it was a pennant that suited both Tionne's mood and her temperament.

She crossed the rolling deck and peered over the railing into the dark water. Their speed and the chop made it difficult to see anything down below, but every now and again she would catch a silver-blue flicker under the waves. Everything was in order. Their escort would remain hidden until Tionne found what she was looking for or until she was ready to sink the ship, whichever came first.

As the Direwake came alongside, the pirates threw heavy hooks onto the deck of the Imperium vessel. They showed no thought or consideration to the passengers. Those who didn't get out of the way fast enough risked being impaled by the wicked three pronged hooks. Heaving in the lines, they drew the ships closer together and lashed them down. A wide plank was laid across the gap between the ships.

Tionne leapt atop it, balancing like a cat as she scampered across the makeshift gangway. Her long black dress, cut too low in the front to be modest and too high on the thighs to be proper, caught the reluctant gaze of some of the men. When they were at sea, she kept her long, raven-black hair in a braid that swished around the small of her back like a serpent, ready to strike. Her eyes were cut emeralds, and just as cold. She scanned the deck looking for the captain and found no one who looked as if they'd play the part.

"You there," she said, her long finger singling out a portly man at the front of the crowd. "Where's the captain?"

"I...I think he might be below, uh, Miss."

"You *think*?" she asked, her voice sickly sweet. It oozed from her lips like pus from a festering wound.

"I...I don't know!"

Oh how Tionne wished that the sea didn't bar her from commanding the Quintessential Sphere. She wanted to call forward memories of fire and flame, of a conflagration so great that she could roast the fat little man like the pig he resembled. She wanted to hear him squeal and beg. It was always so much fun when they started to beg.

There were always promises of what they could do or provide, or how they would make themselves useful. Little did they know that the best way they could make themselves useful was by being a source of the panic and fear she found so intoxicating. Their piteous cries were better than the finest liquor.

I guess I'll settle for the dagger, she thought with a sigh. While it had its own appeal, in general, the blade was much less fulfilling than her magic. Magic was so much more versatile. The blade was so *mundane*. She slid her hand into the slit of her dress and withdrew the obsidian dagger from the sheath strapped to her thigh. The serpentine blade curved back and forth then tapered to a needle fine point. It pierced skin with the slightest pressure, as if it was as happy as its owner to be coaxing agony out of hiding.

Realizing too late that he was in danger, the man tried to step backward, but the crowd wouldn't let him flee. If someone were going to pay the price of vengeance, it wasn't going to be any of them. Someone in the back shoved him forward, and he stumbled, falling to his knees at her feet. He raised his round face to her, his little, red piggy eyes watering.

"Puh-please," he managed to gasp and she put a pale hand under his chin. He tried to pull back, but her men, the pirates from the Direwake, had followed her over. One of them, a beast of a man standing at nearly seven feet tall, grabbed piggy's arms and wrenched them back.

"Poor piggy," Tionne said with mock sympathy, her hand caressing the folds of his abundant neck. "No one wants to help you."

Tionne took the blade and drew it across the side of his neck, and he began to scream. It was a high-pitched, bleating sound, more appropriate to an animal than a full grown man. Her knife sliced easily through the flesh, as if she were carving a yuletide roast. The slightest bit of resistance on the blade told her she was about to breech the artery in his neck and she slowed her hand. His screaming became frenzied as blood poured from the open wound, as if he knew how close to death he truly was. With a flick of her wrist, she severed the blood vessel. Blood sprayed from his neck, covering the crowd in a fine crimson mist. His cries turned to whimpers, and then came to an abrupt end as the last of his life gurgled from the wound. The pirate dropped him to the deck, and the crowd tried to back away as far as the confines of the ship would allow.

"You've seen what we'll do if necessary," Tionne said, wiping the blade on the hem of her dress before sheathing it again. "If you do exactly as you're told, I promise we won't hurt you."

To the pirate standing nearby she said, "Take them up on the rear deck and keep them there. I'm going below to see if it's here."

"Aye, Cap'n."

The pirate began bellowing orders to the frightened passengers, herding them like sheep onto the upper deck. Tionne paused just a moment to ensure that the passengers were going to comply, and then she slipped below. Open portholes provided patches of light that she passed through into longer stretches of darkness. She wasn't worried about what might be waiting for her in the dark. What down here could possibly hope to match the black within her heart?

She heard a sound from the end of the corridor and stopped to listen. Someone was there, ransacking a cabin by the sound of it. There was a loud thud, followed by a string of curses. Tionne put her back against the wall and made her way to the open door.

The captain was inside, his blue waistcoat open and spread out behind him like a blanket. The wide black belt that circled his waist was askew and the gray wisps of hair that circled his bald patch like a wreath stuck out in every direction. He was so consumed with rifling through a footlocker that he hadn't heard her approach. In fact, she wasn't even sure he'd heard the screaming that piggy had done only moments ago. His singular attention was on something in that chest.

Her heart skipped a beat and she put a hand to her breast. Her pulse quickened and she felt a flush creep over her, spreading out from the pit of her stomach and filling her with a warm glow. *Is this it?* she wondered. *Is all my fruitless searching about to come to an end?* She drew her weapon and took a step into the room. If she'd been paying more attention, she would have seen the tin snuffbox near her feet. In her haste, she kicked it aside with a loud clatter.

The captain whirled, his eyes wide with fear. He clutched at his belt, fumbling under the fall of his coat before producing a short saber. Tionne narrowed her eyes. If they'd been on land, this wouldn't have even been a fair fight. She could have disarmed him without much effort at all. Out here, on the water, she was in danger. The dagger in her hand had only a third of the reach of the sticker he held on her.

"I'll kill you," he snarled and lunged forward without hesitation.

Tionne spun to the side, but not before hearing the fabric of her dress tear under the tip of his blade. *Too damn close*, she thought as she side-stepped around the small cabin. *And no room to maneuver in.* The captain flicked his blade this way and that, trying to anticipate where she'd be next. She continued around the edge of the wall, working her way toward the far corner and the chest where the captain had been standing. Perhaps she could put it between them.

Her back was against the narrow chest of drawers when he attacked again, the point of his sword aimed at her heart. Throwing herself sideways at the last moment, she slashed out with her blade and was happy to hear him yelp in pain. When she looked closer, she saw a dark crimson stain spreading up one arm of his waistcoat. He wasn't badly wounded, but perhaps it would prick his confidence.

The captain's next strikes came in rapid succession, and Tionne realized, almost too late, that he was driving her into the corner. That would make her more vulnerable, true, but there might be something she could use to her advantage. She let him drive her toward the bunk and the corner beyond. She'd allow him to believe he had the upper hand for now. *Just a little further.*

She settled back against the bunk and his blade twitched again toward her heart, as if it were drawn there. His eyes narrowed and he lunged, pressing in for a killing blow. Before he could reach her, Tionne wrenched the linens off the bunk and threw them toward him, fouling the sword and covering his face. Before he could react, she dropped to the floor, kicking hard at his knees.

He went over backward, losing his grip on the saber. She was atop him in an instant, stabbing him over and over again. Tionne rained a fury of blows down upon him, refusing to stop even after he'd gone still. It took a full minute or more for the haze of bloodlust to leave her, and for her to realize that her hands were covered in his blood. Her dress was soaked through.

Tionne stumbled up on unsteady legs and grabbed the edge of the bunk for support. She cleaned herself up with the linens that had granted her victory and made a cursory inspection of her hands. They were mostly clean, though the blood would remain under her nails for days.

She replaced the dagger in its sheath and went to the footlocker at the end of the bunk. She mimicked the dead captain, rummaging about inside it and tossing things aside that held no interest for her. Tionne was here for one thing, and one thing only. If the manifests she had stolen were to be believed, it had to be here.

The nearer she got to the bottom of the locker, the more agitated she became. It *had* to be here. They needed it. The consequences of failure were too great. Yet it appeared that it was gone. Maybe someone had found it before her, or maybe it had never been here at all. A black cloud of rage began to form behind her eyes and she fought to push it back, lest it consume her with its creeping tendrils. She slammed a fist into the bottom of the locker in frustration and heard a hollow echo.

Oh, how could I be so stupid? Tionne's fingers traced the bottom of the footlocker. It was an age old trick. One she'd used herself when she was still in the Academy. It should have been the first thing she thought of. There, in the corner, a thread out of place. Almost impossible to see. She took it between her slender fingers and pulled. A small section of lining came up with it. She grabbed it and gave it a tug.

With just a little force, the false bottom came out of the locker. She sat it aside and peered into its depths, scared of what she might find.

Tionne's heart skipped a beat. Nestled in a custom-made chamber at the bottom of the footlocker was what she'd spent weeks searching for. The journal was smaller than she'd expected, clad in thick leather and carved with a master's hand. Seashells and fish made up a border that encircled the cover, and a handful of sirens sat upon a rock at its center. She reached in and lifted out the book, letting her fingers trace over the hills and valleys of the etching.

It wasn't at all what she'd expected, but it was *beautiful.*

~ ~ ~

Going up on deck, Tionne held the journal out in front of her like an idol. In a way, it was. From what she'd been told by Stryne, the last remaining dragon in all of Solendrea, the book she held now was the key to their domination of the entire planet. Within its pages lay the secret location of the Horn of Requiem, a weapon so powerful that they would be able to take entire cities in a single fell swoop.

Their tentative allegiance with the Siren King hinged on the location of this journal and now they had it in hand. She dashed up to the deck to where the passengers were being held in a tight knot, herded together by the sharp swords of the pirates in her employ.

At her appearance with the book, a shout went up from the men. Their mission was well known and now that the journal had been found, they could put many long weeks at sea behind them. Though Stryne wasn't fond of parting with any portion of his amassed treasure, he would be glad to pay out the wages that had made their excursion into the Siren's Sea such a success. That was, of course, if Stryne opted to pay them. He might decide just to slaughter them all. Such was the whim and temperament of a beast that commanded power bordering on the might of a demi-god.

Tionne went to the rail and gave it a solid kick with the heel of her boot. The wood splintered, but did not cleave. She kicked it again and again, until it broke and opened a hole in the railing. Peering over the edge, she saw the silver-blue flashes just under the waves. There were more of them now. That was to be expected. Feeding time was almost upon them.

"Put them in," she commanded, clutching the journal to her chest.

"Wait! You said you wouldn't hurt us if we obeyed you," someone brave, or incredibly foolish, called from the crowd.

"And I did not," Tionne said with a sweet smile. She stopped hugging the book long enough to point over the edge of the ship. "I never said anything about them."

An earnest panic broke out then, but the passengers were gentlefolk, unaccustomed to the predatory nature of the pirates they were now at the mercy of. One by one, either conscious or not, the commoners were dragged to the hole in the railing and pushed over the edge. The water below erupted in a frenzy as the sirens fed.

Overcome with curiosity, Tionne looked over the railing. The sea around the ship had turned an ugly shade of crimson. Every now and again part of a body would bob to the surface, only to be dragged down under the choppy water. A swish of a tail here and flash of pale blue flesh there were the only indications that the sirens were the ones committing the carnage. Once or twice Tionne saw a Grobin surface, only to disappear again. Aquatic cousins of the gnomes, Grobins were well known for their ferocity, but not for their intelligence.

Now that the last of the passengers were off the ship, Tionne turned to her crew.

"Loot what you will, then get back to the Direwake. Anyone left here when the Grobins board is food."

The men streamed down the steps and all but ran to the forward hold hatch. They'd have the ship stripped of anything worth a few crowns in short order. She had no need of plunder. The most valuable object on the ship was the book that she cradled in her hands with reverent awe. She retraced her steps across the gangplank to the Direwake. A distinctive coppery tang hung in the air. With so much flesh to sate them, the sirens should be in a very amiable mood.

Tionne climbed the stairs to the top deck of the Direwake, nodding to the navigator and helmsman as she passed. Only the most essential crew remained aboard when they took another vessel. They nodded back, but said nothing. Just as well. She wasn't interested in a conversation. At least not with them. She went to the edge of the deck and let out a piercing whistle. A silver-blue body broke off from the sirens teeming just under the surface and streaked toward the Direwake. A female siren broke the surface, seeming to balance herself in the water by her tail. Her sucker-like mouth was full of teeth, stained red with blood by the recent feeding. Black eyes seemed to take up a full half of her face and gill slits took up the space where a human's cheeks would be. The pirates were terrified of them and considered them some of the most hideous things they'd ever seen. Tionne thought they were beautiful.

She held the journal out over the edge so the siren could see it. The sucker mouth withdrew, expelling all its fangs outward in the siren equivalent of a grin. She leapt into the air, the iridescent fall of her tail unfurling for a split second above the surface, and then she was gone. Tionne waited. With news this important, she expected a male to be along in short order. Stryne had taught her a great deal about siren society before they'd begun this mission. They were a patriarchal society. Yargen, the Siren King, was thought to have sired more than half their current population.

Tionne hadn't been allowed to attend the meeting between the great dragon and the Siren

King, a fact that still annoyed her when she thought about it. Still, with the journal in hand, there was little to stand in the way of her getting to converse with these strange, beautiful creatures that had been escorting their ship for the last several weeks. Stryne had said they would be able to communicate when the time came, but so far, they hadn't had any real need for a discussion. The sirens waited until Tionne and her pirates unburdened the ships they encountered, then they sent Grobins aboard to tear the vessel apart from the inside out.

As she waited for her contact, Tionne wondered, and not for the first time, if she might be able to domesticate a Grobin and keep it as a pet. They were ferocious to be sure, but somehow the sirens kept control of them, and perhaps that was something that she'd be allowed to learn once she returned the Horn of Requiem to the Siren King. Her ruminations were interrupted by a large male siren bursting from the water. He executed an impressive flip, his long, stringy black hair sending whips of sea-spray into the air. After he landed, he broke the surface and stood poised on his tail as the female had.

He was much larger, his skin mottled with black splotches that oozed green puss. His once smooth flesh was withered, drawn back against the bones in such a way that he looked almost skeletal. Tionne winced. To see such a regal creature reduced to such a state made her heart ache. His hair was strung with tiny shells that caught the sun, and around his neck, he wore an intricate necklace of carved coral. His gills quivered and he dipped below the water for a moment before he spoke.

The sound that came from the sucker-mouth was the most beautiful music Tionne had ever heard. Something about the sound made her restless. She wanted to move toward it, to get closer so she could hear it better, but she knew if she followed the sound, she'd fall.

"Be still and hear my true voice, Daughter of Darkness. I am Yargen, Lord of the Siren's Sea, Master of Waves."

His voice wasn't carried by the music that issued from him. Instead, it resounded in her head. Tionne could hear him clearly between her ears, but not with them. Regardless, as soon as he'd spoken to her, the intense pull of his voice stopped, as if cut off with a pair of shears.

"You honor me with your presence, Lord Yargen." She showed him the journal she'd taken from the merchant ship. "I've found the journal you described to Lord Stryne."

The Siren King's laughter sent waves of pleasure coursing down her spine, and she had to stop herself from writhing under its sensuous caress.

"Well done, Daughter of Darkness! Well done. My people are ill with a great plague, as you can see." His webbed hand indicated the sores that covered his body and Tionne winced. "The Horn will restore us to health, and we will rebuild all we have lost."

"How can I help?"

Yargen dipped under the water, wetting his gills before he again broke the surface.

"You've already done us a great service, Daughter of Darkness. The life force of the humans you've delivered to us will sustain us…revive us…for a time. Find the Horn of Requiem and return it to us."

"How will that help?"

"With each human soul we devour, we get stronger. We turn back the plague we are cursed with. We will empty their cities and feed upon their souls. We will once again rule the seas as we ought." Yargen regarded her with his bottomless black eyes. "May we rely on you, Daughter of Darkness?"

How could she deny them? She had the opportunity to help save the noblest creatures she'd ever met. Of course they could rely on her.

"You have my word. I will find the Horn of Requiem, Lord Yargen, and return it to your people…no matter the cost."

Yargen shot out of the water in a leap that Tionne wouldn't have believed if she hadn't seen it. He was almost level with the deck she stood on when he performed a perfect somersault and plunged beneath the waves. Then he was gone. Tionne turned to the navigator.

"Call the men back and set course for Solorest. Best possible speed."

CHAPTER FOUR

Tiadaria was grateful that they waited until after a goblet of wine and a few Dragonwings before they settled down to the business at hand. Properly sated, she wouldn't have to worry about her stomach embarrassing her in front of the Princess. Her thoughts tumbled back and forth, rarely pausing long enough for her to make sense of any of them.

She'd heard of Greymalkin's daughter from Faxon and from chance words caught while she was inside the Palace, but Tiadaria hadn't known that she was in Dragonfell. Or in the Palace for that matter. From the way she was spoken about, Tiadaria had always assumed that the Princess was in some far off land attending to matters of great importance. To find out that she was here, in the Palace, tucked away in a room high above the servants' chambers, was disturbing. Felyn, for her part, seemed at ease with her role, whatever it was. It was something that Tiadaria couldn't understand. If she'd been shoved away in some remote part of the Palace as Princess...well, the results would *not* have been pretty.

After they'd been refreshed, Felyn led them to a small hearth and the four of them retired to plush chairs around the meager fire. Though she couldn't see outside, Tiadaria guessed that the sun had set. The fire kept Felyn's chambers warm, but not stifling.

"Father has been very ill lately," Felyn said. Her voice was quiet, reflective. "He has good days and bad. On the good days, he's just as he's always been."

"And on the bad?" Faxon prompted.

Felyn shrugged and looked into the fire, the dancing sparks reflected in her red eyes. Tiadaria found her gaze drawn to them again and again. She knew she was being rude, but she just couldn't help it. She'd never seen anything like it before in her life, and it was both strange and a little unnerving. Every now and again, Felyn would catch her looking and Tiadaria would quickly look away. But when she looked back, there was always the ghost of a smile on the Princess's face. As if she were delighted by Tiadaria's reaction.

"On the bad," Felyn said at last, "he hardly recognizes me anymore. He rants and raves and it's all the stewards can do to keep him from disturbing the court. I fear that his time may soon be at an end."

"I hadn't realized things had gotten so bad," Faxon said. "Are you prepared for that day to come?"

Felyn shrugged again, but this time she looked at Faxon. She gave him that same sad, little ghost of a smile she'd given Tiadaria on several occasions.

"As ready as I can be, I suppose. Do you really think the citizens of Dragonfell are ready to have me as their Queen?"

Faxon shifted in his seat, as if the deep cushions had suddenly become hard with spikes. Tiadaria had rarely seen the Quintessentialist unsettled. It was strange to see him so. Felyn rubbed her hands together and leaned forward toward the fire, as if she took strength from its warmth.

"Perhaps they will surprise me. We can't know the future for certain, can we Master Indra?"

"No," Faxon said with a sigh. "We can't. Things are always changing. Unfortunately, that's why we are here."

"Yes, Princess," Jena chimed in. Tiadaria wondered if she was trying to keep herself awake. "We have important matters to discuss."

"And since your father won't see us..." Tiadaria said with what little tact she could muster. Faxon glared at her. She glared back. "What? It's true."

Felyn laughed, a light tinkling sound that put Tiadaria in mind of clinking glasses and fancy parties. Tiadaria felt her cheeks and ears start to burn again. Faxon knew better than to put her in a situation like this. Formality and the rules of court were not her strong suit. She was much more at home with a blade in her hand and mud under her fingernails.

"You speak your mind," Felyn said to Tiadaria. "I enjoy that. So many of my visitors feel the need to dote upon me. It's tiresome."

"Oh, you'll love me then," Tiadaria said with a wry grin. Felyn answered in kind, revealing her perfectly straight, white teeth for the first time since they'd entered the chamber. After a moment, Tiadaria's grin felt out of place and she dropped it.

There was something about the Princess that made her uncomfortable. Tiadaria didn't feel like Felyn was a threat. She was pretty good at assessing a threat. There was just something…off…about the girl. She couldn't put her finger on it. No, girl wasn't the right word. She was small, but she was a full-grown woman. Probably older than Tiadaria herself, by a year or two.

"Well then," Felyn said, smoothing over the lengthy silence. "Tell me how I can help you. What troubles does the realm face now?"

Faxon and Jena both started talking at once, stopped, then started again. Faxon held up a hand and told Felyn what he suspected about Tionne and the pirates. Jena added the details she felt were appropriate. Together they wove together the entire tale and spared no detail in the telling. Tiadaria sat back in her chair and watched the Princess's eyes dart from Faxon to Jena and back again as they talked. When they'd finally finished telling their tale, Felyn sank back into the plush cushions and steepled her fingers under her chin.

"Do you really believe that there is an imminent threat to the Imperium, Faxon?"

"I do. You saw what Tionne and her allies did to this city the last time they were allowed to roam free. I can't let that happen again."

Felyn shook her head, her eyes dark and sad.

"No. Nor can I." She stood and went to the fire, and then prodded the embers with a charred wooden poker. "Nor can I take your information to my father. He is paranoid of late, and I fear that if I take this information to him now, he'll only feel as if you came to me specifically to circumvent him."

"That's stupid," Tiadaria blurted.

"It may be stupid," Felyn said as her shoulders sagged, "but it is also the truth. However, there may yet be something I can do for you."

The Princess placed the poker back in its stand and went to one of the shuttered windows. Faxon burst out of his chair as if he'd been fired from a cannon. Tiadaria was on her feet a second later. She wasn't sure what had alarmed Faxon, but Jena had done one better and was crouched beside Tiadaria with a dagger in her hand. Tiadaria hadn't even known the agent was armed. The dagger seemed to have appeared as if by magic. The girl was full of surprises.

"Felyn!" Faxon cried, lunging for the window.

Felyn laughed and held up a hand, forestalling Faxon's panic.

"Relax, my friend. The sun is set. I'm in no danger." Felyn pushed open the shutters and revealed that twilight had indeed fallen. The western sky was tinged with the pastel colors of sunset. She turned to face them, the dying day lighting her hair like an aurora. "You may sheath your weapon, Agent. No one is in any danger. Faxon is just very protective."

"Of what, exactly?" Tiadaria asked, her suspicions not the slightest bit allayed.

"The sun burns me just as surely as that fire would burn you, Lady Tiadaria. But a moment's touch and I'd be a mass of red flesh and blisters." She gave Tiadaria her almost smile. "This is why I dread my ascension. Do you think the people of Dragonfell will understand why the Queen hasn't seen the light of day in more than two decades?"

Tiadaria didn't answer, and Felyn shrugged. She pointed out the window and Faxon, Tiadaria, and Jena went to stand beside her. They were looking out over the harbor, nearly level with the watchtower. From up here, the ships at anchor looked like half-size models and the people scurrying about the docks looked smaller still. Following the direction of Felyn's finger, Tiadaria saw a warship sitting low in the water. It was flanked on either side by smaller, but no less deadly looking vessels.

"I cannot provide you with the full might of the Imperium Navy. Only an Order of the Court, signed by my father's hand could give you such power. But those three ships, the Nightingale, and her sister ships, the Hawk and the Falcon, are mine. Paid for from my coffers, manned by my men, devoted to my interests. Those three ships are at your disposal."

"Planning a coup?" Faxon asked the Princess with a raised eyebrow.

"I like ships," Felyn said without batting an eye. "And anything that keeps me out of trouble is in father's best interests."

The Quintessentialist laughed, and then he turned to Tiadaria.

"So, Tia, want to go sailing?"

~ ~ ~

Even with the full power and influence of Princess Felyn behind their operation, it required several days for the Nightingale and her sister ships to be outfitted for voyage.

On the morning of the third day, Tiadaria and Faxon stood on the dock overseeing the last of the preparations. Jena had excused herself after their meeting with the Princess, begging off on the fact that she had to get back to her duties with the Imperium Information Service. It was a shame,

Tiadaria thought. Jena would have made an excellent traveling companion.

Primrose stood nearby, her arms across her chest. The dark-haired beauty had acted as Felyn's proxy during the loading, recommending to Tiadaria the men she thought would best suit her needs. The woman was quiet. Tiadaria couldn't quite put her finger on the strange sense of power that seemed to emanate from her like a beacon, but she would have liked to have Primrose on the voyage, as well. Alas, her duty was to protect the Princess and no amount of discussion would persuade her to join the mission.

Tiadaria scowled. That only reminded her that Faxon had just told her he wasn't coming on her first trip out at sea.

"I can't, Tia, as much as I'd like to," he'd said after she asked him for no less than the fifth time in as many hours. "With Greymalkin in the condition he's in, someone needs to be here. As much to keep the peace as to protect the Princess lest things get worse."

"What about Torus?" she'd asked, though she feared she already knew the answer.

Faxon had dismissed that suggestion with a flip of his hand.

Torus was busy. Very busy. With near constant incursions by the Stavanshi elves along the southwestern border of the Imperium, it seemed that another war was inevitable. In fact, most of the Grand Army had already been moved out across the mountains, past Havenhedge. The Imperium Navy would soon follow, sailing almost halfway around the continent of Mizdan to drop anchor on the Crescent Sea. Torus's hope was that the navy could make contact with some of the other tribes of elves that were rumored to live in the southern mountains and forestlands. Tiadaria thought he'd be better off hoping for help from the Pheen.

Now that Tiadaria was watching the last of the supplies being lifted aboard the Nightingale by a dock crane the size of a dragon, she was having serious misgivings about having so blithely signed on for this mission. It had seemed like a good idea at the time. Now it seemed like a whole lot of unknowns wrapped in a neat little bundle.

"I don't know if I can do this, Faxon." She gnawed at her lower lip and looked at him sidelong. "I may have jumped the gun."

The elder Quintessentialist chuckled.

"Too late for that now. You're going. You'll be fine. Just remember that you're not going to be able to use any of your…ah…talents when you're on the water. You'll need to rely on your weapons until you make landfall somewhere."

"That's what I'm afraid of."

Faxon gave her an appraising look and shrugged.

"The best steel is forged in flames, Tiadaria. Look at it as an opportunity to broaden your horizons. Maybe you'll learn something about yourself."

"Like I don't like being cut in two?"

"That's the spirit."

There was a loud call from atop the Nightingale's rear deck. Captain Odeon was waving at them. It was time to board. Tiadaria pretended not to see him, even though his dark skin and silver hair stood out against the backdrop of the morning sky. Faxon nudged her and pointed in Odeon's direction. Faxon waved back and Tiadaria blew out a gusty sigh.

"It's not going to be that bad, Tia. You've faced Tionne before. Find her before she locates the journal and everything will be fine."

"Easy for you to say. You'll be here."

"True." Faxon looked at her, breaking into the boyish grin that made him seem so much younger than he was. "Well, don't screw up. If you don't stop Tionne, we'll all die. You'll never live *that* down."

"You're not helping."

"I wasn't aware I was trying to help."

Faxon took her by the shoulders, wincing a little as faint link-shock danced between them. He turned her to face him and looked at her with such a serious regard that Tiadaria had to fight not to turn her face away.

"Seriously though, you'll be fine. I have the utmost faith in your abilities. Stop Tionne before she finds the journal. Actually, scratch that. Stop Tionne. I don't care if she finds the journal or not, but she needs to be stopped. If you can return her to Dragonfell, so much the better. She has a lot to answer for."

"Again, easy for you to say."

"I'd do it myself if I could, Tiadaria." Faxon shifted his eyes over her shoulder, toward the cavern that held the King's Palace. "It's a critical time for the Imperium right now. I fear that the home you return to may not be the one you are leaving."

"All right. All right. I get it. Do it for the good of King and country and all that rot."

"No," Faxon said, giving her a little shake. "Screw King and country. Do it for the hundreds of thousands of innocents who will die if Tionne gets her hands on the insanely powerful weapon she's searching for."

Tiadaria could easily imagine what Tionne would do with such a weapon, and the images it brought to mind sent a shiver up her spine. A tremor that Faxon felt. He nodded.

"See? You understand full well what's at stake here. I know you'll do fine."

The men aboard the Nightingale began drawing up lines. There wasn't any more time to dawdle here, no matter what her misgivings about the mission might be. It was time to go.

"That's my cue," Tiadaria said, ducking out from under Faxon's grip. She hoisted her carryall from the planks by her feet and slung it over her shoulder. The sack contained every possession she'd have in the world for however long it took them to find and dispatch Tionne and her pirates.

Halfway up the gangplank, she stopped and looked back at Faxon. Standing alone on the dock, he seemed so isolated. An ancient relic in ivory robes. As if he recognized the timbre of her thoughts, he stuck out his tongue and waggled his eyebrows. She couldn't help but laugh.

"Bring me back souvenirs, Tiadaria. It's only polite."

Tiadaria made a rude gesture at him and scampered the rest of the way up the gangplank, past a surly looking seaman who drew it up behind her. He also lifted a pair of rope boarding ladders that had been thrown down alongside the ship, allowing the most nimble of the crew to board without walking up the steep incline.

Reaching inside her armored tunic, she took a rolled piece of parchment tied with a silken purple ribbon. She carried her orders up the steps leading to the rear deck and found the captain standing beside his navigator.

"Strong winds and good sailing, Captain Odeon," she said to the Theid, managing to remember what Faxon had told her about sailors and their traditions.

"Fair journeys to be had, for certain, Lady Tiadaria." His brilliant white teeth gleamed behind dusky rose lips. His silver hair, woven and pulled back in a series of tiny braids that fell almost to the back of his neck, bobbed when he laughed. "No need to be so formal. I'll take those."

His black fingers, thick with pale callouses, tweaked the scroll from her grasp. He slid the ribbon off and glanced over the orders, his cyan eyes tracing the flowing script that Princess Felyn had put down with her quill. Tiadaria had watched her write out the orders and knew what they said by heart. Tiadaria was nominally in command of the entire mission, ships and all. When Tiadaria had protested, Felyn had held up a hand, explaining that Odeon would know what to do. Tiadaria had been forced to trust her.

Captain Odeon tilted his hand so the navigator could read the message, then rolled it up and tucked it in a pocket of his blue waistcoat.

"You're in command of this mission, Lady Tiadaria, but if I might make a suggestion." He laid a finger alongside his nose, and then pointed out toward open end of the bay on the distant horizon. "The men are used to taking their orders from me. Perhaps it would be best if you give me my orders and I pass them along?"

Tiadaria breathed a huge sigh and the butterflies in her stomach settled a trifle. Captain Odeon and his navigator tactfully disguised their chuckles in a well-timed spate of coughing. She grinned at them.

"Captain Odeon, that would be perfect. We need to find Tionne and her band of pirates. Do you know where we might start looking?"

"The Siren's Sea is vast and wide, Lady Tiadaria, but I imagine we can track down your pirates easy enough. We've already laid in a course. All we need is your word."

"The word is given, Captain."

As soon as Tiadaria had spoken, Odeon's voice boomed out over Dragonfell's harbor, carrying not only to his men on the Nightingale, but also to her sister ships beyond. Tiadaria watched in amazement as the massive blue-and-crimson sails were unfurled. The gentle breeze from over the Dragonback Mountains caught the sails, filling them with wind and making them billow out to the full reach of the lines that held them.

A moment later, there was a rumble underfoot as seamen cranked the giant wheel that brought the anchors up off the bottom of the harbor. All of a sudden, they were moving.

Tiadaria rushed to the edge of the deck, peering down over the railing at the dock beyond. Faxon was still standing there and he waved with his whole arm as the vessel slipped away. Then they were free of the moors and in the open water. Tiadaria went to the rear of the deck and looked back toward Dragonfell. They hadn't picked up much speed yet, but it seemed that they were pulling away from her adopted home at an incredible rate.

It wasn't long before Faxon was lost to the distance. The buildings of the harbor became smaller and smaller as they made their way toward the mouth of Crystal Bay. Captain Odeon made no note of her vigilance, other than to mention that it would be at least an hour before they were no longer able to see Dragonfell.

That was all right with Tiadaria. The longer she could keep Dragonfell in sight, the longer she felt she was in familiar territory.

The waters that lay ahead were dangerous and uncharted.

CHAPTER FIVE

Looking back over the past couple of days, Tiadaria would have been perfectly happy if the only discomfort she'd had to contend with was the unsettling feeling of being so far from home and being without anyone she could call a friend. As it turned out, she had more immediate concerns. She'd never been on a sailing ship before. Not even the long boats the Clansmen used to go from one ice island to another in the Frozen Frontier. It had never occurred to her that life aboard a ship would be anything different from life on dry land. Oh how very wrong she'd been.

In addition to the disorientation of being cut off from the Quintessential Sphere, it hadn't taken very long for the nausea and vomiting to set in. When the rocking of the ship first overwhelmed her, she was in the middle of the mess hall with the full complement of sailors surrounding her. She hadn't quite made it to the head in time and subsequently had to accept the help of a seaman with a mop and bucket to clean up the mess she'd made. Since then, she'd put as much distance between herself and the rest of the crew as she was able.

As bad as was coping with the void in the back of her head, the seasickness was worse. The morning of the third day saw her as miserable as she'd ever been in her life, and that was saying something, she thought. She was slumped against the forward rail. The wind and sea spray from their passage felt good against her flushed skin. Plus she was close to the side if she felt the need to be ill again. Her stomach roiled at the thought.

"Please," she whispered in a prayer to any of the Eternals who would listen. "Please, not again. I can't take any more."

"Legend says that Wrynett created the sickness to weed out any who were unworthy of sailing on his seas," a mellow baritone voice said. She opened her eyes.

A tall, lanky man was standing just beyond her feet. He was well outside the danger zone, she noticed. A fact that made her less charitable than she might otherwise have been.

"I'm unworthy. I admit it. Put me back on land. I'll go gladly."

Her visitor ran a hand through his short beard, giving his chin a good scratch before he replied.

"Not much land out here, I'm afraid. Unless you want us to put you on the bottom."

"No, thank you. As bad as this is, I'd rather not drown."

"Well, you know you're only making it worse, right?"

She peered at him. His brown eyes were light, the color of golden oak. He was lean, but not skinny. Muscular without being a wall of flesh. Tiadaria couldn't tell if he was making fun of her or not. If, however, he was serious about making the illness worse, she needed to know what he meant.

"No. How am I making it worse?"

"Stand up and I'll show you."

Tiadaria stood up. As soon as she was on her feet, she pitched forward, only avoiding having a face full of decking by the sailor's quick reaction. He caught her under the arms and rolled her against his chest, keeping her upright.

"Easy there, let's not add a head wound to your worries," he said with a laugh.

She hated him for laughing. She hated him for having seen her weakness, but most of all, she hated him because she knew she couldn't stand on her own. Tiadaria was completely at his mercy. Her knees were just too wobbly to keep her upright on the swaying deck.

"Okay, now," he said with a grunt, pushing her up onto her own feet. "Grab the rail and lock your knees. Now pick a spot on the horizon and watch it. Try not to look out of the corners of your eyes."

Tiadaria felt ridiculous, standing like a statue adhered to the rail. She wanted to look at him, but he'd told her to keep her eyes on the horizon.

"Who are you?"

He laughed and the sound sent a faint feeling coursing through her. Something that she hadn't felt in a long time. Something that had nothing to do with how angry she was or how foolish she felt. *That's enough of that,* she said to herself, squashing down the feeling before it could gain any traction.

"My name is Jonathylathian, son of Marinylathian, descendent of the Great Bear."

Tiadaria turned to look at him now, regardless of how sick it might make her. Her blue eyes were like saucers and he laughed again.

"What?"

"That's a clan name!"

"Indeed it is," he agreed with an inclined head. "As is Tiadaria, unless I'm very much mistaken. I detect a very faint accent. I'm going to guess west of the Ice Fields, which would make you a descendent of the Great Elk."

It had been a very long time since Tiadaria had thought of the clans. Longer still since she had thought of herself as a descendent of anyone, much less the daughter of her father, who had sold her into slavery for no more than a handful of coin and a couple of beasts. Her throat felt tight and her voice cracked when she spoke.

"I haven't been a descent of anyone for a long time," she said, and the hardness of the northern ice was in her voice.

"I meant no offense, Lady Tiadaria. I apologize."

Tiadaria stared at the horizon and found that, either through her anger or his advice, she wasn't feeling as ill as she had been.

"Hey, your trick is working. I don't feel as awful."

"Excellent. We'll make a sea dog out of you yet," he paused, as if he was weighing his next words. When he spoke, Tiadaria knew why. "I really meant no offense. Dragonfell has been my home almost my entire life. You can call me Jonah. I just thought…"

"It's all right. It's just--"

"Not something you talk about." He nodded, his eyes never leaving the horizon. "I understand."

Jonah turned to leave, and Tiadaria found that she was able to loosen her death grip on the railing and not fall over. As he made his way back up the deck, Tiadaria called out to him.

"Hey! Thanks for the advice."

He stopped and looked back over his shoulder, showing his lopsided grin.

"Anytime."

Tiadaria watched him until he stepped into the darkness of the stairwell that led below deck. Then she turned her attention back on the horizon. She took a deep breath, wincing as her stomach muscles protested the injudicious movement. She was going to be sore for a few days, but at least now she didn't feel like retching. Tiadaria wondered how she was going to keep her eyes on the horizon while in her cabin. *Oh well*, she thought. *I'll cross that bridge when I come to it.*

Now that her stomach had settled somewhat, her thoughts could turn to other matters. Like Jonah. What was a clansman doing on a sailing ship in the employ of Dragonfell's Princess? Most of the clansmen Tiadaria had ever met were dour souls without much humor. Jonah had a ready smile and an infectious laugh. He certainly wasn't like any clansman she had ever known.

Something familiar tickled the back of her mind and she shoved it away. She didn't want to think of Wynn right now. Jonah and Wynn were nothing alike, anyway. Wynn had been quiet and reserved, depending on Tiadaria to make every move and lead every dance. Jonah didn't seem to be very reserved at all. Not that it mattered.

Tiadaria's experience with love was that it only prolonged and worsened loss. Not that she loved Jonah. She didn't even know him. Still, that faint voice in the back of her head wouldn't shut up, and it had a point. Jonah was a fine looking man. She tossed her head. She was reacting to his looks and not the content of his character. He could be as brash and uncaring as the rest of the clansmen she'd been exposed to. A single conversation and a bit of advice didn't make him anything special.

The sun was beginning to climb toward its zenith. Odeon had said they would be passing out of the Strait of Seralt and into the Siren's Sea soon. Tiadaria hadn't asked him to specify what soon meant to him. He was in command of their fleet and she had faith in his abilities.

She glanced back across the water. The Falcon and Hawk were still back there, keeping pace with their larger sibling. Though the sea breeze was fresh and warm, tinged with just a hint of brine, Tiadaria shuddered. She couldn't shake the feeling that they were all waiting for something to happen. The ships themselves sat low in the water, as if crouched, watching for events to unfold.

Tiadaria turned her eyes back to the horizon and tried to ignore the feeling of dread that had settled like cold lead in the pit of her stomach. Her discomfort had nothing to do with the sea or its motion. This was something different.

~ ~ ~

By the evening of the fifth day, Tiadaria was confident that her seasickness wasn't going to return. She even joined the men in the mess hall for the evening meal and listened with incredulous ears as they swapped stories that had to be equal parts fact and fantasy. A number of times while passing laden bowls and platters, Jonah had caught her eye. He always seemed to have that lopsided grin on his face, as if everything in life was amusing in its own way.

Tiadaria turned away from him whenever he caught her in his stare. There was a mission to attend to and getting distracted was doing a disservice to both of them. Captain Odeon needed to be able to rely on each of his men, and not have one of them getting all moon-brained over the new woman on the ship. It wasn't as if Odeon's crew was lacking women. In fact, Tiadaria was surprised by the number of crew who were female. She'd always assumed that a sailing ship was work that men would be more drawn to. She'd been forced to distance herself from that notion when watching one of the ladies nearly break the arm of a sailor who said something slightly off color.

She hadn't heard the remark, but from the instant and furious reaction of the lady sailor, it must have been bad. Bad enough to wrench the man's arm up behind his back until his wrist nearly touched the back of his neck, anyway.

Dipping her hunk of crusty bread in the rich broth they'd been served, Tiadaria focused on fueling her body instead of her mind. The distracting buzz that came from disassociation with the Ethereal Realm had faded to an almost subliminal hum, but it still set her teeth on edge. It was no wonder that Quintessentialists who were censured either went mad or took their own lives. It was like having a constant itch you just couldn't scratch. Instead, she turned her attention to chewing and swallowing, the mechanics of keeping well fed. It was much more pleasant now that she wasn't in constant fear of going through the process in reverse.

Movement in the air beside her drew her back to the present as Jonah, a bowl balanced in one hand and a wooden spoon and hunk of bread in the other, seated himself across from her. Perfect. Now it would be all but impossible to ignore him without seeming rude to the others sitting around them. Fortunately, she was almost done with her meal.

"Good evening, Lady Tiadaria."

"Good evening, Jonah." She kept her voice as stiff and emotionless as possible. It was best for both of them if he'd just drop whatever thoughts he had about her.

Jonah gave her a quizzical look and then turned his attention to his food. Tiadaria finished and, excusing herself to those around her, returned her implements to the cook's assistant and fled to the open deck.

The sun had just touched the western horizon, coloring it with oranges, purples, and blues. Catching the colors, the sea threw them back in a haphazard pattern. Forward of the mainsail, the deck was empty. Most of the seamen were below deck, having dinner. The rest were tending to their duties and paid no attention to her flight.

Tiadaria made her retreat to the fore deck and leaned over the rail, watching the sea flash by. It was a retreat and she knew it for one. She wasn't sure why Jonah unsettled her so. It might have been because she didn't find him unsettling at all. From the time he'd approached her on the deck, they'd crossed paths half a dozen times. On deck or in a corridor, or even in the mess hall. There was something in the pit of her stomach that dropped every time he flashed that ridiculous grin at her. Something she hadn't felt since…well, something she hadn't felt in a long time.

She didn't want to feel that way again. Not now. Not ever. That only led to pain and suffering. It was easier to pull those feelings out by the root, like one would a weed, and never let them take hold. That Jonah seemed like a fine, upstanding young man only made it worse. If he'd been a scoundrel, it would have been easier for her to dismiss his casual attention. Perhaps that's all it was. Casual attention. With luck, as soon as they were off the boat, he'd be keen to go his own way.

"Hiding from me?"

Tiadaria jumped. Jonah's voice was soft and she knew that if she turned to face him, he'd be wearing that infuriating grin. She sighed. The ship just wasn't big enough to keep running away.

"If I say yes, will you leave me alone?"

Her voice sounded bitter, even to her. She winced at her own tone, but didn't dare look at him. There was a pause so long that for a moment she thought he'd gone away. If that was all it took, she should have done the first time they met. She felt movement and Jonah came to stand at the rail beside her. Damn. No such luck.

"Probably not. I'm persistent that way."

"Isn't there someone else on the ship you can bother?"

"No one as interesting as you."

Tiadaria sighed. "I'm not that interesting, I'm just new."

"And that makes you interesting. Why are you so reticent to get to know me? Most women jump at the chance."

"Go try your luck with one of them," Tiadaria said, spinning on her heel.

His reflexes were lightning fast as he grabbed her arm before she knew what had happened. Tiadaria ripped her arm out of his grasp. Her open hand flashed toward his face, but he put up an arm at the last second, their wrists colliding into each other with a painful slap.

"You're not most women," Jonah said, rubbing his wrist. "That's what makes you so interesting. Besides, I never said I was interested in anyone else. Just that they were interested in me."

"That's too bad for you," Tiadaria said with a sigh. "I'm not interested either."

"Come on," he flashed that damned grin again. "Not even a little?"

Tiadaria sighed again. "You *are* persistent, aren't you?"

"It's one of my best qualities."

"If you say so." Tiadaria turned to face him and felt that flutter again. She ignored it. "What will it take for you to go away?"

"Just for you to tell me so, and mean it."

"Go away," she said without hesitation. Somehow she didn't think it was going to be that easy.

"Okay. Fair enough."

Jonah turned away from the railing and made his way down the deck. His head was hung low, his hands stuffed in his pockets. He looked like a kid just caught raiding the cookie table. No matter how much she wanted him gone, there was a part of her that hated being the reason he looked so dejected. She groaned, pounding her fists into the railing.

"All right, come back. Stop acting like you lost the last of the cake."

Jonah whipped around, his eyes bright in the light of the lanterns that the sailors were lighting throughout the rigging. He bounced back up to her. *Faker!* She seethed at him. What a manipulative little weasel!

"I knew you'd change your mind," he said as he returned to the rail beside her. "Just get to know me, that's all I ask."

"And then if I tell you to go away?"

His smile faltered, as if it had lost its footing on a treacherous precipice.

"Then," he said, the picture of earnestness, "I'll leave you alone. For good. For real. I just think we're not that different, you and I."

"Really? I think we're as different as night and day."

Jonah shook his head, his eyes cast down toward the deck.

"I don't think so. We're both a long way from where we were born and we're both probably better off for not being there. We both want to do good things. We're both here, now. I think that's a fair amount in common."

"Are you this tenacious with everyone?" she asked him, marveling at his ability to be disarming. She wished she had such social graces.

"Only for the ones that deserve it."

"How do you know I deserve it?"

Jonah stared out over the sea for a long moment. So long that Tiadaria thought he might not have heard her. Then he turned to her, his eyes wide and bright.

"Call it a hunch," he said with his signature grin. He leaned in toward her, his lips dangerously close to hers.

She put both palms on his chest and shoved him back, hard. He hit the rail and almost tumbled backward over it, only keeping his balance by virtue of what she suspected were many years spent on the sea.

"What are you *doing?*" she yelped, calling the attention of a few men still up in the rigging. There was a loud round of snickering from above, and Jonah had the good form to turn bright red. His embarrassment was visible, even in the dim light.

He recovered quickly and took a step back. Tiadaria shoved past him and clomped across the deck, down the stairs, and toward her cabin. Only when she was inside with her back against the door did she stop to breathe. What in the name of nine hells had he been thinking?

CHAPTER SIX

Lying flat on her back, Tiadaria counted the number of knots in the planking above her bunk. Thirty-seven. It had been the same number the last twenty times she'd counted and had remained comfortingly constant while she tried to ignore what had happened up on deck hours ago. It was dark outside her porthole, and the oil in her lantern was burning low. It had to be the middle of the night. If she fell asleep right now, she might get a few hours before the morning routine of the ship roused her from slumber. Not bloody likely.

With a sigh, she sat up and swung her legs over the edge of the bunk. She hadn't bothered taking off her armor. If she wasn't going to sleep anyway, she might as well be dressed. Tiadaria almost wished they would come across Tionne and her pirates this instant. It would give her something to do that didn't involve brooding over Jonah and his ill-timed show of affection. He didn't even know her! Damned if she was going to be some kind of conquest.

Great. Now I'm getting all riled up again. She wanted to stomp around and work off some of her frustration, but the other sailors on the ship had the right to get some sleep. They didn't need her rampaging around like an angry child. Being as quiet as she could, she left her cabin and wound her way through the corridors and steps that led her back to the deck.

The night air was cool on her face and it braced her as she stepped out of the stairwell. A light breeze fluttered the sails above, making them snap against their lines as they took up the slack. The first few days at sea, Tiadaria was certain she'd never want to be on a ship again. Now, she wasn't so sure. There was something uniquely serene about being out on the open, endless expanse of water. Tiadaria went to the port side rail and looked aft across the water. Bobbing along behind them were the lights of their sister ship. The Falcon, she thought. Or maybe the Hawk. She wasn't sure. They looked pretty much interchangeable to her. Maybe she could get Jonah transferred to one of those ships. She'd have to inquire with Captain Odeon.

"You're up, too?"

It wasn't hard to recognize Jonah's voice. Tiadaria groaned. She whirled to face him and he took a step back, hands held up to stave off her aggressive glare.

"Of course I'm up," she said, her voice as cool as the wind blowing across the deck. "After that stunt you pulled this evening? I've been too angry to sleep."

Jonah lowered his head, shaking it slowly from side to side.

"Listen, Tiadaria, I'm sorry. I really am. I don't know what got into me, and you're right. You've got every right and then some to be mad. I know you don't owe me anything, but can you give me a second chance? Please?"

Tiadaria had a speech all ready to tumble from her lips. It was laced with venom, but the desire to sting him died as soon as he asked her forgiveness. She'd expected him to be brash about it, to brush it off as just another failed line on yet another girl. That he'd been contrite about his actions surprised her. It wasn't what she expected from him at all. She took a deep breath while trying to sort her thoughts and blew it out in a long sigh.

"All right," she said, waggling a finger at him. "A second chance, but if you screw it up this time…"

She let her words fade into the night, leaving the dire consequences of her fury remain unspoken. Jonah ducked his head and gave her a sheepish grin. He didn't look like a dashing sailor just then. He looked like a little boy all dressed up in his father's sailing gear. Tiadaria's heart jumped in her chest. Maybe she hadn't handled things all that well either. She was used to acting first and thinking later. Sometimes it got her into trouble.

"I guess I probably could have handled it better myself," she said at last, filling the lengthening silence. "You just took me by surprise. You're lucky you didn't get an elbow in the gut."

Jonah laughed, his rich voice breaking the stillness of the night.

"I suppose you're right. I'll count my blessings then." He thrust out a hand toward her. "To second chances, then, and not making enemies of new friends."

His grin was infectious and Tiadaria found herself smiling as she took his hand and gave it a firm shake. His hands were strong and well-muscled, but not as rough or calloused as she would have expected of a seaman. He must have noticed her puzzled look, for a flicker of something passed over his face as he withdrew his hand.

"What's wrong?"

"Nothing," she said. Then blurted, "Your hands aren't as rough as the others."

Jonah chucked again and this time the low sound sent a shiver up her spine.

"No, I don't haul lines or trim sails. My duties on ship are different." He took a step backward and folded his arms across his chest, tucking his hands under the opposite elbows. There was the faintest whisper of a sound and when he withdrew his hands, he held a six-inch dagger in each hand. The blades were black as midnight, and what she could see of the hilts were crisscrossed in a dark leather wrapping. He flipped the daggers over the backs of his hands, making them dance across his knuckles before rolling them back into his palms in a single fluid movement. "I answer directly to Princess Felyn. Along with Primrose, I guess you could say that I'm her personal Royal Guard."

"You're an assassin," Tiadaria said with a gasp.

Jonah shrugged, sliding the daggers back into the special pockets in his thick leather jerkin. "I prefer to think of myself as a problem solver. Although, I'll admit, my solutions to most problems tend to be rather...permanent."

"And you're here because?"

"Because the Princess thought you might be able to use one more set of skilled hands, and she needed Primrose with her. Odeon and his crew are a good lot and they're right deadly on the open water. They're not soldiers though. Get 'em on land and put a sword in their hand, and they're going to be worse than even the greenest of Torus's men. Princess Felyn wanted to make sure you had every opportunity to complete your mission."

Tiadaria gnawed on her lower lip as she thought that over. The Princess had given her no reason to distrust her. In fact, Faxon's behavior made it seem as if they were old and good friends. She'd given her ships readily for the mission to find Tionne. If there was any indication that the

Princess was on their side, that was a good one. If she felt that Jonah could be an asset, maybe it would do Tiadaria well to go along with it.

"And you're willing to listen to my orders and carry them out?" Tiadaria half expected him to balk at the implied confirmation that she was in charge. She was almost disappointed when he nodded with enthusiasm.

"Your wish is my command, Lady Tiadaria. That's why I wanted to ensure that we got off on better footing than we had this evening. The Princess made me swear to support you as if I was protecting her, so I'm bound by duty and honor to see that through. It wouldn't be impossible if you hated me, but it sure would make it harder."

"I don't hate you, and really, I'm thankful to have someone aboard who isn't a sailor. It makes me feel less like I'm the only one in the dark."

Jonah winked at her, his eye catching the faint light from the lanterns overhead.

"Oh, I wouldn't say that. I can find my way around a ship fair easy if I've got a mind to. I just don't very often. Too much work."

Jonah wrinkled his nose as if the concept of work was something best left to others. If he was in the direct employ of Princess Felyn, he probably didn't have to do too much to earn his keep. Tiadaria didn't suspect that there were many threats to the Princess while she was in Dragonfell.

"Well, I'll expect you to work when we find Tionne and her pirates." Tiadaria turned back toward the rail and gazed out over the sea. "*If* we ever find them."

Jonah stepped beside her and placed his hands on the rail, far enough from hers that she was sure it was a deliberate action. He looked out in the same direction and jerked his head toward the dark water.

"We'll find them," he said with more confidence than she felt. "If there's one thing you can count on in a pirate, it's greed. The shipways are lush with merchant vessels this time of year. I'll be very surprised if your pirates haven't stopped to take advantage of the rich waters along their way."

"Any idea where they might be headed?"

Jonah shrugged. "I'm with Captain Odeon on this one. I think they're probably holing up someplace along the Solorest coast. If we don't find them on the open water, we should be able to track them down once we reach Solorest."

"I hope you're right," Tiadaria said with a sigh. "For all our sakes."

~ ~ ~

It took Tiadaria several minutes to realize that the pounding she was hearing wasn't a function of her dream and was, in fact, someone pounding on the door to her cabin. She opened one eye and glanced about. She'd thrown an extra blanket over the porthole to block out the sun, but bright rays slipped in around the edges making motes of dust dance and swim in their brilliant illumination. At some point, she'd undressed. Her armor lay in a heap on the floor, and under the bunk's thin sheet she wore only her underthings.

"Just a minute," she called, rolling from the bed and snatching the blanket from over the porthole. Light flooded the cabin and she squinted against its sudden assault. "Great Gatzbin's gonads!"

She threw the blanket over her shoulders and cinched it around her body as best she could before she opened the cabin door. Jonah was standing there, peering at her with the most curious look on his face. He was fully dressed, clad head to toe in the supple leather armor he wore.

"You weren't still asleep were you?" he asked, a grin tugging at the corner of his mouth. He seemed to think better of it and schooled his features into something more neutral.

"Yes, I was still asleep," she snarled. "We were up until nearly dawn and then it took me another hour to fall asleep in the first place."

Jonah worked his jaw and Tiadaria was certain he was doing his best not to laugh at her. If she hadn't been clutching the blanket to protect her modesty, she'd have made damn sure he had nothing to laugh about. As it was, he gave a little nod of his head in the direction of the stairwell.

"Cap'n wants you on deck on the double. He thinks he's spotted smoke on the horizon. Might be the first sign of your pirates."

"Why didn't you say so?" Tiadaria tossed the blanket on the bed and rushed to the heap of armor on the floor. Jonah, to his credit, looked away as she slid into her breeches and tunic. Tiadaria adjusted the fall of the witchmetal rings and jammed her feet into her boots. She had to get down on her hands and knees and feel under the bunk for her sword belt, which she looped around her waist and fastened with nimble fingers. She brushed her long blonde hair back from her face and tied it in a crude knot at the base of her neck. She wouldn't be winning any beauty contests, but it was enough to keep it out of her face if things got interesting.

Tiadaria barged past Jonah and made for the stairs, getting a few steps before she realized that he wasn't following. The cabin door banged shut and he turned toward her. Now it was her turn to laugh.

"Well? Are you coming?"

Jonah recovered his composure quickly and they raced down the corridor and up the steps that led onto the deck. Tiadaria leapt over the railing to the deck stairs and took them two at a time. When she reached the top, she almost bowled over Captain Odeon who was standing just short of the stairs, peering through a long brass looking glass. Tiadaria skidded to a stop, narrowly avoiding running the Captain down. Jonah put a hand on the small of her back to keep her from going down the steps backwards. She glanced at him and smiled, giving him a little nod of thanks. He shrugged.

"There will be no running on my ship, young rapscallions," Captain Odeon said without lowering the glass from his eye. "Ships are dangerous places. Twice as much when you're carting weapons around. Kindly treat the Nightingale with the respect she deserves."

Jonah rolled his eyes and it was all Tiadaria could do to keep from laughing. Instead, she took a little breath to steady herself and answered as politely as she could.

"Of course, Captain Odeon. Jonah said you might see something?"

Odeon lowered the scope for the first time and locked her in his piercing gaze. There was something in his eyes that made her feel insignificant. As if he was weighing all her deeds, past, present, and future, in that one look.

"Too early to tell, Lady Tiadaria. We've changed course to investigate." He handed her the looking glass and extended a dark finger toward the horizon. "Just there, that haze above the water may be smoke. May be nothing, but it's the best lead we have at present and we're going to take it."

Tiadaria raised the glass to her eye and swept the horizon. It took her a minute or two and several sweeps of the glass to find the smudge that Captain Odeon was talking about. It didn't look like much to her, but as the captain had said, it was all they had to go on. She passed the glass to Jonah while she spoke to Odeon.

"How long?"

"As long as it takes, Lady Tiadaria." The captain shook his head. "Hard to say this far out, but we'll make the best time we can. I'd advise you to remain vigilant."

There was a snap as the sails that weren't already lowered unfurled. The ship crouched low in the sea on the starboard side as the navigator spun the wheel to take them toward the spot on the horizon that Captain Odeon had indicated. Jonah passed the looking glass back to the captain, who collapsed it and tucked it into his waistcoat.

Captain Odeon turned his back on them, shouting orders to the men up in the rigging in between hurried spates of instructions to the navigator. Jonah took her by the hand and led her down the stairs onto the main deck. He pulled her off to one side where they wouldn't be in the way.

"I guess we were dismissed," Tiadaria said with a laugh, freeing herself from Jonah's hand.

"Captain Odeon runs a tight ship. There aren't many captains in the Imperium fleet better than he is. Plus, he's a Theid. They're always a little aloof to start with." He paused, looked at her, and shook his head. "What's wrong with you?"

"Nothing, why?"

"Because you're bouncing."

Tiadaria hadn't realized it, but she *was* bouncing. She was up on the balls of her feet, shifting from one foot to the other. She was worried. She was nervous. Now that they might actually have to fight, the constant buzzing in the back of her head that reminded her of her lack of magic seemed to be twice as loud. It threatened to drown out everything else. She shook her head, trying to drive it back, but now that she had recognized it, it seemed content to stay where it was, mocking her every moment.

"It's nothing," she lied. "I've just got some nervous energy, that's all."

"Well save it," Jonah said. "Battles at sea can be tricky. There are a lot of moving parts."

"I'll do my best."

"Just follow my lead if things get ugly. Princess Felyn told me I'm personally responsible for your safety, and I don't plan on falling down on the job."

Tiadaria knew what he meant but couldn't resist needling him just a little bit.

"Is that all I am to you? A job?"

Jonah jerked back as if he'd been slapped. He blinked and then realized that she was joking. A slow smile spread across his face and he shook his head. "No. Not at all."

They both jumped as the ship's bell tolled above them. Once, twice, thrice it rang. In the distance, they heard the bells from the Hawk and Falcon answer back. Three chimes. Jonah looked out to sea, leaning over the railing to get a better look. He took her by the hand again and pulled her behind him, further up the deck.

"Come on, you're going to want to see this."

She followed him up to the rise in the foredeck where they could see alongside the massive ship. A rumble under her feet told her something was happening below the deck. As she watched, the doors on the side of the ship began to open one by one, starting aft and moving forward. Once the doors were open, the snub black noses of cannons emerged from their ports. There was a loud thud that reverberated through the ship as the guns were locked into position below.

"Guns ready!" came the shout from the officer of the deck. Above, on the rear deck, Captain Odeon stood with his hands resting on the rail.

"Guns ready, aye," the captain replied.

Across the water, Tiadaria could see that the other ships had readied their weapons as well. Tiadaria wondered if Captain Odeon knew more than he was letting on. She looked out across the bowsprit toward the horizon. There, looming ever larger, was a black cloud making its lazy journey into the sky.

Whatever was out there was burning, and they were going to meet it ready for war.

CHAPTER SEVEN

Tiadaria wasn't prepared for what they found when they finally pulled up short of the burning wreckage of a large passenger ship. Tongues of orange and red flame leapt into the air as if chasing the plume of smoke that had risen like the pall of a funeral pyre from the doomed ship.

Captain Odeon ordered his ships to maintain a safe distance from the burning hulk. There was nothing to be done but wait for the sea to claim the last remnants of the crippled vessel. A few bodies bobbed obscenely on the surface, but there were far fewer than Tiadaria would have expected from a ship that size. She supposed that there might be more bodies inside, but they'd never know.

As if sensing her thoughts, there was a mighty crack and the ship's hull gave way under the strain of the burning timber atop it. A fissure raced across the ship as it broke in two, like a cracked egg, and allowed seawater to flood inside. A loud hiss, like a thousand vipers, filled the air as the elements did battle with each other. Fire versus water, neither winning but both being transformed into something different altogether. A column of steam rose where the smoke had been, clearing the ash from the sky.

Jonah's mood had changed the instant they'd arrived. He stood at the rail, looking out over the water and drumming his fingers on the arms of his jerkin. Tiadaria could appreciate his agitation. There was nothing to be done here except mourn the dead. She wasn't sure that this scene would take them any further in their quest to find Tionne and her pirates.

Captain Odeon called for the long hooks and a few men gathered on deck and lowered the tools over the side. With as much care as the sea would allow, they snagged a body on the blunt hook and drew it up onto the deck. No sooner had it landed, when the men jumped back with a chorus of shouts. Some pleaded with the Eternals for mercy, and some made protective signs of hedge religions long dead. From her vantage on the rear deck, Tiadaria couldn't see what had upset them so.

She started toward the steps when Jonah grabbed her by the shoulder, holding her back.

"Wait a minute, Tia."

"I want to know what's going on."

"As do I, but there are things that are done a certain way on ships. Just wait for Captain Odeon to go on deck first."

Tiadaria shook her head. She couldn't understand why there were so many rules and traditions standing in her way. When she wanted something done, she did it. She didn't have to wait for someone to make a big deal out of it first. Still, if Jonah thought it was important, she could play along. She was relying on these people to get her to Tionne. She gained nothing by stepping on their goodwill.

Captain Odeon descended the stairs and motioned for the men to stay back. Not that they needed any encouragement for that. If the deck had been twice as wide, they'd probably still have been lined up against the opposite rail. As soon as Odeon's foot touched the deck, Tiadaria started down the steps. She thought she might have heard Jonah sigh, but she wasn't sure and she wasn't about to wait any longer to find out.

As she approached the body, she understood why the men had reacted the way they had. The body was a shriveled husk, its skin drawn back against the bones so that they appeared as hard lines under the taught skin. The eyes were rolled back, showing only white, and protruded from their sockets. That alone would have been gruesome enough for even the most stalwart stomach. Add to it that the body was covered with some sort of strange sores, and she could forgive the sailors their reaction.

As Odeon said some words over the body, Tiadaria crouched down next to it. Jonah joined her, but didn't seem overly inclined to get any closer than he had to. She hovered a finger over the body, not wanting to touch it both because of the sores and for fear of what the flesh would feel like. If it felt as waxy as it looked, she was certain she didn't want to experience it firsthand.

Tiadaria had never seen sores like this before. There was a dark ring on the flesh, almost like a bruise, though it was clear that little if any blood remained in the corpse. Inside the ring were a series of deep punctures, almost as if someone had driven a nail into the flesh around the inside perimeter of the ring.

"Have you ever seen anything like this, Jonah?" She didn't look at him. If she had, she would have seen that he'd gone pale under his sun-weathered tan.

"I've seen it. Too many times. I wish to the Eternals I didn't know what it is."

Jonah, who hadn't shown a hint of fear or uncertainty in the time they'd been on the ship together, sounded like a boy confronted by a nightmare in his closet. She wondered if the waver in his voice was real or if she just imagined it because his reaction was so visceral.

"What? What is it?"

"That, Lady Tiadaria," Captain Odeon replied for Jonah when his voice faltered, "is the worst thing you can encounter while at sea. Those are the bite marks of sirens. Many of them, by the look of it."

Tiadaria drew her hand back as if by proximity the sirens might find her as well. Not everyone got to go to sea on a fine warship such as the

Nightingale, but everyone had heard of the sirens and the horrors inflicted by them. Adept in commanding the forces of the Ethereal Realm in a way that even the Quintessentialists couldn't understand, sirens could beguile the senses and cloud the mind, luring men off passing ships and feeding on their very souls.

The tales were as old as recorded history and all ended with the same dire warning. Where there were sirens, there was no safety. Kill all you encounter without hesitation or mercy, for the denizens of the deep would show none to you. Tiadaria backed away from the corpse. Her skin felt as if it were covered in ants. She scrubbed her palms against her thighs, trying to rid herself of the dirty feeling.

"We need to get the body off the ship," Jonah blurted, finding his voice again. "It's bad luck."

This time, Tiadaria wasn't inclined to argue with superstition. She wanted to be as far away from the body as the sea would allow. At the same time, she didn't want to be the one charged with moving the corpse. It seemed indecent to just dump it back into the water, but there were no good alternatives.

Captain Odeon called to his men and for a moment, Tiadaria was sure they were going to revolt. Instead, they hesitatingly came forward with the hook and maneuvered the body over the rail and into the water. The body entered the sea with a splash, and the hair on the back of her neck stood on end.

Tiadaria stared at the spot on the railing where they'd pushed the body over the edge. It'd be easy, so easy, to follow the corpse down into the depths. In a few short moments, her worries would be over. All she had to do was breathe in the sea and wait for it to consume her. So easy. So quick. So safe. Before she quite knew what she was doing, she wandered toward the rail, the soles of her boots shuffling across the deck planks.

One of the men tending the hook reached the rail before she did. He climbed atop it, balanced there for a moment like a bird on a branch, and then stepped off the edge. In that moment, Tiadaria envied him. His long journey would be over soon and he would be at peace.

Her cheek stung and she put a palm to her face, turning toward the pain. Jonah's face was inches away from hers, his features twisted in a mask of fear and rage. She saw him raise his hand again, but didn't understand its meaning until he hit her again, rocking her head back with the force of the blow.

All at once, the world seemed to speed up. Men were shouting and a horrible high-pitched keening assaulted her ears. She tried to put her hands to her head to shut it out, but Jonah had her by the shoulders and was shaking her so hard that she thought her neck might break.

"Tia! Snap out of it! We're under attack!"

Those last three words cut through the fog like nothing else. Her alertness came flooding back, and she realized, belatedly, that she now knew firsthand what the enthralling magic of the sirens felt like. If Jonah hadn't been there... She pushed that thought out of her head. She couldn't think about that now. She had to focus. At least now she was aware of the danger. She could be more vigilant for it and fight it.

She'd have to. A quick glance across the water told her that men on the other ships had fallen to the dangerous lure. Bodies thrashed in the water, and she caught a glimpse of blue-green shapes flashing under the waves. Her hands fell to her scimitars and pain lanced up her arms, settling into her chest like a deep ache that threatened to consume her.

The fire within her breast would take her one day, but not today. Today she would stand and fight. The Nightingale bucked as if slapped by a giant hand. The acrid odor of burnt flashpowder filled the air. Cannons belched flame and smoke, and a hundred spouts of water leapt up from the sea as the canister shot tore into the waves.

A shout from the forward deck dragged her attention away from the cannon fire, and she saw a tiny blue body fly over the railing and land on the deck. It unrolled itself from its crouch and stood on stumpy blue legs. Its black eyes were huge and seemed to drink in the light. Short fingers tipped with black claws were perfect for rending flesh, and when it snarled, Tiadaria could see three rows of sharp teeth.

"Grobins!" Captain Odeon shouted, drawing his saber from the belt slung low across his hips. "Kill them all!"

That was an order Tiadaria could get behind. She spun her wrists, testing the weight of the blades she'd inherited from her mentor. The heft of them was them familiar. They were old friends who would eventually turn on her, but for now would serve as faithfully as they could.

Tiadaria tightened her grip on the blades and entered the fray.

~ ~ ~

Combat was one of the only things that made sense to Tiadaria on an instinctual level. She understood it. She could feel it in the pull of her muscles and the jarring impact of her weapons on enemy flesh. It was a deadly dance in which she was a skilled entertainer. At least, that's how it felt when she was in tune with the Quintessential Sphere. Out here on the ocean, she felt like a drunken fool, slipping and sliding through steps meant for another performer.

What came effortlessly to her through her connection to the Ethereal Realm took a monumental effort to reproduce without it. Her muscles ached, her bones felt brittle, and the constant fear of death loomed over her like a black specter perched on her shoulder.

Tiadaria forced herself to focus on the here-and-now, doing her best to ignore the protests of body and mind. She found a rhythm and stuck with it. The first Grobin to land on the deck was far from the last. As soon as she cut one down, it seemed as if there were two more there to replace it. At one point, looking down the length of the ship, she thought there must be dozens of them on the Nightingale.

Every now and again the flow of battle would slow as another wave of siren magic washed over the boat. Tiadaria got adept at anticipating these attacks, forcing herself to block out the impressions that bombarded her. She found that if she kept the image of the lifeless corpse they'd drawn out of the water in her head, it was harder for the siren magic to get a toehold.

As soon as she shook herself free of the intruding thoughts, she was back in the fight, her blades slicing through Grobin flesh as fast as she could swing her scimitars. Others had joined the fight with various degrees of effectiveness. For as clumsy and awkward as Tiadaria felt, Jonah appeared every bit the consummate artist. His motions were fluid, his body shifting from one foe to the next and seeming to bend at impossible angles.

Jonah's daggers weren't weapons, they were extensions of his hands. Warm flesh fused with cold metal to deal death with staggering efficiency. It wasn't long before the deck was awash in blood, both human and Grobin. Periodically the cannons would roar, firing their projectiles at the siren warriors who were circling the ships and flinging their Grobin minions onto the decks.

A number of Grobins had gotten into the rigging and were tearing through rope and sailcloth at a frightening rate. A boom swung free of its mast and Tiadaria only managed to avoid being swept off the ship by the narrowest of margins. She ducked under the speeding timber and rolled out from under it, allowing it to pass over her. A sailor behind her wasn't so lucky. He caught it in the chest and went sailing over the edge of the deck with a scream. The sound stopped as he hit the water and was dragged under by blue webbed hands.

Flames streaked past her and Tiadaria turned to see a siren, balanced on its tail, hurling magical fire at the ship. A fireball streaked toward her and Tiadaria turned her scimitar broadside to meet it. The projectile dispersed, bathing her in warmth. A second later, a sailor with a spear gun appeared beside her. He put one foot on the railing and took aim at a siren below. There was a thump as he pulled the trigger, the flashpowder driving a wicked trident from the end of the weapon. It struck the siren dead center, sending blue-gray ichor spraying from the wounds. The sailor crowed in triumph, shaking the spear gun over his head in both hands before kneeling to reload.

Tiadaria spun away from him, her blade slicing into the leg of a Grobin that was attempting to sneak up on the gun-wielding sailor. Another slice of the blade opened the Grobin's neck, ending its fight.

"Well, this is exciting, isn't it?" Jonah grunted as he threw one of his blades sidearm across the deck. The weapon buried itself in the eye of a Grobin who fell backward with a spasmodic lurch.

"How long can this go on?" Tiadaria said between panting breaths. She was exhausted and every moment longer was one where she might come dangerously close to faltering.

"I don't know." Jonah said. "Hopefully not long. Look."

He jerked his head toward the horizon and she saw either the Hawk or the Falcon was in flames. The other ship had pulled alongside and was trying to offer assistance as best they could, but it was clear, even from this distance, that they were overwhelmed. Across the din of battle, Tiadaria heard the ship's bell toll on the stricken ship. Five times it tolled, then five again, and a final five times. Jonah jerked upright.

"Oh, no," he said, his voice catching.

Tiadaria put her boot on the Grobin by her feet and yanked her blade free of the gaping wound she'd made in its chest. She looked up and found Jonah's eyes locked on the Nightingale's sister ships. They had drawn apart somewhat, as the flames on the burning ship had gotten too intense to allow for any sort of rescue to take place. Another five tolls on the bell.

"What? What does it mean?"

"She's lost," Jonah muttered. "Damn it. She's lost."

Before Tiadaria could ask him what he meant, a massive explosion tore through the stricken ship, sending a wall of shrapnel out from where the vessel had been. The Hawk, for she could see its markings now that it had turned away from them, took the worst of the damage with pieces of planking from the other ship tearing into her hull. Flaming pieces of debris fell on both the Hawk and the Nightingale, and men scurried to push the flaming wreckage off into the sea.

What was left of the Falcon slipped under the waves as the passenger ship had done not long before. The panicked cries of sailors in the water were too often cut short by the ravenous frenzy of the sirens who encircled them. They didn't have much time to consider the fate of the doomed ship. Another wave of Grobins had been launched onto the forward deck and they were trying to tear open the hatch that led below. Tiadaria didn't want to think what kind of damage they'd do if they got in among the cannons and flashpowder.

"Come on," she said, grabbing Jonah by the shoulder and spinning him away from the carnage and devastation out at sea. They had enough to deal with here. "I need you to fight. Are you with me?"

Jonah wiped the back of his hand across his mouth and nodded. His eyes had taken on a steely glint. They were almost as dark as the dagger he carried. He knelt to retrieve the knife he'd thrown earlier and wiped the blood off on his thigh. He nodded again.

"I'm ready."

They waded into the chaos side by side, blades flashing in the afternoon sun. Sweat poured down her face and into her eyes. She blinked it away, but moments later it was back, stinging and threatening to put her in danger. Her hair flew out behind her like a cape, having come loose from its knot in the heat of battle. She spun and dove, sliced and stabbed. One by one, the Grobins fell at their feet, laid low by one of the two fighters who were pouring everything they had into the battle.

It almost came as a surprise when they ran out of enemies to fight. Tiadaria spun in a slow circle, unable to believe that there were no more Grobins on the deck, yet it was true. None were left alive. Her arms and shoulders ached unlike anything she'd felt since Royce had first begun her training. He'd pushed her past her limits then, just as she'd done today. There wasn't a part of her that wasn't beaten, bruised, and sore.

Even so, she was proud. They'd come through the battle. She hadn't been able to rely on the power of the Quintessential Sphere and she was still alive. Maybe there was something to Faxon's assertion that she wasn't just the sum of her powers after all.

"I think that's all of them," Tiadaria said, her voice weary. She slid her scimitars, their Pegasus-shaped hilts stained with blood, into the scabbards. As soon as she released her grip on the weapons, she felt some of the terrible lethargy wane. She might not be able to control the Quintessential Sphere out here, but it still held her in its grasp.

"Good." Jonah slumped against the forward mast, rubbing his left shoulder. They hadn't even had a chance to breathe yet and Captain Odeon was rushing across the deck to meet them. Tiadaria groaned. What else could possibly go wrong?

Somewhere beyond the Nightingale, a ship's bell tolled five times. Tiadaria grimaced. Not another one. How many lives would be lost today? She listened for the rest of the bells that had foretold the doom of the Falcon, but they didn't come. Perhaps things weren't as dire as they appeared.

Captain Odeon skidded to a halt in front of them, digging his heels into the planks on the deck. He looped his saber through his belt and gave a jerk of his head toward the rear of the ship.

"Lady Tiadaria, the lookout reports ships on the horizon. Three ships, all flying the Bloody Cross. It might be your pirate crew, but the Hawk is in bad shape. She's likely to go under any moment. What do you want to do?"

CHAPTER EIGHT

"We have to catch those ships, Captain. No matter the cost."

"Aye, Lady Tiadaria." Captain Odeon gave her a long, appraising look, before he spun on his heel and began shouting orders to the men on deck. He climbed the steps to the rear deck as fast as his lengthy legs would allow.

Men scurried along the spars like squirrels in a tree, adjusting the rigging and trying to make repairs to the Grobin-inflicted damage as best they could. The main sails came down with the thud, fluttering for a moment before taking up the wind and billowing out to their full size. Tiadaria felt the ship begin to move and she ran to the railing.

As they pulled away from the scene of the battle, sailors aboard the Hawk rushed to the rail, shouting for help. The Hawk was beyond redemption. Its masts had been snapped and the main sails were ablaze. She had gone so low in the water that it wouldn't be long before the sea began to pour into the open gun ports. Once that happened, it would only be a matter of time before she started a one-way trip to the bottom.

Tiadaria closed her eyes. She wished there was a way to save everyone and still be certain of catching Tionne and her men. Even now, the odds were stacked against them catching up with the pirate vessels. If they did catch up with them, Tiadaria wasn't sure what was going to happen. It was their brave Nightingale against three ships of unknown strength. Who knew what horrid tricks Tionne had up her sleeve.

As the Nightingale pulled further away, the shouts from the Hawk increased in fervor and intensity. Jonah grabbed her by the wrist. His fingers were digging into her and she tried to pull away.

"You're hurting me."

"You can't do this," Jonah said, seeming not to hear her. "They'll die. Haven't we lost enough good men today?"

Tiadaria wrenched her arm from his grasp, rounding on him.

"We've lost too many! I'm trying to keep us from losing any more!"

"The Hawk is sinking. If it goes down, those men are doomed. Everyone left aboard that ship will die. They'll drown, or worse yet, the sirens will get them. That'll be on you, Tiadaria."

"Don't you think I know that?" She was shouting, and the men were looking at them. She didn't care. "What would you have me do? Save one ship and sacrifice the Imperium?"

"We can save both!"

"No, we can't!" Tiadaria took him by the shoulders and gave him a little shake. He'd look at her, damn it. This was important. When his eyes finally met hers, she held them. "You don't understand. If Tionne escapes, the entire Imperium could be in danger. Everyone. Every man, woman, and child."

"One woman can't wipe out the entire Imperium," Jonah replied with a shake of his head. "I don't care how powerful she is. It isn't possible."

"It is. You have to trust me. Tionne is evil. Pure, unfettered evil. She must be stopped. If we don't stop her, no one will. I need your help, Jonah. I need you to help me stop her before she brings about the end of the world as we know it."

"She's one girl," he snapped at her. "She can't possibly be that dangerous."

Tiadaria sighed.

"She is, Jonah. How much do you know about what happened in Dragonfell a few years ago?"

"Enough to know it was bad," he admitted slowly. "I stayed with Princess Felyn until it was over. I heard that they nearly breeched the palace."

"The city almost fell, Jonah. We lost a lot of good people then, too."

Tiadaria's voice broke as memories of Wynn came flooding back to her. She spent so long pushing them further from the surface of her mind, keeping them at bay. She was raw now, exhausted, and didn't have the strength to push them back. Images bombarded her. Wynn's body on the table in the hospital. His internment. Those first few mornings after the city had gotten back to normal when she had felt anything but. She'd kept expecting him to walk through the door with a witty turn of phrase or that boyish grin he'd always used to disarm her. He didn't. He never would again.

She swallowed hard against the lump in her throat and went on.

"Some of us lost more than others, which is why I have to make the right decision now. I have to do what's best for the Imperium. The whole Imperium. Not just the men on the Hawk. I mourn for them, Jonah, I really do. If there were any way to save them, I would. But there isn't."

Jonah stiffened and she was sure he was going to fight her. She could do it without him, but she didn't want to. She'd seen him fight. He could be an invaluable ally, but he needed to understand what was at stake. Really understand it, the same way Tiadaria did. His eyes softened and some of the rigidity left his frame. His eyes searched hers, and she wanted to turn away from that penetrating stare.

"Who was it, Tia? Who did you lose?"

"He was…" She trailed off with a sad smile and a shake of her head. "It isn't important. What's important is that I need you with me. Will you stand by my side? Will you fight with me? Will you mourn with me?"

Sudden inspiration struck her and she paused. They shared a common heritage. Even if it was something they were both removed from, they spoke the same language. In a more formal tone, she asked, "Will you speak the tales of the honored men who died here today?"

Jonah shot her a surprised look. It was clear that he hadn't expected her to ask that particular question. It was a matter of clan pride. To invoke that question was to confer the honor of being Lorespeaker. The Lorespeaker was a powerful spiritual member of the clan, responsible for keeping their oral traditions, and second in prestige only to the Folkledre. To ask Jonah if he would speak the tales of the honored dead was akin to asking him to bear their souls with him into the Ethereal Realm.

He nodded. Slowly at first, then with vigor, as if in making the decision he'd come to fully understand what was at stake. Tiadaria doubted he would truly understand it until much later, but she'd take what she could get.

"Yes," he said, his voice rough. "I'll stand by you. I'll fight with you. I'll mourn with you. I'll speak the tales of these honored dead, that none may forget the sacrifice they made for their people."

Tiadaria threw her arms around him, folding him into a hug that he couldn't have escaped from if he had wanted to. Her face was pressed into the crook of his neck. He smelled of man and sweat, of hard work and battles fought. She didn't care. He'd sworn an oath of sorts and she knew he'd stand by it. The hardest part was over.

"I just need you to trust me," she said into his neck. She felt him nod, and then she released him from her grasp. She pushed him back with a gentle touch, nothing like the shove she'd given him before. "Thank you."

Jonah's cheeks went red at the simple statement of gratitude and he ducked his head. Tiadaria reached out and put her fingers under his chin, forcing his eyes to meet hers again.

"Jonah. Thank you."

"It's fine. Don't make a big deal out of it."

He pulled away from her, pushing through a knot of sailors who had been watching them with undisguised curiosity. Tiadaria felt the weight of eyes on her and she glanced up to the railing around the rear deck. Captain Odeon was there, looking down at her. If he'd heard their conversation, he gave no indication of it. He stood, and he stared. He looked at her until Tiadaria, feeling self-conscious, looked away.

Jonah had made his way as far forward as he could go and was helping the sailors throw Grobin bodies overboard. He needed some space. *Got it,* thought Tiadaria. *No worries.* She crossed to the other side of the deck and helped another group of men there clear the bodies from that side of the ship. Some of the older sailors had brought mops and buckets from below and were swabbing the blood from the deck.

The knot of men who had been watching her interaction with Jonah had their heads pushed together, speaking in low tones. Tiadaria could only imagine the gossip they were engaging in. She was sure she'd have quite the reputation by the time they got back to Dragonfell. If they got back to Dragonfell.

The bodies cleared, she looked around for something else to do. Almost everyone was busy with some task or other. It wouldn't be long before they had the ship set to rights. Soon enough, the rigging would be mended, the sails patched, and the deck free of blood and bodies. All would be as it had been, clean and in good fashion.

Just in time for them to face Tionne and her pirates, plunging them into chaos all over again.

~ ~ ~

Tiadaria pounded the rail so hard that pain flashed up her arm all the way to the shoulder. How? How could they have lost the only glimpse they had of Tionne's ships? She'd given the order as soon as Captain Odeon had provided her with the information. They'd set out at once. It wasn't like her argument with Jonah had cost them any time. They were already underway when that happened. Yet somehow, like a wisp of smoke on the wind, Tionne had just vanished.

She scowled at the horizon as she prowled the width of the deck just behind the bowsprit. There was nothing for her to do but wait and hope they encountered the ships again and Tiadaria hated that. She liked problems she could face head on. Tionne was skilled at coming at you sideways. She always had been. Like a snake, that one. Slip right up to you and bite you in the ankle before you ever knew what happened. Tiadaria cursed violently under her breath and the one sailor who had been nearby working on the rigging retreated as if he'd suddenly remembered something more important to do elsewhere.

The men on deck were wisely giving her a wide berth. No one had said a word to her since Odeon had brought her the news that the lookout had lost their quarry. They were going to stay on the same course, Odeon had said. It was possible, but unlikely, that Tionne's crew had seen the Nightingale in pursuit. The haze of battle would make them difficult to see, and it was possible that Tionne's pirates would assume all hands lost in the siren attack.

Odeon gave her no indication of whether or not he agreed with her orders. Tiadaria was fine with that. She didn't need his approval. She knew the men would judge her for leaving the Hawk behind. That was their prerogative. Maybe, someday, they'd understand how near they had come to the bottom of the sea themselves. It was still a distinct possibility. They were outnumbered three to one. What happened next could end all of their problems very quickly.

She turned on her heel, deciding to go below and try to eat something even though she wasn't very hungry, and nearly ran down Jonah who had come up on the deck behind her. She stopped and took a step back.

"Sorry," she said, though Tiadaria knew full well it didn't sound as if she was sorry at all.

"It's all right," Jonah said, a faint smile tugging at the corner of his mouth. "I was wondering if we could talk. About before?"

"Listen, I'm sorry. I know I kind of shouted you down, but I needed you to listen to me and—"

Jonah reached over and gave her a little shake. "No, Tia. I was wondering if we could *talk*. You know, that thing were I say something, and you listen and think about it. Then you'll say something and I'll do the same. You've convinced me. You've rallied me to the cause. Now I just want to *talk*, okay?"

Tiadaria felt her ears go red and her cheeks burn. She was so intent on making him see that she'd only had one right decision that she'd failed to understand that he could have accepted it as she did. She nodded.

"Okay."

"Odeon told me that the lookout lost track of the pirate ships—"

"How?" Tiadaria interrupted. "How does that happen? How can they just be there one minute and just…just…not the next? I mean—"

Jonah reached out and put his finger across her lips and she stopped, jerking backward at the touch. Tiadaria considered slapping his hand away, but she had to admit that he was right. She'd gone off again. There wasn't much thought or consideration in that.

"Sorry," she said, somewhat meekly.

Jonah laughed.

"It's all right. What I was going to say was that we should go up in the secondary watch and see what we can see."

Tiadaria craned her neck, looking up past the rigging to the top of the foremast where the secondary watch was. The main crow's nest was at the top of the main mast and was very much off limits to anyone not a designated member of Odeon's crew, but if there wasn't anyone in the secondary, she saw no harm in it.

"Up there?" she asked, trying to guess how high the mast might be.

"Up there. You're not afraid of heights, are you?"

"Heights? No. Falling? Yes."

"You'll do fine, come on."

Jonah took her by the hand and led her to the forward mast. His grip was warm and inviting, nothing like it had been earlier in the afternoon when they'd nearly come to blows. He laced his fingers together, offering her a boost to the first set of pegs that ran up the mast. She climbed up a bit, and then looked down to see him leap up and catch the pegs on his first try. Jonah shimmied up the pole until he could get a good foothold, then grinned up at her. Tiadaria was impressed.

It didn't take long to climb up to the trap door that let them into the secondary watch. She had to take a hand off the pegs to push the heavy door up and over, allowing them to crawl inside. Tiadaria didn't care for that part much at all, and her stomach felt like it was filled with cold lead as she grabbed the edge of the opening and swung out over empty air before pulling herself through. She might not mind sailing, but she'd never make good crew.

Jonah followed her into the crow's nest and kicked the hatch shut with one foot.

"Wow," Tiadaria said, drawing out the word into a long sigh. She couldn't help it. The view was amazing. She could see for leagues in every direction. She almost thought she could see Dragonfell's harbor from up here.

"Quite the view, isn't it?"

"It's beautiful."

Tiadaria almost felt bad, that she could enjoy the rapture of such natural wonder in a scant few hours from when dozens of men had given their lives. It wasn't fair that she got to live and they didn't. It was even less fair that the responsibility for their deaths hung on her shoulders like a shroud. She shook her head, trying to drive off the negative thoughts.

"You did what you had to do," Jonah said, his voice soft.

"Am I that transparent?"

He shrugged.

"I think it's natural…and for what it's worth, I'm sorry I made it harder on you than it had to be."

"You didn't understand." She sighed. "I'm still not sure you *really* understand, but you trust me, and that's enough."

They stood together in silence for a long time. When Jonah's hand found hers and circled her fingers with his own, she didn't pull away. Thoughts of Wynn tried to push their way back into her mind, but she forced them away. Wynn was dead. She was living. That was the way the world worked. If they were lucky, someone would always be left to carry on. Tiadaria cut off that melancholy line of thought. The last thing she wanted was to be morose while perched precariously at the top of a mast.

Jonah dropped her hand and Tiadaria almost scolded him for his abruptness before she realized that he was leaning way too far over the edge of the lookout for it to be safe or prudent. She grabbed him by the back of the jerkin, worried that he'd tumble over and take both of them to their deaths. If they died falling from the top of the mast, who was going to save Solendrea?

"Easy!" she said as he leaned out. He jammed a finger toward the horizon.

"There! Do you see that?"

His excitement was contagious. She scanned the sea and saw nothing.

"No. Where?"

Jonah grabbed her hand and pointed it where he was looking. She saw nothing but a wispy white smudge on the distant horizon.

"There."

"All I see is a little smudge."

"That's it!" Jonah cried, quite pleased with himself. "That's what you were looking for. Those are clouds."

She looked again and saw what he meant. Far off, almost lost in the reflection of the sun, there was a white scattering of clouds in the distance.

"Clouds. Great," she said with little enthusiasm.

When Jonah turned to her, his face was lit by a wide grin.

"It *is* great, Tia. Clouds mean land. Land means I think I might know where your pirates are heading."

"Where?" she asked, plainly dubious.

"There's an old legend common among thieves and scoundrels, of an ancient city atop an island mountain. The city of Am'Corr is said to hold a great treasure, but as far as I know, no one has ever found it. There are hundreds, if not thousands of islands off the coast of Solorest. It would take ten lifetimes to check them all."

"And?"

"And what if the pirates have found it? What if Am'Corr is where the Horn is hidden?"

That spurred Tiadaria into action. They went down the mast twice as fast as they climbed up. Tiadaria paid no attention to the possibility of falling. She went down the pegs at a breakneck pace and skipped the last several altogether, leaping to the deck and racing for the rear stairs.

When they reached Odeon and the navigator, both Tiadaria and Jonah tried to speak at once, their words tumbling over each other to the point where neither of them made any sense.

"Quiet!" the Captain roared, shocking the pair of them into silence. "Now, one of you, tell me what's gotten into you."

"I need to see the navigation chart," Jonah said in a rush. "I think I might know where the pirates are headed."

Odeon peered at Jonah for a moment, then motioned to the navigator's shack standing off to one side of the rear deck. When Jonah pulled Tiadaria into the shack and in front of the table where the chart was tacked, Odeon followed.

Dotted lines, scribed with a charcoal pencil, traced their serpentine route from Dragonfell through the Strait of Seralt and down into the Siren's Sea. There were figures and notations scrawled around the edges of the chart, and though they appeared to be in the common tongue, Tiadaria couldn't decipher them. She assumed that it was terminology only a seaman would understand.

Jonah's fingers hovered over the chart, taking care not to smudge the notes that had been taken with such meticulous care. He dropped his finger from the 'X' that marked their current position and traced it south and west. The tip of his finger stopped on one of the islands off the coast of the southeastern continent.

"That's where we're going, Captain," Jonah said with a grin that Odeon did not share. "If I'm right, the ruins of the city of Am'Corr are on that island."

CHAPTER NINE

There was a knock at the door, and Tionne shoved the sketch she was working on into the desk and slammed the drawer. It wouldn't do to let the men see there was anything more to her than the bloodthirsty witch they'd come to expect.

"Enter."

Brait, her first mate, opened the door and took only a single step into the room. He held his black skullcap in his hands and the gold hoop in his ear swayed as he came to a stop.

"The siren wants a word, Cap'n. Your orders?"

Tionne liked Brait as much as she could like anyone. He was direct, loyal, and shared a taste for the brutal that made their domination of the Direwake complete. She lowered her head, running her long black hair between her fingers. Brait didn't stir. There was no indication he was even breathing.

They were maybe a day outside the island spoken of in the journal. She wanted nothing more than to sail full speed toward the island with no distractions, but Brait had said *the* siren wanted to speak with her, not *a* siren. That meant that Lord Yargen was keeping pace with the Direwake. If he wanted to speak to her, it would do her well to listen.

"Bring us to a stop and drop the anchor. Halt the fleet. I'll speak to him directly."

"As you say, Cap'n."

Brait left her as he'd come, silent and efficient. He pulled the door to her cabin closed behind him. Tionne went to the large casement window that graced the rear wall of her quarters. There were distinct advantages to being the Captain. The fine appointment of the cabin was one of the most tangible. She lifted the catch and pushed the window open.

It took some time for the anchors to be readied and dropped. Longer still for them to bring the impressive ship to a halt. Throughout the process, the water to the stern churned with unseen movement. Tionne found herself wondering if Lord Yargen had ordered some of his people to follow her ships. The Siren King had nothing to worry about. She wanted to see the Horn of Requiem returned to him as much as he wanted it back. There was something poetic about it.

The sirens had lost the Horn hundreds of years ago when the Shyraan, a slave race created as thralls for the sirens, had revolted and attempted to overthrow their masters. Though the sirens had prevailed in the subsequent conflict, the Shyraan had managed to steal a few very precious artifacts. Among them, the Horn of Requiem. The Horn was crafted by the finest craftsmen of the siren people. It was indestructible by human standards and Tionne suspected that the Shyraan found it likewise hard to dispose of. So they'd hidden it away somewhere that the sirens could never go. The top of a mountain.

Crafty creatures, the Shyraan, Tionne thought. They knew that sirens could only control a thrall within a certain distance from themselves. By hiding the Horn where they had, they'd made sure that the agents of the sirens wouldn't be able to get to it. A Grobin might have been able to make the journey, but they were of limited intelligence. Sending a Grobin could just as easily have resulted in the Horn being lost forever.

Lord Yargen broke the water, his deep blue skin tinged an unsightly gray. When he spoke to her, his words echoed inside her head like a voice down a long canyon.

"Daughter of Darkness, how proceeds the search for the Horn?"

"It proceeds well, Lord Yargen," Tionne replied, trying to disguise the irritation she felt at being called off task for this impromptu meeting. "We should reach the island soon, and be able to retrieve the Horn shortly thereafter."

"Make haste, Daughter of Darkness. Even now there is a ship in pursuit of you. You must not let them interfere."

"A ship? Just one? You're sure?"

The Siren King ducked under the water before he replied. Tionne sagged against the wall of the cabin as an image materialized in her head. Yargen was making her see what he had seen. A fierce battle between the sirens and three ships. Two of the ships had been sunk, but the sirens had been too weak to take on the third. It had escaped and was now chasing them across the sea. She gasped as the image faded away.

"A single ship only. It should be no match for your vessels."

All the same, Tionne wanted to be on the island before that ship managed to catch them. The sooner she was climbing to the top of that mountain, the happier she'd be.

"Understood, Lord Yargen. If you'll excuse me, we must set sail for the island at once."

"I would have you tarry a moment longer, Daughter of Darkness. There is something you must see."

Tionne ground her teeth. Lord Yargen had the same infuriating lack of urgency that afflicted Stryne. The dragon failed to understand that every moment wasted was a moment lost. If the ship that was in pursuit managed to close the distance between them in the time that she was catering to Yargen's whim, it would make things more difficult than they needed to be.

"Lord Yargen, with respect—"

"Lord Stryne told me that you would be amiable to my terms," Lord Yargen said, his mouth displaying the full ring of teeth around its inside edge. A sudden dread filled Tionne; a feeling unlike any she'd felt since that day so long ago when the Xarundi had invaded her village and slaughtered every man, woman, and child...save one. Her spine felt as if it were wrapped in ice. As her knees buckled from fear, she caught herself on the windowsill and managed to stay upright.

"I'm sorry! I meant no disrespect, Lord Yargen. I just wish to complete task I've been assigned."

"And complete it you will, Daughter of Darkness. As soon as you've done what I ask."

The terror that had filled her lifted like fog burned off in morning sun. Although she was no longer gripped by fear, Tionne felt cold and distant, as if there was still something inside her watching from the inside out. She shook her head, trying to dispel the unsettling feeling.

"As you wish, Lord Yargen."

"Secure your ship. I would have you join me in Selethrion."

The word meant nothing to Tionne. She shook her head. "I don't understand."

"Our greatest city, your..." his voice trailed away and she felt the presence in her mind move, like cold fingers poking into the dark recesses of her brain. An image came to her then, of Dragonfell in flames.

"Your capital," she said, trying to shut out the image. "Okay, I understand."

The presence withdrew. Tionne wondered if that's what being in a thrall felt like. If it was, she understood why the Shyraan had revolted. It was unsettling, at best. She went to a heavy brass chain that hung from a hole by the door. She gave it a tug and heard the distant chime of the bell on deck. She could count on one of the men to be down shortly for her orders.

While she waited, Tionne tried to rid herself of the feeling of being watched, but failed to produce any meaningful result. She couldn't very well demand the Siren King withdraw from her mind. In fact, she probably just had. She quickly thought that an apology was in order. She'd never tried to tame her thoughts before. It was harder than she would have expected.

A knock sounded at the door and Tionne opened it to see Brait standing there as he'd done not long before.

"Aye, Cap'n?"

"Brait, I'm leaving the ship. You have command of the Direwake until I return."

Something akin to disgust passed across the man's features before he managed to school them. He gave his head a little shake.

"Don't go, Cap'n." He lowered his voice to the barest whisper. "They can't be trusted."

If only he knew that Lord Yargen was very likely overseeing his betrayal for himself. Tionne wondered what Brait would say then.

"Your concerns are noted, Brait. I'll be fine. Please keep things in order until I return."

For a moment, Tionne expected him to defy her order. The men liked Brait and had served under him for a long time before Stryne had managed to exploit his contacts to put her in command of the Direwake. If he chose to try to take control, there was no telling what could happen.

"As you wish, Cap'n," he said at length and retreated into the darkness of the corridor. Tionne shut the door and returned to the open window.

Yargen was circling just below the surface. Tionne couldn't help but think of the predatory fish they'd seen earlier in their journey. Killing machines full of teeth and deadly intent. The sirens weren't all that different.

Putting the thought out of her head, she stripped off her flowing black dress and tossed it on her desk. She could only imagine all that material getting waterlogged and dragging her down below. Clad only in her underthings, she boosted herself up onto the window ledge. Her pale skin stood out in stark contrast to the dark wood of the Direwake.

"Come, Daughter of Darkness."

The time for hesitation, if there ever was one, was over. Tionne pushed off the ledge and dropped twenty feet to the water below. Pain like sharp knives pierced her as she plunged into the cold water. She tried to shout for help and found her throat filled with briny water. On the verge of panic, Tionne thrashed about, trying to find purchase. Strong hands lifted her from the water, holding her above the rolling waves.

She gasped for breath and felt a wave of comforting thought roll over her. It pushed the panic aside as a summer storm pushes the heat of the day away before it.

"Breath normally, child. I am here."

"I can't do this," she blurted. "I can swim, but not that far!"

"You needn't worry."

A strange feeling passed over her, starting at her feet and spreading up her body like a warm bath. As the feeling reached her head, she found she couldn't breathe. Her chest rose and fell, but no air entered her lungs. The first tendrils of panic gripped her again and the Siren King dragged her under the surface.

As soon as her head slipped beneath the waves, she was able to breathe again. Her hands went to her neck and slipped into soft folds that had appeared there. Tionne took her hands away from her neck and looked at them. Thick webbing had appeared between her fingers. Her feet, too. She looked at the Siren King and realized that the water wasn't murky at all. In fact, she seemed to see with a clarity unlike any she had ever experienced.

"Worry not, Daughter of Darkness. The transformation is temporary."

Tionne kicked forward, gliding through the sea as if she'd been fired from a cannon. She felt weightless and free. She tumbled head over feet, then returned to where the Siren King floated just under the surface. Tionne had never felt more complete.

"Does it have to be?"

~ ~ ~

Selethrion was nothing like Tionne had imagined. She had expected it to be as far from the human idea of a city as the siren's appearance was. In reality, the similarities to Dragonfell were striking. Homes and shops lined avenues that ran through the city. Gardens of sea grasses were tended by attentive workers. Young sirens chased each other around a large sculpture in the center of the city, swimming around, under, and through the structure in pursuit of their friends.

"Not what you were expecting, Daughter of Darkness?"

"Not at all," she admitted with uncharacteristic candor. Then she turned to look at the Siren King. "Why do you keep calling me that?"

"I found it fitting. You were born of darkness. I can see it in your mind. A tight black space from which you had to be freed before you could find yourself. Do you prefer another name?"

"Tionne. You can call me Tionne."

She looked at the ornate statue in the center of the square. The young sirens had drifted away, their games taking them elsewhere. They were alone. She wasn't sure why Lord Yargen's succinct appraisal of her early life bothered her, but it did. It felt like there should have been more to say.

She pushed the unpleasant thought away, instead focusing on the sculpture before her. It was easily twenty feet around and depicted a group of sirens in mid-battle. Ribbons of coral extruded in long thin fronds represented the surface of the sea. Beyond the coral sea, the shadowy forms of men armed with spears and nets loomed over the sirens' struggle. Scattered about the base of the sculpture were human bones. The meaning was clear.

Lord Yargen was watching her, but his pitch-black eyes gave no indication of emotion. He could be angry, bemused, or frustrated. She'd never know from his appearance. Tionne wondered if the telepathic nature of the siren's communication precluded the need for body language.

"You find the sculpture interesting?" the Siren King asked her as she swam to the other side to get a better look at the human side of the scene.

"I find it beautiful. I sympathize with your struggle."

"That isn't a very human feeling."

"Most days I don't feel very human." Something moved just outside her peripheral vision. She turned to see what it was. A group of three sirens were carrying another toward a building at the edge of the square. The siren being carried was an ugly shade of greenish gray and white fungus stood out in stark relief against the dark scales. Her stomach tightened. She wasn't sure if she was worried for Lord Yargen, afraid she might contract the disease, or both.

"What's happening there?"

"The plague offers no mercy based on station," the Siren King said, and Tionne could feel his grim amusement. "Worry not, Tionne. The plague is deadly only to my people."

"Time is of the essence," Tionne said, annoyed that the Siren King had brought her to Selethrion when she could be sailing toward the Horn and their salvation. "Why bring me here?"

"I have a gift to offer you. Come with me."

The Siren King led her down a wide avenue between buildings shaped from the seabed. She could feel curious eyes on her as they passed, but saw no one. She wondered if the sirens had been ordered to remain in their buildings until she was gone. The thought annoyed her almost as much as Yargen's instance that she come here. She wasn't a threat to them.

"They are afraid, Tionne. You are the descendant of a savage race. They do not understand you the way I do."

It was interesting, Tionne thought, that every story she'd ever read about the sirens portrayed them as the aggressors. Called *them* the savages. It felt strange and uncomfortable that such noble creatures could view her the same way. She was very quiet until they reached a large building that was obviously a royal residence.

Carved from white sandstone, the palace extended up as far as the eye could see. Polished rocks and crystals, as well as seashells of every type imaginable, were embedded in the walls of the palace. Flat crystals were set into window openings, flickering with muted magical lights. Outside the entrance were two huge sirens, perched atop the largest turtles Tionne had ever seen. Their sharp, hook-shaped beaks looked as if they'd have no problem cutting her in half. They wore reins of a sort, braided sea grass that the sirens held in one hand while wielding wicked tridents in the other.

As Yargen approached them, the sirens pulled back their mounts, clearing a path to a huge stone door that seemed to open of its own accord. Tionne wondered if telekinesis was a talent of the sirens as well. As they slipped past the door, she saw a much more mundane explanation. A siren with long white hair stood inside. As they entered, the siren pushed the door closed again and followed Tionne and Yargen into the palace.

The walls themselves seemed iridescent. They sparkled in shades of blue, purple, and green, lit by magical lanterns that hung from short chains in the ceiling. Alcoves held statues and trinkets, treasures that tugged at Tionne's imagination as they passed. She was, at once, torn by the need to leave as soon as possible to complete her task and drawn in by the desire to stay and learn more. Like every other human being, she'd heard stories about the awesome power of the sirens, but somehow in her mind that didn't equate to having built an entire civilization below the sea, complete with artists, craftsmen, and this wonderful palace.

They turned down a long corridor and descended further into the residence. Tionne tried to drink in every new thing she saw, painfully aware that the experience would be over all too soon. They reached a doorway, the doors themselves the gargantuan shells of some animal Tionne never hoped to meet. The siren who had been accompanying them opened the doors and waited for them to pass through. Then closed the doors behind them.

The lighting in this chamber was more subdued than the rest of the palace had been. Sparkles drifted down from the ceiling, floating serenely around the finely appointed room. Sculptures as ornate and detailed as the one in the center square were nestled in alcoves around the walls. Chests were piled high with all manners of treasure. Glittering gold in one, sparkling gemstones in another, and a shimmering substance that Tionne didn't recognize in yet a third.

"What is this place?" she asked once she felt as if she could breathe again. She'd forgotten altogether that she was hundreds of feet below the surface of the sea. *Poor Brait,* she thought, *he must be beside himself.*

"This room holds the amassed treasures of my people. Do not worry about your men. I sent an envoy to keep them apprised of your location so that they might have the ship ready for your departure upon your return."

"Begging your pardon, Lord Yargen, but why are we here?"

"As I said, I have a gift for you, Tionne."

The Siren King went to a chest and lifted the lid. From inside, he withdrew a coral box, no more than the width of her hand on all six sides. Opening the box, he lifted from it a length of fine gold chain crafted from links so small they were almost impossible to see. From the chain hung a pale blue, teardrop shaped crystal that seemed to pulse with a life all its own. As if somewhere deep inside it there was a flicker of light trying to escape.

She was at once flattered and irritated. No matter how beautiful the bauble was, surely it would have kept until after she had returned the Horn of Requiem.

"This is no mere bauble, Tionne," Lord Yargen said. She wondered if she would ever get used to having unspoken questions answered. "In fact, this is a powerful siren artifact that will aid you in your quest."

He opened the chain and motioned toward her. Tionne put her hands up to lift her hair out of the way only to find it floating up around her like a cloud. She laughed, the noise strangely lilting in the abyss. Lord Yargen placed the chain around her neck and closed the clasp.

As he did so, Tionne felt the full power of the Quintessential Sphere come flooding back to her. It coursed through her, waves of pleasure and pain flowing out from the base of her spine and dispelling the subliminal buzz that had been a constant annoying reminder of her handicap while at sea.

"Oh how marvelous," she breathed. She opened her palm and brought to mind memories of light and brightness. A will-o-wisp formed in her hand, bobbing gently in an unseen current. She snuffed out the light with a flick of her hand.

Tionne glanced at Lord Yargen and found his teeth aquiver. She wondered if that was the siren equivalent of a smile. She wished she had more time to find out. Right now, her duty to Yargen acquitted, she had a job to do.

"I release you to your task, Tionne. May you find that Wyrnett's Tear assists you on your journey."

She had the full power of the Quintessential Sphere at her command, she thought, almost giddy with excitement. There was *nothing* she could not accomplish.

True to Lord Yargen's word, the ships were ready to depart as soon as she returned. Brait himself hauled her aboard with a sour look at her new accessory. His disapproval was made clear by his silence. She gave the order to depart, and they set sail for the island where she would reclaim the siren's weapon.

CHAPTER TEN

"There! See it that time?"

Jonah was pointing at a darker purple smudge on the horizon. Tiadaria thought she might have seen something that time, like a yellow-orange glimmer at the very limit of her vision. If she was actually seeing something, and her brain just wasn't making things up, whatever it was had to be very far off in the distance.

"Maybe? I think so. A glimmer of light?"

"Yes!" Jonah's face lit up under the pale circle of light cast by the lantern hung on a hook above the forward lookout. "Those are your pirates out there. I told you they'd be heading for land."

Tiadaria was dubious. As much as she appreciated Jonah's enthusiastic reassurance, the fact of the matter was that they had no way of knowing if those were Tionne's ships or not. It could have just as easily been a distant storm on the horizon or even another vessel. It was a big ocean, but surely ships passed in the night on occasion.

"I hope you're right," she said, not wanting to dampen his excitement but feeling she needed to be realistic as well. "If they are, hopefully we'll be able to catch up with them soon."

"We will. If we are close enough to see their lights, that means we'll be able to catch up to them within a day. We're almost there, Tiadaria."

Jonah took her hand and she let him. He was positive that the little flicker of light they'd seen would be the culmination of their pursuit across the waves. Tiadaria didn't have the heart to point out that neither of them knew what would happen when they finally got Tionne backed against the wall. She might be young, but her youth did not at all diminish the danger she represented.

"Let's wait and see," she said, deciding that the cautious approach was best. He dropped her hand and gaped at her. Tiadaria sighed. She could always tell when Jonah was about to go off. He'd get this glint in his eye and once that happened, the only thing there was left to do was go along for the ride. His outbursts were like a sea squall, sudden and violent, but usually short-lived, and they were always followed by the return of his sunny, happy-go-lucky disposition.

"Why is it so hard for you to see the bright side, Tia? I mean, honestly. Isn't this why we're out here, to find those ships and stop them?"

"In my experience, the bright side is usually bright because there's something burning," she said with an apologetic smile. "I'm very glad that we may be near to reaching our goal, I'm just worried about what will happen when we get there."

Jonah frowned. He looked out to sea and then back to Tiadaria.

"I don't like that you don't believe we can stop her," he said. "It feels like you've already decided the outcome of the battle before the first blow is even struck."

"I haven't," she said, taking his hand and giving it a squeeze. "I promise. I'm just being cautious. That's all."

"I've heard a lot of things about you, Tia, but never that you were one to be cautious."

He hadn't meant anything by it, but his offhand comment rocked her back on her heels. It must have shown in her face because an instant later he had a panicked look on his face.

"Hey, what is it? What did I say?"

"It's nothing," she lied. It wasn't exactly nothing. She wondered who he'd been talking to, or more accurately, who'd been talking about her. It was true that she wasn't exactly known for her patience or forethought, but thinking those things about yourself was one thing. Hearing them echoed as fact by some distant third party hurt more.

"Tia, I'm sorry."

"It's nothing, Jonah. Forget it. They're right. I'm not known for my caution, but Tionne has taken enough from me in the past that it bears being careful this time."

Tiadaria looked past Jonah's shoulder out toward where the sun had slipped below the horizon not so long ago. The sky was still painted with pink and purple. Soon those colors, too, would fade into the inky blackness that was night on the open sea. The dark didn't bother Tiadaria. She was used to facing the monsters there, but she wondered how long the ghosts of the Captain and Wynn would continue to follow her around.

"Are you all right?"

Jonah's voice brought her back into the here and now. She gave him a little smile. For all his bravado and considerable skill as a fighter, Jonah had a good soul. For someone so adept at putting his blade in the heart of any who dared oppose him, he was very considerate of hers.

"I'm fine. Just thinking." She leaned in, kissed him on the cheek, and was pleased when he turned red, even in the dim light of the lantern. He dropped her hand and turned away from her. Tiadaria frowned. *Great! What'd I do wrong now?*

"I wish you'd tell me what you were thinking," he said, still looking out to sea. "I might not be able to help, but I can listen. I'm not stupid."

Tiadaria wasn't sure what to say. She knew that she'd been keeping those thoughts, the painful ones of Wynn and Royce, at bay because she didn't want to talk about it. Talking about it didn't do anything but reopen old wounds. The more they were opened up, the longer they'd linger and the more scars they would inflict.

Even so, it wasn't as if she could ignore that part of her life. Those experiences, no matter how painful, were a part of who she was. If Jonah was going to fight, and possibly die, beside her, didn't he deserve to know who she was? Good and bad? Light and dark?

"You're right," she said after a long moment of reflection. She heaved a sigh that seemed to bubble up from around her ankles.

"I just— wait. What?"

"I said you're right. I don't talk to you because I don't want to talk about it and that's not fair. I know you're not stupid...and you should know."

"Know what?"

"Everything there is to know. You said you wanted to get to know me better. Think very carefully before you answer my next question because there's no shutting this door once it's been opened. Do you really want me to talk to you? To tell you everything?"

"Yes!"

Tiadaria wished he had taken a moment to think about it. To consider the possibility that he wasn't going to like what he heard. Instead, he charged full-speed ahead in his typical fashion. If nothing else, she had to admire his steadfast belief that everything would work out in the end. She didn't know if she'd ever be able to be as positive about anything.

Still, he'd said he wanted to know, so she told him. Huddled together on the floor of the forward watch, they watched the stars appear overhead as they talked. As the night got colder, they clung to each other for warmth, and Tiadaria told him everything. Everything except for the clandestine truth of what she was. She justified that by thinking of it as an omission, not a secret. Jonah would be safer not knowing what she was. If anyone ever found out about her powers, it could be bad for anyone else who knew and failed to act on the information.

But she told him everything else. She told him of her father, and his betrayal. She told him of Cerrin's violation and her rescue by the Captain. She told him of her training and how she'd been expected to become a very different person in such a short amount of time. She told him of the changes and the challenges she'd faced. She told him of battles waged and won and the battles she had lost.

Finally, at long last, she told him all about the Captain and Wynn. She told him about how she had lost the only men she'd ever loved. Royce as a man who was more a father to her than the Folkledre had ever been, and Wynn, who had somehow managed to touch her heart even though they were so different. Perhaps in spite of it.

By the time Tiadaria was done telling her tale, the eastern horizon was tinged with pink and she was exhausted. It wasn't the lack of sleep that made her feel so utterly drained. She had laid out everything she was for Jonah and she almost felt bad for him. There was no way he could have known what he was in for when he'd asked her to tell him everything. In her defense though, he *had* asked.

Jonah was quiet for so long that Tiadaria checked to make sure his eyes were still open. They were. He was awake and alert—he just wasn't saying anything. She waited for him to say something, but he didn't. The silence lengthened and became a gulf, spanning the distance between them as the first rays of dawn breached the horizon and touched the sky with brilliant blues and oranges.

"Are you going to say something?" she finally asked, more than just a bit of a hard edge to her voice.

He looked at her and when his eyes touched hers, she saw something there, something that hadn't been there before. Jonah, who was usually so easy to read and wore his emotions like a badge on his sleeve, was inscrutable. Tiadaria wasn't sure what that meant, but she was fairly certain that it wasn't good.

"No," he said.

Great, Tiadaria thought. *That clears things up.*

Before she could lay into him, he leaned across the distance between their shoulders and put his lips to hers.

In that instant, there was something deep inside her that wanted to pull away, but every other part of her responded to his kiss with such urgency that the deep worry about the danger was drowned out. She wasn't thinking now—she was feeling. A sudden surge of warmth passed through her body, starting at her navel and spreading to the tips of her toes and the top of her head.

There was an electricity in his touch that was like link-shock, but so much better. He'd heard everything she had to say and this was his answer. He'd given himself to her, body and soul, heart and mind, and this was the only way he could show his utter commitment.

He'd said they would stand and die together. Tiadaria believed that now. More than anything, she knew that Jonah would be there no matter what happened…and there was a part of her that was more scared by that than any horror Tionne could dream up.

~ ~ ~

When they finally descended from the forward watch, Tiadaria and Jonah got some curious looks from the crew. None of the sailors said anything to either of them though, so she was content to deal with the furtive glances and whispers. Let them think what they wanted. It didn't matter to her. Jonah didn't seem to mind the extra attention, so she resigned herself to ignoring it. It was going to be a long enough day without adding anything she didn't really need to be worrying about to it.

They'd gone below for something to eat when Tiadaria felt something familiar wash over her. Her head swam and she had to lean on the table to keep her legs from going out from under her. A quick look around the mess hall and it was clear to see that everyone had experienced it. Trays were dropped from lifeless fingers and some of the men and women seated at the tables had slumped forward into their uneaten meals.

Tiadaria shook her head from side to side, forcing the intruding thoughts out of her mind. There were sirens nearby. She took Jonah by the shoulder and gave him a little shake. The cloudiness in his eyes disappeared and he was alert once again.

"Sirens," they said at the same time.

Almost as soon as they'd said the word, the bell above began to toll its alarm. The strident sound penetrated the mess hall and snapped those who hadn't recovered yet out of the stupor. Tiadaria had time to wonder at the marked difference of the siren's magic for just a moment before Jonah grabbed her by the wrist and all but dragged her up on deck.

When they burst out into sunlight, they were greeted by pandemonium. A few Grobins were already up in the rigging, tearing with razor sharp claws at whatever they could get their hands on. The forward sails had been torn from their mast, the shredded remnants fluttering in the ship's headwind. Near the far forward end of the deck, one of the seamen was protecting himself as best he could with the end of a mop handle.

Jonah jerked his head toward the man and Tiadaria fell into step beside him. As they ran, Jonah reached under his arms and withdrew the deadly blades he carried there. Tiadaria dropped her hands to her sides and stopped short. Jonah's momentum carried him for several paces before he stopped and turned to her with a quizzical look. She spread her hands across her waist and he grimaced, realizing what she had only just noticed herself. Her sword belt was still in her quarters. She'd taken it off last night before they ascended the forward watch and she hadn't been back to her cabin to retrieve it.

It was a stupid, amateur mistake and it grated on her. With a shrug, Jonah flipped one blade in his hand and offered her the hilt. Tiadaria took it, feeling the familiar bite of steel against her flesh.

"It doesn't have the reach of your scimitars, so be careful," he said, then turned back to face their common enemy.

Tiadaria hefted the blade, testing its weight. It was lighter than she would have imagined, but then, she was used to her swords that were at least four times the size. She wasn't confident in her ability to cut a steak with Jonah's dagger, much less defend the ship, but it would have to do. She couldn't very well go below to retrieve her weapons. Not while there were men on deck fighting for their lives. Tiadaria knew one thing for certain, this would be the last time on this adventure or any other that she went anywhere without her sword belt wrapped firmly around her waist.

As it often did, the battle took on a sense of time all its own. She waded into the fray with Jonah's dagger and did her best to dispatch the Grobins that were appearing over the deck rail at an alarming rate. The dagger was long, but even so, this was a style of fighting that was far too up close and personal for Tiadaria's peace of mind. She preferred the comfortable distance that her scimitars placed between her body and the enemy. It felt safer and less intimate.

A Grobin streaked past her, headed for a group of unprotected sailors aft of the main mast. Reacting without thinking much about it, Tiadaria stuck her foot into its path, tripping the stocky little creature and sending it sprawling on the deck. It whipped its head around to hiss at her and when it opened its mouth, she could easily count every triangular tooth in its gaping maw. It tried to scramble to its feet, but Tiadaria stopped it by plunging the dagger into the back of its neck, just above where it joined the stout body. The creature jerked once, and then was still.

Jonah had moved forward, almost to the great winches that drew up the anchors. There were Grobins attacking the chains with single-minded intensity. A swift kick with his booted foot and Jonah sent one of the attackers through the chain port and back out to sea. His dagger sought out another, sending a spray of blood across the deck as he nicked an artery.

"Jonah!"

Tiadaria only had time to shout his name. Two Grobins had appeared from the other side of the forward mast and were too close to Jonah for her to reach them in time. They leaped in unison, and a moment of fleeting panic flashed across Jonah's face as he realized that he wouldn't be able to avoid them both in time. The assassin threw himself to the deck, trying to flatten out his body as much as possible. It was almost enough, but not quite. One of the Grobins sailed over him with room to spare, but the other caught his jerkin with its sharp claws and clung on. Arresting its forward motion with Jonah's body, it raked its claws down his face.

Bloody furrows opened on Jonah's face and Tiadaria winced at the scream of pain that burst from his lips. He struck over his shoulder though the blood pouring down his face blocked his sight on that side. The blade only just nicked the Grobin, but it was enough of a distraction that Jonah could shake it free. By the time he'd done so, Tiadaria was beside him. She finished the creature off, plunging the dagger she held into its chest and giving it a savage twist for good measure.

She took a quick look around, and seeing that they weren't in immediate danger, helped Jonah to his feet. Tiadaria took the dagger and cut a strip off the bottom of her tunic, folding it into a pad that she used to mop the worst of the blood away. The wounds were long, but shallow. They'd missed his eye, which was good, but Jonah was bound to end up with some interesting scars.

"How bad is it?" he asked, recoiling from her touch as she prodded the wound to assess the extent of the damage.

"You'll live and have some fetching scars to add to your tales of adventure. I'm sure they'll be a hit with all the ladies."

He grimaced and gave a shake of his head. "The only lady I'm worried about is you."

"Well, then you're safe there. I'm hardly a lady."

Jonah didn't have time to reply. The lull in the battle had ended and more Grobins were being launched aboard the ship. Tiadaria noticed something different about this wave. They were slower than the first attackers had been, and their blue skin had a slight gray tinge to it. They weren't quite as fierce either. They still pressed the attack, but they seemed listless, almost distracted.

"What?" Jonah asked with a quirked smile, and then cursed as the motion pulled on his wounds. "Did they run out of front line fighters?"

"You noticed too?"

"How could I not? These little beasties did not bring their best game."

Cutting through the attacking Grobins took little time and as Tiadaria looked aft across the deck, she saw that the others were driving the attackers back easily. Seizing a moment's break, she rushed to the rail and looked over the edge. There were a few sirens in the water. She could see their blue-green bodies just under the surface, but none of them had breached the waves to attack the ship directly.

The Nightingale lurched to one side as the order was given to fire the cannons. Great plumes of seawater rose from the surface, climbing almost as high as the main mast. Blood stained the water and Tiadaria watched with morbid interest as half a dozen siren corpses bobbed to the surface, their bodies shredded by the canister shot fired from the cannons.

"Is it just me, or are they not putting up as much of a fight this time?" Jonah asked, appearing beside her at the rail.

"It's not just you. Something's wrong. Why attack us out here? There's nothing to defend."

"Nothing to us," Jonah replied, his tone thoughtful. He tentatively touched the torn skin on his cheek and winced. "Maybe there's something here we can't see. Something below they want to protect."

Tiadaria shrugged. "Possible, I guess, but it's not like we could reach anything down below. It doesn't make any sense."

There was a commotion aft of the main mast and since the battle had appeared to come to an anti-climactic end, Tiadaria and Jonah went to investigate. An injured siren lay on the deck, ichor oozing from what would certainly be mortal wounds if given enough time. It made a hideous screeching sound with its fanged mouth, compounded by the fact that one burly sailor in particular was prodding it with a sharp-tipped spear, opening new wounds.

Before she could say anything, Jonah dashed forward and snatched the spear from the man's grasp. The sailor tried to struggle for it, but Jonah neatly reversed the weapon and used the thick handle to sweep the legs out from under his would be attacker. The man hit the deck, hard, and an instant later, Jonah had his boot pressed against the man's neck.

"Is this how you treat a prisoner of war?" Jonah asked, his voice a menacing growl. "Would you like to be treated that way?"

Tiadaria watched as the group of sailors who had been cheering on their mate seemed to have second thoughts. They looked at her with furtive eyes and she made sure to make eye contact with every man there. She committed their faces to memory. War was one thing. Torture, altogether different.

The siren's screeching had stopped, replaced by a keening that, though alien, was very easy to understand as pain and fear. Tiadaria stepped forward, her hand still wrapped around Jonah's dagger. She knelt beside the hideous face, mastering her revulsion at being so close to such an unappealing creature.

"I don't know if you can understand me, but if you can, I promise to end your suffering as quickly as I can."

She lowered the blade to the siren's neck and with a single, clean motion, cut through the vessels there. It took only a moment for the faint light in the siren's black eyes to fade away. Jonah chased the sailors below deck, threatening them with the spear he'd taken from their leader.

"Wait until Odeon finds out about this. Those men won't see the outside of the bilge for months," Jonah said as he returned from the stairwell. Tiadaria was silent. She was busy looking at the body of the siren she'd just dispatched.

"Look at this," she said, indicating a discolored part of the siren's body with the tip of the dagger. There was a sickly whitish-yellow growth on the mottled skin. Tiadaria was no expert on siren physiology, but she knew when something looked wrong.

Jonah hunkered down beside her and took a closer look at the siren's corpse.

"Looks like it was sick," he said at length. "Maybe that's what was wrong with the Grobins, too."

"Maybe. If so, it would explain why they attacked us. They were desperate."

"But for what?" Jonah asked with a frown. "What could they have hoped to attain from us that would help them?"

Tiadaria shook her head.

"I don't know."

CHAPTER ELEVEN

"I have a working theory. Want to hear it?" Tiadaria asked as she approached Jonah.

He was sitting on an upturned crate with a whetstone in one hand. With the other, he steadied the blade of his dagger, resting on a piece of oilcloth laid across his knee. He looked up at her and narrowed his eyes with a playful smile.

"Don't have much choice, do I?" He waved the whetstone at his gear laid out before him. "I'm something of a captive audience and all."

"That's the best kind."

Tiadaria snagged her own crate and dragged it over next to Jonah. She swung her leg over, feeling the familiar weight of her scimitar resting against her thigh as she took a seat. She'd gone below and retrieved her weapons as soon as she was sure the battle was over. Jonah's daggers were fine weapons, but she never wanted to fight with them again. A wicked thought crossed her mind and she chuckled. Jonah raised an eyebrow at her.

"Nothing," she said with a toss of her head. "Just wondering if it says anything about my fighting prowess that you felt the need to maintain your blade after I used it."

For a split-second, Jonah looked stricken. Then he burst out laughing.

"That has nothing to do with it. I promise. Just routine maintenance."

Tiadaria arched an eyebrow.

"I'm sure you say that to all the girls."

Jonah chose that moment to inspect the edge of the blade he was working on.

"You said something about a working theory?" he asked without looking up.

Jonah was a shrewd man, Tiadaria thought with something akin to approval. He handled her well, even when her acerbic and sometimes boisterous nature got the better of her. He was a good… She'd been about to think replacement, but that wasn't right. Nor was it fair. Jonah wasn't replacing anyone. He was his own man, and a good one at that. If Jonah noticed the toss of her head as she shook off the errant thoughts, he didn't mention it.

"Right. My theory." Now that she was talking about it out loud, she wasn't sure it made that much sense to start with. Oh well. Too late now. She'd already told him about it. "We know the artifact that Tionne is after is some sort of indestructible weapon. What if it's related to the sirens' illness somehow?"

Jonah drew the blade across the whetstone and then peered down the length of the dagger before he replied. "Like how? You think it's cursed?"

"I hadn't thought of that," Tiadaria admitted. "I don't know how. Maybe it's cursed. Maybe they need it because it's a part of some ritual that keeps them alive. I haven't figured it all out yet, but it explains why they're relying on Tionne, of all people. It also explains their most recent attack."

"You're going to need to draw me a map, Tia. I'm not following."

"Well, they'd want to use Tionne because she's ruthless and has no sense of morals. She's killed innocents without provocation. From everything we know about the savage nature of the sirens, doesn't it seem likely that they'd choose those same traits in the person they wanted to retrieve their weapon?"

"That's a fair point. Okay. What about the attack today?"

"I think when they sank the Hawk and Falcon, they used up all their front-line fighters. I think that what we saw today was what they had left. They are in dire shape and that's all they could afford to throw at us. I don't think they were trying to stop us. They were just trying to slow us down. To keep us from catching up with Tionne."

"It's an interesting theory. If we're lucky, maybe they'll all die before Tionne gets her hands on their weapon. It would save us a lot of trouble."

"Jonah!"

He paused sharpening his dagger and gave her a curious look. "What? It's true."

"It might be true, but I'm not sure we should be advocating the extermination of an entire race just because it would be easier on us."

"Why? Isn't that what you said was key in the fight against the Xarundi? Wiping out as many as possible?"

"That was—" Tiadaria faltered. "That was different. The Xarundi wouldn't have stopped, ever. Not until humanity was wiped off of Solendrea."

Jonah uttered a mirthless laugh. "And you think the sirens are any different? You give them too much credit, Tiadaria. You have a strange sense of mercy."

She shot to her feet so fast that the crate she'd been sitting on skittered across the deck and slammed into the rail.

"And you don't seem to have any. I guess you lose your capacity for mercy when you'll kill for the weight of a crown."

Tiadaria stomped off. She heard Jonah's crate move. If he came after her, he was going to be sorry. She was furious with him. Both for his casual attitude toward wiping out all of the sirens they could and because he was right. This wasn't any different than her single-minded obsession with killing every last Xarundi she could find.

She hated it, but at least she'd had a reason for wanting the Xarundi dead. They'd taken Royce from her, before she ever really got to know him. He was a good man. A good teacher. She had learned so much from him, but there was so much more she could have learned. Like how to balance being a merciless killer for the good of the Imperium with compassion.

Tiadaria slammed into her cabin. The door hit the adjoining wall so hard that a muted objection came from the other side. She ignored it and kicked the door shut with one foot. She plopped down on her bunk and took a deep breath. It wasn't that long ago that her state of mind would have brought on tears. She didn't want to cry. Didn't need to cry. She was angry. What she wanted, what she *needed*, was to hit something. They couldn't catch up with Tionne's ships fast enough.

~ ~ ~

She wasn't sure how long she'd been sitting there when someone knocked on her door. Tiadaria really didn't want company. She ignored it, hoping whoever was calling would just go away. Especially if it was Jonah. She didn't want to face him just yet. He might have been right, but she didn't have to like it. The knock came again. They were persistent, whoever they were. With a sigh, she got up and opened the door. Jonah. Of course it was Jonah.

"Can I come in?"

Tiadaria had half a mind to close the door in his face, but she couldn't bring herself to add another insult on top of what she'd already hurled at him. She shrugged and stepped back from the open door. Jonah entered the cabin and paused, as if he wasn't sure what was going to happen when he crossed the threshold. After a moment's hesitation, he closed the door with a soft touch.

"Tia, I'm sorry."

"I know," she blurted. "I shouldn't have said— wait...what?"

"I said I'm sorry."

"What are *you* sorry for?" Her tone was incredulous. She'd been expecting him to lay into her about what she'd said. Not to come in and lead with an apology.

"For not understanding. You're trying to be fair. You want to see the good in people, even after you've seen so much evidence to the contrary. I shouldn't have tried to snuff that out...so, I'm sorry."

"I'm sorry, too. I don't really think you lack a sense of mercy. I was angry."

"I noticed."

They descended into silence. In that moment of respite, Tiadaria's mind was a tumult of thoughts, each racing around the other. It wouldn't be long before they reached Tionne's ships. When they did, they wouldn't have a moment of peace until things had ended, one way or other. Jonah was here. He'd come to apologize with his hands still covered in oil. He hadn't stopped to clean up before he'd come to her cabin. She rose in a single fluid motion and went to him. He took a step back.

"Careful," he said, showing her the backs of his hands. "I'm still covered in muck."

Tiadaria wrapped her arms around him, drawing him close. She brushed her lips against his ear. He smelled of brine and oilstone, of leather and old steel. It was comforting. She liked having him near her, so close that she could almost feel the beating of his heart.

"I don't care," she whispered in his ear, laying her head on his shoulder.

Jonah wrapped his arms around her, trying to keep his hands off her armor, and she laughed. Then he laughed, too. In that moment, things were right between them again and the world seemed to make sense.

"I really am sorry," she said into his neck, not for a second releasing her hold on him.

"I am, too. Truce?"

"Truce."

It was the first time in a long while that Tiadaria felt as if she could let her guard down and just be herself. It was nice. Jonah didn't expect anything from her. She could just be Tiadaria.

Something she could rarely, if ever, do in Dragonfell. When she invited him to stay, Jonah declined, seeing himself out.

"I want to stay," he'd said, standing at the door.

"Then why don't you?"

"Because it isn't the right time."

Tiadaria wanted to ask him when the right time would be, but she knew she wouldn't get anywhere. Jonah would decide when his 'right time' was, and there was little she could do to persuade him otherwise. Accepting defeat with a sigh, she bade him goodnight and closed the door to her cabin. She listened as his footfalls moved away from her door, and then she collapsed on her bunk.

She'd forgotten how exhausting men were.

~ ~ ~

Tiadaria was shaken awake by the roar of cannon fire. Her bones seemed to vibrate as the timbers overhead creaked and groaned. A moment later, someone was pounding on her door. She rolled out of her bunk still fully dressed. She snagged her sword belt off the floor and tied it around her waist as she went to the cabin door. She was unsurprised to find Jonah on the other side.

"We've caught up with Tionne's ships. We're about to engage. Cap'n wants all hands on deck."

Two more cannon volleys had been fired by the time Tiadaria and Jonah arrived on deck. An answering volley from one of Tionne's ships sailed past them and detonated in the water, sending spouts of seawater skyward.

"Nice of you to finally join us," Captain Odeon called down from the top of the rear deck. "Seems as if we've found your quarry, Lady Tiadaria."

Tiadaria jumped up the steps to the rear deck. She peered out across the water at the ships they'd been chasing for what seemed like years. They certainly fit Tionne's personality. All black sails and angular lines, with the pirate's crimson cross slashed diagonally across the black flag.

"We fired a volley of warning shots across her bow, Lady Tiadaria. She's turning broadside to aim her guns. If you're going to give orders, now would be the time."

"Send them to the bottom, Captain."

Odeon gave a mirthless chuckle. "We're still outnumbered three to one, Lady Tiadaria. But I'll see what I can do."

Hours seemed to creep by as Odeon's ship played mouse to the more agile cats of Tionne's fleet. A lucky broadside had sent shrapnel tearing through the mainsails of one of Tionne's smaller ships. It wasn't enough to take the ship out of combat, but it made it harder for the pirates to put the ship where it could be the most threat against the Nightingale.

Odeon wasn't the only one getting lucky, unfortunately. Shots from Tionne's flagship had slammed into the bow of the Nightingale, tearing open a wide gash in her side and destroying the three forward cannons on the starboard side. The damage was well above the waterline, so they didn't need to worry about sinking, but a small panic ensued as the men dashed around below to ensure that no errant spark reached the flashpowder magazine.

Tiadaria hadn't moved from the rear deck in all the commotion. She wanted to see those ships sink and to round up any of the men who survived as prisoners. They would take them back to Dragonfell to face the punishment they deserved. She was only partially aware that Jonah was standing nearby. He hadn't said anything since the battle had begun. Part of her wanted to ask his council, but the larger part was too consumed with the battle playing out to want to bother.

"Enemy ships moving to intercept, Cap'n!" the navigator cried. His grip on the ship's wheel was so tight that his knuckles were pale ghosts.

"Game's up, Lady Tiadaria. If those ships close off our route to Tionne's flagship, she'll escape and we're done for."

Tiadaria glanced up at the mainsails. They were full of wind. She had an idea, but Odeon wasn't going to like it.

"Can we make the ship any faster, Captain?"

"I can cut the anchors and the cannons free, but we'll be defenseless."

"We'll have to risk it. Bring the bow to bear on Tionne's flagship and make your run."

"Aye, Lady Tiadaria."

As Captain Odeon relayed the order, Jonah stepped up beside her and whispered in her ear.

"You mean to ram her! You can't be serious!"

"I do, and I am," she said without bothering to lower her voice. "We have to stop her. You heard the Captain. If those ships intercept us, we're done. As it is, we have to make it through their net before we can make a run at Tionne's ship. It's damn dangerous."

"Don't worry, Lady Tiadaria. We'll make it," Captain Odeon said with a grim smile. "Best crew in the fleet, I've got."

"Yes, Captain, you do."

There was nothing left to say. Given their orders, sailors scurried up the deck with wide-headed axes. They loosed the winches, allowing the anchors to drop into the sea, trailing their chains behind them. There was a jerk as the chains hit their limit, fastened to the winches by thick ropes that the men attacked with the axes. A moment later, the anchors were free and the ship jumped forward.

Tiadaria looked alongside the ship and could see the men in the gun bay pushing the cannons toward their ports with heavy levers. One by one, the cannons dropped into the sea and sank out of sight. Soon, the ship was almost empty of her guns. Tiadaria noticed that the last two cannons on either side of the ship were still aboard, but she didn't mention it. She wasn't sure the weight of four more cannons would make that much of a difference. As it was, the Nightingale seemed to dance across the surface of the sea.

Captain Odeon stepped up to the ship's wheel and took it from the Navigator, who stepped aside with minimal protest.

"My ship, my duty," Odeon said simply. "Go below and tell the men to rig the flashpowder magazine for a long burn. Then ready the boats, but keep them inboard until we hit. I don't want them getting fouled, and this is going to get messy. Get as many of the men to shore as you can."

Tiadaria had been so focused on Tionne's ships that she hadn't really looked at the island. They weren't too far off. If the men were able to get into the boats and away from Tionne's ships, they'd have a reasonable chance of making it to shore.

They were about to pass through the shrinking passage made by Tionne's two smaller ships.

Tiadaria held her breath. If they didn't make it through this narrow pass, all was lost.

It seemed like only a moment later and they were between the two ships.

"Fire!" Odeon cried, and thunder erupted from both sides of the Nightingale.

Tiadaria wasn't sure what the cannons had been loaded with, but it was clear that it wasn't normal shot. Great gouts of fire splashed out from where the shots impacted the enemy ships. Men and material alike were set ablaze. There was a low rumble and the last of the Nightingale's cannons were pushed into the sea, hissing like angry snakes as they disappeared below the waves. Both of the smaller ships were awash in flame and the Nightingale passed between them without incident.

"Impressive, Captain," Tiadaria said without a hint of irony.

"Don't be impressed yet, Lady. We still have to run the gauntlet."

Tiadaria looked toward the bow of the ship and her breath caught in her throat. They were on course, the bowsprit lined up with the middle of Tionne's flagship, but her cannons were pointed right at them. The bores on the weapons gaped at them like a dozen hungry mouths.

Tionne's ship rocked back as the cannons were fired, smoke and flame belching out from the gun ports. Instinct told her to duck, so Tiadaria did, dragging Jonah down with her. Facing Tionne's ship directly, the Nightingale presented a smaller target, which allowed some of the projectiles to pass by without harm, but they couldn't avoid all of them. Tiadaria watched as chains attached to the heavy shot ripped through the rigging, tearing down sails and cutting through masts like a saw.

The men on deck did their best to get out of the way of the falling debris, pushing it over the side where they could. To their credit, they were doing everything they could to keep the Nightingale moving swiftly toward her destiny. They were getting close now. Tiadaria could clearly see the men on the deck of Tionne's ship scurrying this way and that, shouting orders she couldn't quite make out over the din of their passage and the pounding of her own heart in her ears.

They were close enough now that she could see men through the gun ports of Tionne's ship working feverishly to load more shot. They'd never get the chance.

"Brace for impact!" Captain Odeon roared over the wind and sea and sounds of battle. "Prepare to abandon ship!"

The actual impact seemed to take forever, but happened all at once. It was as if time had stopped for a brief moment before impact, giving both ships a final breath before all hell broke loose. The

Nightingale slammed into Tionne's ship almost at the precise midpoint. Timbers shattered, sending jagged chunks of wood through the air in a deadly rain.

The Nightingale's bow seemed to fold in on itself before bursting at the seams. Tiadaria could hear seawater gushing into the lower decks like a waterfall. They'd almost split Tionne's ship in two, but not quite. Tiadaria looked over at the far deck and caught a glimpse of Tionne atop the stern, climbing to her feet with the help of the rail.

"Thank you for your sacrifice, Captain. Get to your boats. I'll keep them busy as long as I can."

"We'll keep them busy," Jonah corrected.

Captain Odeon nodded. He turned toward the deck and gave his final order aboard the Nightingale. "Abandon ship!"

Tiadaria and Jonah jumped down the stairs. Their feet barely touched the deck as they ran headlong toward the place where the two doomed ships were tangled. Tionne's men were milling about the deck as if dazed by the unexpected attack. Good. That would work to their advantage.

Reaching down, she clasped the scimitars and felt their familiar pain lancing deep into her chest. She took a breath and skidded to a stop near the wreckage of the joined ships.

"Ready?" she asked Jonah, indicating Tionne's ship with the tip of her blade.

"Ready as I'll ever be."

A running start seemed prudent, so Tiadaria backed up a few steps and hurled herself across the chasm of twisted planks and broken rigging. She landed hard on the other side, tucking in her shoulder and rolling across the deck to absorb the worst of the damage. Tiadaria paused just long enough to make sure that Jonah was across. She needed him.

Jonah landed on the deck more gracefully than she, taking a few steps to slow his stride and check his momentum. He reached under his arms and his daggers appeared. Two of Tionne's pirates tried to flank him, but he spun in a deadly dance of flashing steel.

Tiadaria had little time to admire his fluid attacks. Men were descending on her as well. She took a deep breath and prepared to fight.

CHAPTER TWELVE

Mortally wounded, the ship shifted and rolled underfoot, making it almost impossible for Tiadaria to keep her footing. Every time she turned to fend off an attack from one of Tionne's pirates, her balance was threatened. Timbers creaked and groaned around them, threatening to splinter and send her tumbling into the bowels of the ship. A dark, writhing shape streaked past her, and Tiadaria only just managed to avoid the bolt of ethereal energy.

Her eyes went to the broken rail of the ship, and Tiadaria half expected to see sirens in the water, aiding the pirates with their magic. Another bolt came toward her and she turned her blade to block it, protecting herself from the vile magic with the enchanted metal. She glanced up and saw a familiar form. Tionne was there, her flowing black dress billowing out behind her. Dark bolts of energy coalesced in her hands before being flung toward them from above.

Tiadaria didn't have time to ponder how Tionne was performing magic, but the question nagged at her. They were still at sea. They should have been on even footing. Yet, somehow, Tionne had found a way to channel the power of the

Quintessential Sphere. The sorceress brought her hands together and a black shadow sped across the deck. It hit Tiadaria like a wave, lifting her off her feet and throwing her back. She sailed through the open air before her back slammed into the broken shaft of a mast. Her breath left her in a rush. Jonah hadn't fared any better. He was laboring to get to his feet and retrieve the daggers that had been knocked from his grip.

When Tiadaria looked back to where Tionne had been, she was gone. The bow of the ship was pitching downward, making the deck tilt at a precarious angle. Most of Tionne's pirates had scampered away, working to lower boats from davits they swung over the side.

From the rail, Tiadaria could see many boats already rowing toward the distant shore. It was impossible to tell which of those boats Tionne's men were in and which were the Imperium sailors from the Nightingale. They would need to go ashore to figure out who was who.

Before she could turn to find Jonah, a massive explosion ripped through the Nightingale, pelting Tiadaria with flaming debris. For the second time, Tiadaria found herself thrown through the air. Her body screamed in protest as she managed to grab the railing with one hand. Her muscles burned with the incredible stress being put upon her body. As she dangled there, her eyes went to the churning sea below. Tiadaria threw her other shoulder toward the ship, groaning as her fingers scrabbled for purchase on the slick wood.

With great effort, she managed to pull herself back up onto the deck. She wouldn't be able to stay there for long. The Nightingale, the last of her structure shattered by the explosion, had pulled free of Tionne's ship and had almost disappeared from view. Tiadaria knew that Tionne's stricken ship would soon follow. Water was lapping over the front deck rail and Jonah was struggling to climb up the steep incline toward her.

Hand over hand, she lowered herself down along the railing toward him.

"We need to get off this boat before we go down with it," he called as she got close. She nodded, unsure of how they were going to suit words to action. Then she saw a number of men huddled near the most damaged part of the ship, trying to free a shore boat that had become fouled in its own davits.

"There," she said, pointing to the panicked men.

Jonah nodded and they made their way across the deck. Consumed with their task, the men didn't even notice Tiadaria and Jonah approach. She poked one of them in the back with the tip of her scimitar. Yelping, the man whirled on her, then stopped short, his jaw going slack. He must have realized they were no match for the weapons arrayed against them. He backed away, his hands in the air.

"Jump, or die," Tiadaria said, flicking the tip of the blade toward the water beside the stricken ship. "Your choice, but I won't say it again."

Tionne's men didn't seem terribly inclined to argue. One after another, they took the short drop into the water, leaving Tiadaria and Jonah with the entangled boat.

"Help me cut it free," she said to Jonah. Together, they were able to free the boat from the lines that held it fast to the davits. It was heavy, but not impossible for them to manage together.

"Other side," Jonah grunted as he pulled his end of the boat toward the far side of the deck. Looking down at the water, Tiadaria could understand his concern. The wreck of the Nightingale had left a field of burning debris below them that would be hell to navigate.

Tiadaria put her shoulder against the aft of the shore boat and pushed as hard as she could. Little by little, they managed to get the little boat to the opening in the rail on the opposite side. They heaved it over the edge and Tiadaria watched with baited breath as the boat slipped under water. When it bobbed back to the surface, she breathed a sigh of relief.

"Time to go," she said to Jonah. Without waiting for him to reply, she stepped out into the abyss and was falling.

Though the ship was already in the process of sinking, the time it took for her to slam into the water seemed immeasurably long. Cold seawater drove the warmth from her body and it took every ounce of her self-control not to scream as the ocean closed over her head. She kicked hard, pulling at the water to try to overcome the weight of her armor and weapons. She broke the surface and slipped below again. Tiadaria put her arms up, reaching for the little boat and finding no purchase.

A strong hand grasped her by the wrist and wrenched her upward. Jonah was in the boat, helping her board. He was soaking wet, too. *How had he managed to get inside the boat so fast?* Tiadaria decided she didn't care. With his help, she was able to roll into the boat, gasping for breath. While she recovered, Jonah pulled the oars from their rack under the bench.

"On your feet, soldier. We're late to the party."

Tiadaria struggled to sit up and took the oar he offered her. Somewhere across the water, there was another muted explosion. They were too far away to even feel the concussion wave. It must have been one of the smaller ships the Nightingale had disabled before ramming Tionne's ship.

Jonah was right. They were going to be the last of the boats to reach the shore, which meant that Tionne would have a considerable head start on them when they finally landed on the beach. Putting their oars to water, Tiadaria and Jonah rowed as fast as they could, trying to make up for lost time. No energy was wasted on talking. They both knew what was at stake and how many stood to die if they didn't prevent Tionne from retrieving the weapon.

They landed well down the shore from the rest of the boats, and Tiadaria was thankful for the moment's respite. As soon as they'd touched land, the unnerving buzz in the back of her head had snapped like a thread cut by sharp scissors. She felt the power of the Quintessential Sphere wash through her and breathed a sigh of relief. Jonah gave her a curious look, but didn't mention it. He probably just thought she was glad to be back on solid ground. He wasn't wrong about that.

Looking out to sea, Tiadaria took a quick tally and her heart ached. The Nightingale was gone. Where the gallant ship had been, now there were just bits of wreckage bobbing among the waves. Soon the tide would bring in what was left of the ships and deposit it upon the shore. The burning hulks of Tionne's other ships had been abandoned and were drifting along with the current. It wouldn't be long before the ocean claimed them as well.

Turning her attention to the beach, Tiadaria took a quick accounting of the sailors she saw there. Most of the men and women she knew by face, if not by name. She would have thought that there would be more unfamiliar faces among them, pirates from Tionne's ship who had also come to shore. In fact, she saw no one who looked as if they'd come from the doomed pirate ship. Even their boats were gone.

"Jonah," she said, a cold hard pit forming in her stomach. "Where are Tionne's men? Where are the boats? Where did they go?"

"What? They have to be…oh, how odd."

"We have to find them, Jonah. Fast."

"They can't have gotten far, Tia. We'll find them. They're probably just further down the shore."

They made their way down the beach as fast as the sand would allow. It was a constant battle to keep from slipping and sliding as the ground shifted under their feet. They were exhausted by the time they reached the makeshift camp the sailors from the Nightingale had started putting together. Odeon was perched on top of a salvaged crate, his waistcoat soaked through with seawater, barking orders to the men.

"Captain," Tiadaria called. "Have you seen the pirate's boats?"

"Aye, Lady Tiadaria." He motioned down the beach, toward a rock outcropping that jutted into the water. "They disappeared beyond the jetty. They had help getting their boats to the beach."

"Help?"

"Sirens," Odeon replied with a grim shake of his head. "And if I never see another, it'll be too soon."

~ ~ ~

As they made their way down the beach, Tiadaria wished she had a proper army. The men were brave enough and followed orders well, but they were poorly armed and armored. In fact, out of all of them, the only proper weapons were her scimitars, Jonah's daggers, and Odeon's saber. The rest of the men were armed with small folding knives of the sort that were popular with seamen. They were short blades, more suited to slicing fruit than flesh. Those who hadn't kept hold of their knives during the fight and landing had to make do with clubs crafted from tree branches or bits of debris that had washed up on the shore.

Odeon had picked the seven men who he thought would be best for their goal. He left the navigator in charge of the survivors left behind, ordering them up off the beach and as far away from the influence of the sirens as they could get. The navigator gave a quick salute and promised the Captain that he'd return to a camp in better condition than he left it.

Tiadaria didn't have the heart to tell him that she wondered if any of them would see the camp again. Realizing, in this instance, that discretion was the better part of valor, she kept her mouth shut. The look Jonah gave her told her everything she needed to know about his feelings on the matter. His eyes were dark, with no trace of the wry wit and quick humor that she'd come to expect from him. That alone was more than enough reason to worry.

The men were anxious and ready to fight, so Tiadaria gave the order to move out. They kept to the edge of the jungle as much as possible, taking advantage of the surer footing of the loam. It was easier to move there than over the shifting sands on the beach. Tiadaria did her best to ignore the sounds that came from deeper in the jungle—the snapping of twigs and the rustling of underbrush--that made it seem like they were being shadowed from deep within the trees. Tiadaria didn't know what kind of beasts made the jungle their home, but they had enough to worry about without adding natural predators to the list.

They reached the jetty and found it to be full of points and sharp edges. Climbing over it was going to take some time, but going deeper into the jungle to get around it would probably take longer still. Tiadaria resolved to go over it, and urged the men to be as careful as possible.

Some of the thinner rocks were as sharp as one of Jonah's daggers. One misstep could send them toppling to the bottom in a bloody mass of torn flesh. Fortunately, the top of the jetty had been worn down by the wind and weather, providing them a certain amount of safety.

"There," Jonah said over the roar of the incoming surf as he pointed down the shore.

Tiadaria could see Tionne's pirates busy setting up their own camp. They'd landed a good distance away from where the survivors from the Nightingale had. Aided, no doubt, by the sirens Odeon had seen. Fires were already burning on the beach and Tionne's men shuttled back and forth from the jungle to the fires like industrious insects.

"They'll see us coming," Odeon said with a frown.

"Not if we stick to the tree line," Tiadaria replied, motioning to the edge of the jungle. "We move faster there anyway. As long as we stay close to the jungle, we should be able to sneak up to the edge of their camp before they catch on."

"Then what?"

Tiadaria eyed the Captain. She'd heard that the Theid were notoriously aloof, unfazed by almost anything. It was hard to believe that they were such a stolid people, but here he was ready to wade into the fray without the least guarantee of how it might turn out. After having dealt with Odeon during the whole of their voyage, she was starting to understand how they got their reputation.

"Then we do our best to take them by surprise. We get as much information as we can, however we can. I need to know where Tionne went. Then I'll deal with her."

Captain Odeon gave her a curt nod, his own kind of salute, and began making his way down toward the beach on the far side of the rock outcropping. A moment later, his men followed, leaving Tiadaria and Jonah to be the last off the jagged rocks.

Working their way back to the tree line, they continued their slow advance toward their adversaries. As they got closer, they could see the work Tionne's pirates had undertaken. Some of the men were driving sharpened spikes into the sand around their makeshift camp. Others were using vines to lash together the boats and sturdy branches as shelters. Still more were knee deep in the surf, armed with spears or the occasional harpoon. A glint beside one of the fires caught her eye and she nudged Jonah in the ribs, calling his attention to the stacked weapons that the pirates had either stashed in the landing boats or liberated from the ship before their departure.

"Oh, good," he said, rolling his eyes skyward. "I was afraid our luck was going to change."

"What luck?" Tiadaria asked.

"Exactly."

"They are better armed, but we have the element of surprise on our side," Odeon said, his voice soft and even. "That may well tip the balance in our favor, provided we don't squander the advantage."

"So we charge them and hope for the best?" Jonah asked.

"Unless you have a better plan," Tiadaria said, hoping that he did. When he shook his head, she did her best to hide her disappointment. "All right. Let's get as close as we can before we reveal ourselves. The closer we are, the better. On my signal, we break and rush the camp. Try to disable them, if you can. We need information and dead men tell no tales."

Odeon nodded and his men indicated their understanding with unenthusiastic bobs of their heads. Tiadaria couldn't blame them. She wasn't excited about their plan either, but it was the best they could come up with in the time they had. The longer they stayed crouched at the edge of the jungle, the more likely it was that they'd be spotted by an observant member of Tionne's crew.

They moved slowly, but with a purpose. Tiadaria was thankful that the pirates hadn't had the time to extend their defenses all the way up to the tree line. Their attack would have been made much more dangerous if they had been forced to try and clear those sharpened stakes before they could get to the pirates. That minor good fortune aside, her misgivings about the plan grew with every passing minute.

Jonah held up a hand and they stopped. There was something moving in the jungle ahead of them. Cracking branches drew the attention of the pirates on the beach and Tiadaria breathed a sigh of relief. If they were focused on the jungle, they were less likely to be aware of the flanking danger creeping up on them.

Her relief was short-lived. A massive body erupted from the trees with an ear-splitting howl. Its thick fur was striped with yellow and orange. Even from this distance, Tiadaria could see the milky white claws that tipped each huge paw. She'd never thought she would see something that put a Xarundi's claws to shame, yet here it was, walking upright on thick legs banded with muscle. When it howled, it revealed a set of fangs that looked as sharp as knives. She wondered if it was too late to change her mind. Maybe Tionne finding the relic wouldn't be so bad after all.

"Is that…" Tiadaria managed to ask before her voice abandoned her. Jonah nodded, his eyes never leaving the creature.

"A feral Shyraan by the look of it."

Tiadaria knew that very few living humans had seen a Shyraan. They were a xenophobic race, not predisposed to allowing intruders on their land to live. She'd heard Torus tell the tale of a time he and Royce had been stranded on a deserted island and encountered them. His story was the only one like it she had heard. For one thing, he'd lived to tell the tale. She suspected not many did.

The pirates ran for their weapons, but the feline creature was terribly fast. It bounded across the sand, preventing them from reaching the blades stacked beside the fire. A huge man, rippling with muscle, was the first to challenge the creature that towered over him. He ran toward it as fast as he could, lowering his head and shoulders like ram. As the man got within arm's length of the beast, powerful claws raked across his abdomen, tearing open the flesh and exposing pink entrails. The man fell face first into the sand, his burbling screams cut short as he died.

Uncertainty spread across the beach like wildfire as the pirates tried to react. The Shyraan paced the sand between the pirates and their weapons. Tionne's men either found their courage, or realized they had no other option. They rushed the monster towering over them.

CHAPTER THIRTEEN

As impressive as the creature was, it was no match for twenty men rushing it at once. Claws flashed and jaws snapped. Blood spurted from wounds, staining the sand an ominous shade of crimson, but for all the damage the beast was able to do, it wasn't enough. A few of the pirates were able to slip past the frenzied Shyraan and grab their weapons. Being armed emboldened them, and they pressed in toward the creature, driving it back toward the forest with a frenzy of their own.

"Now's our chance," Tiadaria said, seeing the chaos on the beach as the pinnacle of their advantage. "Take them down, but try to keep them alive. We need information. They're no use to us dead."

Odeon drove his men down from the edge of the jungle and they careened across the sand, slipping and sliding as they went. Both the pirates and the jungle beast were surprised by this new quarter of attack. Some of Tionne's men tried to retreat, but the beast, more graceful than a human could dream to be on the uncertain footing, caught up with them in two great strides. They were cut down before they got more than twenty feet.

Rallying to the aid of their companions, the rest of the pirates closed ranks and advanced on the creature. In so doing, they turned their backs on Tiadaria, Jonah, and the others. They'd chosen to face the more savage foe, perhaps hoping that Tiadaria and the others would be more likely than the primal beast to let them live. She thought that was a considerable risk to take, but then again, they weren't offered an abundance of choices.

The feline creature's ears laid back across its skull and it hissed with low menace at the men approaching it with drawn steel. As if it recognized the odds against it, the beast wound itself into a crouch and leapt toward the trees with a single massive bound. It crashed through the dense undergrowth and was gone.

Tionne's men stood on the beach, staring at the spot where the Shyraan had vanished. Like Tiadaria, they probably expected it to reappear at any moment. They hesitated for a moment, then turned their attention on Tiadaria and her ragtag force of allies and sailors.

Blade clashed against blade, sending staccato echoes across the sands. The sound seemed to rebound from the edge of the jungle, amplified somehow, until Tiadaria thought that her head would split with the cacophony of battle. A bare-chested man with a red sash tied around his waist swung at Tiadaria, the tip of his blade passing so close that she felt the air move around her. She threw herself backward, into the path of another blade, and dropped to the ground, rolling away from the immediate danger.

She caught sight of Jonah, dancing in and out, under and through the much longer, deadlier blades that the pirate's wielded. His daggers seemed so small and inefficient for a battle being fought with swords and sabers, but somehow he managed to hold his own. He spun on his heel, avoiding the descending blow of a pirate's sword, and buried one of his daggers in the man's chest.

Blood burbled from the corners of wounded man's lips and dripped down his chin as Jonah pulled the dagger free. Then he was off again, ducking and lunging in the dance of death he performed so well.

Something tugged at the edge of Tiadaria's perception, a tingling feeling at the base of her neck. A warning from the Ethereal Realm that something was wrong, or that she was in danger. She assessed the space around her, finding no blade near enough to be an immediate threat. She'd rolled away from the combatants and no one was near enough to reach her.

Sudden pain bloomed in her left arm. Broken witchmetal rings sprung off her armor like startled toads as the damaged metal tried to constrict with the force of the impact. Tiadaria heard a sharp crack and it look a long moment, longer than it should have probably, for her to realize that one of the pirates was crouched behind a makeshift driftwood barricade. There was a smoking hand-cannon clutched in his grubby fist.

"Tia, GET DOWN!" Jonah roared.

In her head, Tiadaria heard the words as if they were echoing down a long corridor. The cobalt blue silk of her armor was stained a deep purple by the blood running down her arm. The arm of the witchmetal overlay, which gave her armor its strength and protection, was mangled beyond repair. An entire section of rings was missing and around its edges, the broken rings twisted outward like briar-thorns.

Tiadaria's brain finally caught up with the rest of her senses and she realized that the pirate was leveling his weapon for another shot. She threw herself to the ground and rolled toward a crate half buried in the sand. She heard the crack of another shot, but felt no pain. He had missed. She flexed the wounded arm, wincing as the injudicious movement pulled on damaged tissues. She'd be able to use it, but fighting with it was out of the question. Tiadaria rolled to the edge of the crate and peeked around it.

With a roar that rivaled that of the jungle beast, Jonah hurled himself at the pirate with the hand-cannon. He slammed into the man's chest, his momentum knocking the weapon from the pirate's hand and sending them tumbling across the sand.

The pirate screamed as Jonah's blades pierced his flesh. Then the screaming came to an abrupt end. If Tiadaria hadn't witnessed, first hand, the savagery of the attack, she wouldn't have believed Jonah capable of such brutality. Even once the pirate was still, Jonah's blades continued to violate the body.

Tiadaria pushed herself to her feet and stumbled across the sand. She stopped to retrieve the scimitar that she didn't remember dropping. It must have fallen from her nerveless fingers in the moments after the shell from the hand-cannon had passed through her upper arm.

Gritting her teeth against the agony that seemed to set her arm and shoulder ablaze, she slipped the blade into the scabbard on her hip and made her way toward Jonah.

A pirate rushed her, the tip of his blade low as if he aimed to skewer her through the middle. Though her left side pulsed with pain, her right was more than ready to attend to the dangerous business at hand. She brought the ready scimitar up, the ornate Pegasus flashing in the sun, and knocked the pirate's blade aside. He lurched to one side and her blade flashed down, raking across the back of his leg. Tendons were severed, blood was spilled. The pirate fell, screaming, face-first into the sand.

When she reached Jonah, he was still in the throes of his maniacal bloodlust. He didn't see her or anything else on the battlefield. He was consumed in his single-minded attack on a man long dead.

"Jonah," she said with some force, trying to snap him out of it. Then again. "Jonah!"

He couldn't, or wouldn't, hear her. He was covered in gore sprayed from the wounds inflicted by his daggers. Yet he continued to strike, again and again. Tiadaria wasn't left with much of a choice. She gripped the hilt of her scimitar as tightly as she could, and slapped Jonah in the shoulder blades with the flat of the blade.

The force of the impact knocked him off the body, sending him sprawling in the sand. The daggers dropped from his hands, sand sticking to the blood on the blades. Jonah gulped air and then forced himself to sit up.

"Tia! I thought you were…"

"I'm fine, Jonah. More or less."

"If you don't mind my saying, Lady Tiadaria, you don't look fine," Odeon said when he trudged up to them. His blue waistcoat was torn and stained, and a nasty gash parted the dusky skin of one forearm. "You're rather white."

"I could use a sit down," she admitted.

"Then do. The men have things well in hand."

Tiadaria glanced over her shoulder and found the battle, violent and bloody as it had been, was over. Odeon's sailors were rounding up the pirates who still lived and binding them to each other at wrist and ankle.

She sank to the sand next to Jonah. Odeon nudged the ravaged body of the pirate with the toe of his boot. His lips were drawn in thin line, but he remained silent, keeping his own council. Instead, he looked to Tiadaria.

"Now what, Lady Tiadaria?"

"Now we find out where Tionne went and I go after her."

Odeon regarded her with undisguised skepticism.

"With that arm? Do you think that's wise?"

"I'll manage," she said, her voice short. "Besides, I'll have Jonah with me."

Odeon looked at the corpse, then to Jonah, and back again.

"Indeed," Odeon said, and that was all.

~ ~ ~

After seeing what Jonah had done to their comrade, it didn't take much convincing for the pirates to turn on the man who had been Tionne's first mate. His name was Brait, a muscular Theid who shared Odeon's brusque demeanor. His bare chest was crisscrossed with the fine lines of old scars. Large gold hoops hung in each ear, and his teeth were alternating bone and gold. Brait was the very vision of a pirate and obstinate to boot. He seemed unlikely to give them the information they were desperate for.

"I guess you'll have to see if you can get anything useful out of him," Odeon said to Jonah as they stood near the prisoners.

That simple comment set off a near riot as the pirates who were bound alongside Brait tried to get as far away from him as their bonds would allow. His dark, weathered skin made it hard to tell for certain, but Tiadaria would have sworn that Brait blanched a bit under Jonah's cold regard.

"I have no use for a pirate," Jonah said, his tone almost conversational. "I could use the gold though. I'll take it out piece by piece and leave the body as a warning."

Jonah hunkered down in front of Brait and took the man by the jaw, forcing his fingers into the hinge and the big man's mouth open.

"Plenty of gold in here. Anyone have a pair of pincers?"

Brait whipped his head to the side, out of Jonah's grasp. The whites of his eyes were very large as he regarded Jonah. Tiadaria wondered if he was judging the man's ability to follow through on his threat. Tiadaria wouldn't have bet against it.

"I'll talk," the pirate said in the thick accent of the Southern Sea. "Just keep that one away from me."

Brait jerked his chin in Jonah's direction and Tiadaria waved him off. Jonah looked as if he wanted to argue, but Tiadaria wasn't in any mood for more delays. Every second they spent on the beach was another that Tionne was getting further away. Tionne had a mountain to climb, and that probably wouldn't be easy, but Tiadaria wasn't inclined to give her any more of an advantage than she already had.

Jonah moved off to the side, his eyes dark. Odeon raised an eyebrow at her, but, again, said nothing.

"Then talk," she said, turning her attention to Brait. "Where is Tionne, and how long ago did she leave?"

Brait jerked his head toward the jungle, too near where the beast had vanished for Tiadaria's peace of mind.

"Path there, leads up to a shrine. The journal we took from the merchant ship tells of a shrine in the center of a forgotten city. A Shyraan city. Am'Corr. In the shrine is the horn the Shyraan took from the sirens." Brait paused to spit in the sand at Tiadaria's feet. "The evil one is going to find it, return it to the Siren King."

The irony of Brait, a man who had no doubt sent countless ships to the bottom of the sea and killed more people than she could even hope to guess, calling Tionne the evil one wasn't lost on Tiadaria. She wondered what Tionne had done to earn that particular moniker among her crew.

There wasn't time to ask and it didn't really matter anyway. She had all the information she needed. If Tionne was following a path to the summit, Tiadaria and Jonah would follow the same path. They'd have to push hard to catch up, but Tiadaria was well motivated. She expected Jonah would be as well. If he thought that facing Tionne would put Tiadaria in danger... The image of the gutted pirate flashed back into her head and she did her best to ignore it.

"Captain Odeon, will you hold the beach until we get back?"

Odeon nudged the captive pirates with the tip of his boot and they shied away from his touch. He nodded.

"Aye, this lot won't be doing much from now on. I'll send a man to bring our people here. These folk were better prepared. More supplies and the like. Easier to stay here than try to take them back to where we landed."

Tiadaria nodded. She looked at Jonah. He shrugged.

"Ready for this?" she asked.

"Are you?" Jonah's eyes flicked to the damaged armor and the blood that had begun to crust around the tattered hole.

Odeon had looked at the wound before they'd started interrogating Brait. He'd said the projectile had gone straight through and cleaned it as best he could with the supplies they'd hand on hand. He'd wrapped it with clean cloth and shrugged, saying it was the best he could do. Tiadaria would have to hope that when it healed, she'd regain use of the arm. That was, of course, if infection didn't set in first. Trekking through a dense jungle on the ass end of the world didn't seem like the best way to treat a fresh wound.

"I'll manage," she said. "Let's go."

There was neither time nor need for a long goodbye. Odeon wished them luck and a few of the sailors waved them off with traditional expressions of speed and goodwill. Then they ducked past the hanging fronds of a huge tree at the edge of the jungle and slipped into perpetual twilight.

The difference on this side of the jungle was staggering. Where the beach had been warm and dry, lit with bright sun and welcoming, save for the battle they'd just concluded, the jungle seemed foreign and hostile. The air was thick and damp, crouching on their shoulders and around their heads like a heavy and ill-fitting cloak. Underbrush crackled and swayed as unseen creatures skittered about underfoot. For the first time in her life, Tiadaria wished she wore the thigh-high boots that were popular with some of the ladies in Overwatch.

As it was, her boots only came to mid-shin and seemed woefully inadequate against the unknown dangers lurking just out of sight. Even with

Jonah's considerable skill at tracking, it took them a few moments to find the head of the trail Brait had spoken of. Once they found it, it was a trivial task for Jonah to follow it. It was also clear that Tionne had passed this way. There were fresh footprints in the thin layer of mud that had settled over the ancient cobblestones that made up the path.

Tiadaria slipped into sphere sight, or tried to. As soon as her spirit form breached the Ethereal Realm, she was assaulted with such a jumble of living memory that pain exploded behind her eyes. It was all she could do not to cry out at the pain, and she quickly schooled her features lest Jonah see something was wrong. She needn't have worried. He was looking away from her, surveying the growth around them.

"Well," Jonah said with a hint of his characteristic humor. "I don't like this at all."

"Believe me, neither do I. Let's get this done and get back into the sunlight. At least in the daylight it doesn't feel as foreboding."

"It might when we've been here for a few weeks."

Tiadaria stopped short, torn between her sudden realization that they were stranded and the urgency of their task.

"I hadn't thought about that." Tiadaria looked at Jonah and he shrugged. "Do you really think it'll be weeks?"

"It could be. Depends on how long it takes Princess Felyn to miss us and how soon the search and rescue crew finds us." He glanced around the jungle, not meeting her eyes. "If they find us."

Tiadaria could have done without that last bit. She'd had enough of rough living when she was in the Frozen Frontier. She could survive, thrive even, on less creature comforts than the average city dweller, but she'd grown accustomed to those comforts and would miss them greatly.

She decided that she'd worry about all of that when they were done with their mission. A few long strides took her up the first gentle rise that would take them further up the mountain. After a moment, Jonah followed.

"Let's stop Tionne and then we'll figure out how we're going to get out of here. We can try to limit ourselves to dealing with one life-changing problem at a time."

"Actually, I thi—"

"Shut up, Jonah."

"Shutting up. Lead the way."

Tiadaria couldn't have guessed how long the path had been there. In places, the cobblestones that made up the trail had been pushed aside by the encroaching growth of the jungle, making it all but impossible to navigate. These were the places that it was easiest for Tiadaria to see the evidence of Tionne's passage. They were also the places that gave her the most hope. If Tionne had to cut her way through the dense foliage on her way to the shrine, all the better. Tiadaria and Jonah would have an easier time passing through and it would slow Tionne down. Though the situation was still urgent, Tiadaria would take all the help she could get.

They'd just pushed through a dense tangle of underbrush when Jonah dropped to a crouch, pulling Tiadaria down beside him. She groaned under her breath as his fingers tugged on the wounded arm, and he glared at her. She glared back, jerking her head toward the wound, still red with fresh blood. He dropped her wrist as if he had been burned, his quiet eyes seeking forgiveness but one finger still resting across his lips. Tiadaria remained quiet with a considerable effort. The pain in her head and the pain in her arm warred with each other for attention.

Straining her ears, Tiadaria listened for what had alerted him. It wasn't the first time she'd wondered if he might not be blessed by the Quintessential Sphere in some way that heightened his senses, but there was no link-shock between them when they touched. His abilities were just human skills honed to perfection. In a way, that made them even more impressive.

At last, she heard what he'd heard moments before. Somewhere up far up ahead she could hear a faint course of cursing. Tionne wasn't having an easy go of her journey through the jungle. Tiadaria couldn't guess how close she was, but if they were close enough to hear her colorful epithets, they were close enough to catch her before she reached the shrine.

Tiadaria unwound from her crouch and started forward. Jonah snapped his fingers once to catch her attention, and then shook his head from side to side with a violent motion. It was clear he didn't want her going forward. She looked at him and shrugged as best she could, trying to convey both her frustration and annoyance. Jonah held up one finger, and then pointed to his ear.

Trying to quash her irritation, Tiadaria hunkered back down and listened. Then she heard it and understood why Jonah was so reticent to move. There was something else out there. Something big lumbering through the forest growth, and Tionne, cursing up a storm like she was, probably couldn't even hear it. Tiadaria's eyes went wide and Jonah nodded.

Up ahead, a scream pierced the stillness of the jungle, startling birds into flight.

CHAPTER FOURTEEN

Tionne was still seething when she entered the jungle. That bitch, Tiadaria, had interfered with her plans for the last time. As soon as she got to the Horn, she'd see to it that the Swordmage, and everyone she held dear, were the first people to fall to its power. How dare she? Tionne took a handful of vegetation and ripped it out of the ground. Writhing pink grubs fell free from the clump of soil held together by the roots and landed on the toe of her boot. She tapped the edge of her boot against the almost hidden cobblestones and then ground the grubs under her heel until they were nothing but wet smears on the stone.

If only ridding myself of Tiadaria were so easy, she thought. Tionne's head whipped around as something snapped in the jungle behind her. There was something out there, something big, making its way between the trees. Tionne played statue, not moving so much as a muscle. There! A glimpse of yellow fur between the trees. There it was again. It was moving toward the beach, away from her. Good.

A howl echoed through the forest and Tionne winced as the sound violated her ears. Screaming from the direction of the sea told her that her pirates had encountered the beast. Tionne retraced the path to the edge of the jungle just in time to see Tiadaria and the others join the fray. Tionne glared at her from the safety of the semi-dark. There she was, swinging those ridiculous swords around. The ones with the stupid winged horses that swept back along the hilts. Tionne promised herself that as soon as she killed Tiadaria, her next act would be to melt them down for scrap.

There was nothing she could do for the men, not that she really wanted to do anything at all. They had served their purpose. They'd gotten her here. That's all she had needed them for. What happened to them now wasn't her concern. Her boot slid a little in the thin layer of soft mud that caked the cobblestones. She'd have to watch her step. The Swordmage would be following soon, so Tionne needed to get moving. She had little hope that the pirates would be able to dispatch Tiadaria on their own, even if the jungle beast were to help. The Swordmage was nothing if not resilient.

Tionne made her way back up the path to where she'd started clearing the undergrowth. She opened a space just large enough to squeeze through and then she was off. It wasn't long before she could no longer hear the sounds of war being waged on the beach, though she didn't know if that was because of the distance or because the conflict had come to an end. It didn't really matter. She couldn't rest. Not until she had the Horn of

Requiem in her grasp and was able to return it to Lord Yargen.

Navigating the ancient path up the mountain took far more time than Tionne would have liked. She wanted to harness the power of the Quintessential Sphere, blasting the undergrowth from her path or withering it at the roots to make it easier for her to pass. However, she found it more prudent to keep her strength in reserve. If she did end up facing off against the Swordmage, Tionne didn't want to be at a disadvantage. Every ounce of her magical ability would be required to end Tiadaria once and for all.

Tionne slipped into sphere sight, hoping to catch a glimpse of Tiadaria if they were in pursuit already, but the tumult of living memory that assaulted her was too much to comprehend. A dull ache formed behind her eyes and she shook her head, trying to rid herself of the last of the muddled impressions. The Shryaan must have done something to this place to protect it from Quintessentialists. Otherwise, it would have been a trivial matter for a mage as skilled as she to find the Horn's impression in the Ethereal Realm and summon it from the shrine.

"All right," Tionne said to herself, her voice low and angry. "The hard way it is."

The next barrier of undergrowth was even tougher than the first. Tionne slipped the curved obsidian dagger from the sheath on her thigh and

attacked the brambles. She found the entire task
was made a little easier if she imagined that it was
Tiadaria she was cutting through instead of a mass
of green and brown vines. She'd gotten rather
involved with it, hacking with glee at the plants
and imagining it was a finger here, a leg there,
when she noticed that the jungle had gone silent.

It had been quiet when she entered, but there
had still been some sound. There were birds
chirping to each other in the high canopy and little
animals scurrying around, hidden by the broad-
leafed plants that covered the jungle floor. Now
there was nothing. All was still. Tionne made a
second attempt at slipping into sphere sight and
the headache she'd been left with the first time
blossomed into outright agony. At the same time,
somewhere to her right, a branch snapped among
the trees. There was something out there.
Something watching. Something waiting.

Tionne turned to try to get a better look at
what was stalking her. A blur of orange and
yellow streaked through the trees toward her and
she screamed, falling backward over a mossy log.
Her knife knocked from her hand, Tionne was
defenseless as the massive feline creature towered
over her. Its claws were almost as long as the
blade she'd held seconds ago. Her long gown had
gotten snagged on the log she'd fallen over,
exposing an immodest length of pale thigh to her
attacker. Blood ran down one leg from a shallow

furrow in the flesh. She must have scraped it against a sharp twig as she fell. She'd been lucky not to be impaled.

The beast twitched its flat triangular nose, and the green eyes, as clear and bright as Tionne's, darted to the blood running down her leg. She was ready. As soon as the beast's eyes shifted, she brushed her palm across the blood. Tionne extended her hand, speaking ancient words of power that called to the darkest memories of the Quintessential Sphere. Memories of plague, suffering, and disease, and of dark, malignant things that grew in damp places.

Black tendrils of ethereal power crept from the palm of her hand, growing and multiplying as they fed upon the power in her blood and the will she exerted over the Quintessential Sphere. Snaking out, the tendrils searched for something to devour, finding the offering of the great jungle beast too tempting to resist. They streaked toward the feline monster, ravenous, and wrapped themselves around it, enfolding it in coils of living darkness.

Howls of rage shifted to a pitiful mewling as the tendrils slipped into soft places. They violated the corners of the eyes, the ears, the nostrils, and finally, cutting off one last pathetic squeak, the mouth.

Tionne watched, eyes half closed in the ecstasy of control, as the tendrils ate their fill. Blood was consumed first, carrying with it the essence of life. Then the organs and soft tissues. The creature's skin drew drum tight across the frame of its bones, leaving a withered husk that stood only under the control of the tendrils of darkness that had ravaged it.

Like a dozen angry snakes, the tendrils whipped back into the blood on her palm, returning to the Deep Void, whence they were summoned. Haggard and dry, like a dead leaf clinging to a dead tree, the corpse teetered for a moment and then fell to the ground. It crumbled where it hit, leaving only a sifting of ashen gray dust to mark the beast's passing.

Unable to move for a moment, Tionne listened to the sounds of the jungle. The chirping of the birds had returned. Once again, small animals scurried across low branches. Predator dispatched, life returned to normal. As normal as it ever was, anyway.

Tionne wiped her palm on the hem of her gown, tugging it free of the gnarled knot it had caught on. She scrambled to her feet, her eyes ranging here and there over the ground until she found the obsidian blade. Though it could be replaced, she'd spent a long time crafting that dagger and longer still imbuing it with the darkest magic from the depths of the Quintessential Sphere. She'd rather not reproduce the effort.

She slipped the dagger into the sheath on her thigh, working her way through the notch she'd cut in the undergrowth. Further down the trail, toward the ocean, she thought she heard a faint cry, but it was too far away for her to know for certain.

It didn't matter. The Swordmage was out there and that was all Tionne needed to know. She turned her attention to the task at hand and made her way up the ruined path as fast as her feet would allow.

~ ~ ~

Once the thundering of her heart in her ears died down to a reasonable roar, Tionne forced herself to slow down. Running headlong through a dangerous jungle was a good way to get herself killed. Besides, who knew how many of those cat-things there were out there. She had one goal and one goal only—to obtain the Horn and make her way back to Selethrion.

She stopped at the edge of a natural clearing, blinking against the brightness of the shaft of sunlight that penetrated the hole in the canopy. Tionne much preferred the semi-dark of the interior. Bright lights and open spaces made her feel far too exposed for her to be at ease.

She had just resigned herself to going around the edge of the clearing to appease her already taut nerves when a small cluster of purple berries near her feet caught her eye. She hunkered down next to the bush, peering between the spear-shaped leaves at the center vine. The main stem was a purple so dark it was almost black. She smiled to herself. Adderberries. Adderberries were a popular poison among assassins. Quick to act and deadly in small amounts, a single drop of juice from the berries would doom a grown man to delirium and convulsions before he slipped in a coma from which he'd never awake.

Glancing around the clearing, Tionne was quick to formulate a plan. She tossed a look over her shoulder, checking to make sure that the path was still empty of her pursuers. She had a little time, and a little time was all she needed. Plucking needle-like spines from a low-hanging vine, she pushed them through the center of a broad leaf and folded it over, making an envelope to carry the brittle thorns. Then she grabbed handfuls of vine and pulled them down off the tree. She set to pulling back thin branches from the sides of the trail, tying them down with the vines. Splitting the leaves of a fibrous creeping plant, she extracted a single long, almost invisible thread, which she strung across the cobblestones. Tionne stepped back, admiring her work. The tripwire was all but invisible.

Returning to the Adderberry bush, she pushed the tips of the needles into the berries with a slow, methodical touch. She was very careful to handle only the thick end of the thorns. The last thing she needed was to be felled by her own poison. When she had a handful of poisoned needles, she pushed them through the thick leaves of the branches she'd rigged on either side of the trail. With a little luck, the Swordmage would fall before Tionne even saw her pinched, ugly face.

There was more rustling in the trees beyond the clearing and Tionne froze, every fiber of her being alert for danger. She tried to slip into the Quintessential Sphere and found such a haphazard jumble there that her consciousness was knocked out of commune with the Ethereal Realm. She shook her head, trying to clear the hazy remnants of the mental assault. Adept in muddling the living memory of the Quintessential Sphere herself, Tionne recognized powerful magic when she felt it. When the Shyraan had hidden the Horn here, they hadn't just relied on the out of the way location to keep it safe. She'd have to be careful.

A brush pig emerged from the trees on the other side of the clearing, and Tionne let slip the breath she'd been holding. She checked the construction of her traps one last time and then began the slow process of making her way around the perimeter of the open area where the brush pig was rooting for food. The wrinkled little gray and brown creature might actually work to her advantage, Tionne thought. If it made enough noise, perhaps it would draw Tiadaria's attention and make Tionne's surprises even harder to notice.

It took her twice as long to go around the clearing as it would have taken her to go through it, especially since it seemed that every bush and twig snagged the fabric of her gown and threatened to tangle her up in her own legs. After the third or fourth such occurrence, she took her dagger and sheared the dress off just above her knees. Balling up the extraneous cloth, she stuffed it under a nearby bush and made her way back to the trail.

Tionne had only gone a few hundred feet and her pale legs were already crisscrossed with a fine tracing of red lines. Thorns and brambles tore at her skin as she made her way along the ancient cobblestones, pin-pricks of crimson welling up where the worst of the punctures happened. She didn't mind the pain. In fact, she rather enjoyed it. It centered her in a way that few things did. The distant sting in her legs helped her shake free the last of the fog that had entered her mind from her brief and disastrous foray into the Quintessential Sphere.

There was a boon in that, as well. If she wasn't able to use sphere sight, the Swordmage couldn't either. Tiadaria would have no way of knowing how far ahead Tionne was, nor the traps that she'd left waiting for them. There would be no surprises from that quarter. At least as far as warnings went, they were on even footing.

The light shifted again up ahead and Tionne stepped out from the jungle onto a broken path carved into the side of the mountain. The land dropped away on one side, giving a clear view of the surf pounding jagged rocks a couple of hundred feet below. Steps carved into the sheer rock face climbed at a dangerous angle and were narrow enough that Tionne wondered if she'd even be able to fit both feet on one at once.

As her eyes traveled up the stairs, Tionne saw that the narrowness of the steps wasn't the worst of it. About halfway up, a rockslide had destroyed the path, leaving only a small pile of boulders and loose shale in its place. Getting over that without sliding off the side of the mountain and being smashed into the rocks below would be an arduous task, to say the least.

She went to the foot of the staircase and looked up its length. She steadied herself with a hand on the wall as a feeling of vertigo washed over her. The clouds streaking past the blue sky overhead made her feel as if she were falling already. Tionne closed her eyes and forced herself to take deep breaths, calming the terror that was rising inside her. She hadn't expected her quest to include hanging in the open air on the side of the mountain. If anything less had been at stake, she'd have turned around and abandoned this madness.

Her throat made a loud click as she tried to swallow her fear, and Tionne was certain that it was loud enough for the Swordmage to hear, no matter how far away she was.

One foot in front of the other. One step at a time, Tionne told herself. Yet her feet didn't move. She was stuck as truly as if she'd been rooted to the spot by magic. Tionne tried again, lifting her boot from the ground and hesitating for a long moment before putting it on the first step. Surely it was only her imagination that the stone felt slippery as ice. Her hand sought purchase on the rock wall and found little in the way of comfort. The ridges along the cliff face were too narrow for even the tips of her fingers to get a good grip.

It took her several minutes, but Tionne was able to get up the first half dozen steps. With each painstaking step, the rockslide came closer to her. She stopped to take a breath and regain her composure. As she paused there, six steps up, a gust of wind blasted around the lee side of the mountain, racing along the cliff and puffing grit into her eyes. Tionne tried to take a step back, away from the unexpected assault, but her foot found nothing but open air.

Time seemed to stop as she threw her body forward, her arms thrown out, pin wheeling, trying to keep from toppling backward down the stone steps. Cold sweat broke out across her forehead and ran in rivulets from under her arms. At what seemed like the last possible moment, Tionne managed to keep herself upright, clutching at the step in front of her with both hands. She gripped it so tight that several of her nails split down the middle. She ignored the pain, refusing to let go. An inarticulate cry of panic and fear burst from her lips, and Tionne hated herself for that moment of weakness. There was scant hope that Tiadaria hadn't heard her cry.

The wind died down and the immediate threat to her safety subsided. Yet still, Tionne was unable to move. Forward or back, both seemed equally deadly. At least the way back wasn't barred by the tumble of rocks that blocked the path ahead. Tionne closed her eyes, resting her forehead against the cool stone ahead of her.

Behind her, she heard shouting from the forest. Her pursuer was getting closer. Tionne was running out of time.

With a deep breath, she took another step.

CHAPTER FIFTEEN

"Jonah, wait!"

He'd taken off as soon as he'd heard Tionne's shout from up ahead, and Tiadaria had lost sight of him through the thick underbrush. She could still hear the thudding of his thick leather boot heels on the path and that gave her some measure of comfort. As she forced her way through the heavy fronds, she heard him yelp in pain.

"I'm all right," he called back to her, as if he knew that her breath had caught in her chest as soon as she'd heard him cry out. "For now, anyway."

Tiadaria wasn't overly fond of the qualifier and increased her pace through the brush to the small clearing where Jonah was sitting on a felled tree. A trickle of blood ran down his arm.

"You're bleeding," she observed as she stepped into the clearing.

"Can't pull one over on you, can I?" Jonah quipped, but there was something strange in his voice, an edge that hadn't been there before.

"What is it?" Tiadaria asked, alerted by his shortness. "What's wrong?"

Jonah had produced one of his daggers and was cutting a throng of leather from his jerkin. He motioned toward the edge of the clearing with the tip of the knife. There was a branch hanging there and it took her a moment to realize there were needle-like spines sticking out of one of the leaves. She stepped forward to get a closer look.

"Don't touch it," Jonah snapped. "They're coated in poison."

Poison. The word sent cold coils of dread circling down into Tiadaria's stomach. Jonah's cry and the blood on his arm. That must mean…no. No. She couldn't lose another one. Not here. Not when they were so close to stopping Tionne and being able to go home. *Not all poisons are deadly, right?* Tiadaria wrestled with the panic that threatened to consume her. She turned to face Jonah.

He'd wrapped the strip of leather around his upper arm so tightly that it bit into his skin. Already the flesh below was taking on a purple hue.

"It's bad," he hissed through a sharp intake of breath. "Adderberry. There," he motioned again with the tip of the knife. "Edge of the clearing. That's where she found them."

Tiadaria couldn't care less about the source of the poison. It seemed that all she could see were the beads of sweat that stood out on his forehead and the pained look in his eye. She went to him, her fingers almost touching the wounds that were still weeping blood. He knocked her hand away, and then inclined his head, seeking her forgiveness.

"It's nasty poison, Tiadaria. Just touching it could be enough to make you sick."

"Are you—I mean, will you…?"

"I'll be dead within the hour, Tia." He shook his head and pounded his good fist into his thigh. "Stupid. I was stupid. I didn't even think to check for traps. I didn't think she'd have time. You need to be careful, there might—"

"Shhh, Jonah. Relax, please!"

Tiadaria wasn't as well versed in poisons and their effects as she could have been, but she knew that the rate of his heart would determine how quickly it spread through his system. She needed him for as long as he could stay with her. He got to his feet, swayed for a moment, then managed to steady himself.

"No time to relax, Tia. Every minute we waste here is another minute that Tionne is getting further up the mountain. I promised to get you to Am'Corr. That's exactly what I'm going to do."

She wanted to scold him and tell him to sit back down and relax, but she knew it wouldn't do any good. Jonah was as stubborn as she was, in his own way. She wondered if it might be a trait that was bred into the makeup of the clans. In any event, the lump in her throat would have made it impossible to argue with him, so she just nodded.

Before they left the clearing, Jonah snapped the branches that held the needles and made a cursory inspection. Finding no more traps, he led the way from the clearing, refusing to allow Tiadaria to go ahead. He'd already been poisoned, he reasoned. If he were struck again, the damage was already done.

Tiadaria thought there was a rather sizable hole in that logic, but she kept her mouth shut. They made their way through the jungle. The further they went, the more haphazard Jonah's footing became. He stumbled along the path in such a drunken manner that Tiadaria thought he might collapse at any moment.

She felt as if there were two of her. One of them knew she had to stop Tionne and prevent the Siren's weapon from falling into the wrong hands. The other one just wanted to sit and stay with Jonah until he had passed. She wanted him to rest his head on her lap. Tiadaria would stroke his hair and be as comforting as she could until he slipped past the physical realm and became one with the Quintessential Sphere.

She was furious with herself for being so ready to accept that he was going to die. Had she really become so jaded to the deaths of the men she loved most that accepting it seemed like the rational thing to do? What was wrong with her that the only men she loved or cared about died or were horribly injured in her presence? Only Faxon had survived, and maybe that was why he didn't come to visit as often as he used to. She wondered if he blamed her for the injuries he'd never quite recovered from. She'd never asked. She wasn't sure if she wanted to know.

It wasn't long before the jungle dropped away on one side, exposing a sheer rock face that plunged down to the sea. Jonah stumbled into the sunlight and, all at once, his legs seemed to go out from under him. He slid to the ground and Tiadaria saw for the first time how pale and drawn his face had become. The skin under the tourniquet was so dark a purple that it was almost black. Tiadaria got her hands under his arms and dragged him to the side of a large boulder at the tree line. She propped him up and his head lolled to one side.

"I'm so sorry," Jonah said, his voice almost inaudible above the roar of the surf below. He closed his eyes as if speaking were the hardest thing he'd done all day. "I'm sorry, Tia. I just can't go any further."

"It's okay," she said, going to her knees beside him. She took his head and pressed it against her chest, trying to convey all the things she couldn't say in that single, simple embrace.

Even though Jonah was in his final moments, her eyes were drawn to the cliff and the rock steps that had been carved there. Tionne was up there now, among the ruins of Am'Corr, seeking the weapon that would bring about a dark age on Solendrea. She loved Jonah. She could finally admit that to herself. But as much as she loved him, she couldn't stay. Tiadaria had to stop Tionne. Jonah would die a hero, but he *would* die. There was nothing she could do to stop it.

"I have to go," Tiadaria said, her voice no louder than his had been. She bowed her head and pressed her lips to his forehead. "I'm sorry."

Jonah opened his eyes and looked up at her. He opened his mouth, as if to speak, and then closed it again. He gave his head a little shake and a small smile tugged up the corners of his pale lips.

"I'll miss you," he said at long last. Tiadaria smiled. Three words, but not the three he was thinking. She could feel it in the air between them.

"I love you, too," she replied, and leaned in, brushing her lips across his.

His good hand caught in her hair and he crushed his lips against hers, as if in that single kiss he could impart all the things he wanted to show her for years to come. It was, as their relationship had been, powerful, short, and painful. Jonah sagged back against the rock, spent.

Tiadaria held his hand for a moment, giving it a squeeze. The flesh was already turning cold. It wouldn't be long before he was gone. Coward though it made her, she didn't want to stay for that, even if she'd had the time. She wanted to remember Jonah as he had been, not as he was now.

"Go," he said, with a forcefulness that belied his condition. "Stop her, before you run out of time."

Tiadaria rose, and with a last, longing look at the man she'd come to love, turned away from him and ran toward the stone steps that led up the face of the mountain. Her feet only just touched the stone steps. She ignored the wind that gusted around her, letting her momentum carry her forward past the resistance. When she reached a small rock fall halfway up, she vaulted it with ease, landing on the balls of her feet on the other side.

She was going to find Tionne, and when she did, Tiadaria was going to kill her.

~ ~ ~

Though his vision was beginning to blur around the edges, Jonah watched Tiadaria's blue and gray form ascend the mountain as if she were a creature possessed. She didn't seem to touch the steps, but rather hover above them as she made the perilous climb seem like no more than a child's game. She rounded a corner and was gone.

With nothing left to focus on, Jonah came to the startling realization that he could no longer feel his legs. He tried to bend his knees and found himself unable to perform even that simple task. *It won't be long now,* he thought. The aching cold that had climbed up through his limbs was working its way under his breastbone. Soon it would stop his heart and he'd slip into the Ethereal Realm.

Jonah managed a chuckle. He was an assassin. He'd dealt death with dozens of poisons and concoctions, but never imagined he'd have an urgent need for an antidote himself. On the mainland, he carried half a dozen vials of poison on his person as a matter of course, but never the cures. He wondered if this revelation might be his final moment of clarity, and then decided not to worry about it. Whatever would happen, would happen. There was little he could do about it now.

His eyes landed on the leather throng that was buried deep in the flesh of his arm. The fingers had gone numb, almost as dead as his legs felt. That tiny piece of leather was the only thing that had kept him alive this long. If he loosened it, it would speed along his descent into the darkness.

Jonah's fingers brushed against the knot, then stopped. If he were to remove the tourniquet, it would be the same as admitting defeat. He'd never done that before and wasn't sure if he could do it now. The tightened band was giving him a fighting chance. A certain pride went through him at the thought of not giving in. Even though there was no one else to know of his struggle, at least he would die knowing he fought until the bitter end.

Jonah blinked, trying to clear the flashes of pink, yellow, and green that invaded his vision. He seemed to be hearing things as well. Fragments of sounds came to him in bursts. Shouts, the roar of the sea, clinking of glasses. The sweet, almost lyrical voice of the barmaid in his favorite tavern in Dragonfell. Grunts and groans, the sounds of death, and a siren's call.

He shook his head, sure now that he was hallucinating at least half of what he saw and heard, if not all of it. That moment of lucidity was a blessing and it allowed him to relax in the final throes of the poison's grasp. No matter what he saw, or heard, or felt, he would be beyond all of it soon and there was a peace in that knowledge that was hard to describe.

Jonah closed his eyes and waited for the Ethereal Realm to call him to its warm embrace. After a few moments, he opened his eyes again. He wondered for a moment if he hadn't already died. No, he was still on the ground near the stone stairs. His back was still pressed against the bolder and there was still a jagged piece of stone pressing into the small of his back.

Black splotches danced across his eyes, fading in and out and making it impossible to make things out clearly. There was a dark shape before him, a towering form that seemed too big to be a man.

Rough hands grabbed him by the injured arm and he tried to protest. Jonah found that his mouth wouldn't work. It fell open, his swollen tongue lolling from between his teeth. A moment later, searing pain flashed down his arm. Somewhere, at the very edge of his consciousness, he realized that the leather band had been removed and blood was rushing down into his arm. Jonah found the strength to scream.

What his body managed to produce, however, was little more than a throaty croak. Something bitter was pushed under his tongue with what felt like a long feather. He tried to spit it out, but powerful hands held Jonah's jaw closed, massaging his throat until he was forced to swallow. He gave in, feeling the bitter mass burn all the way down his throat. New pain assaulted him at his wrists and ankles. Flesh that had only just had circulation returned to it protested at the rough handling.

Though at the very edge of consciousness, Jonah realized he was being bound. He tried to struggle and found that his body wouldn't respond. He was trapped. There was a part of him that wondered if the bitterness in his mouth and throat wasn't another kind of poison. Still, the cold ache in his chest had eased a bit. If this were the price of not dying a painful death at the hand of the Adderberry, so be it.

Something rough was passed through the bonds at his wrists and ankles. With a sudden jerk, the ground fell away and Jonah found himself suspended by his restraints. He tried to scream again and again, but only succeeded in making a harsh gurgling sound. His captors, whoever they were, didn't seem to notice or care.

Although it felt as if he had boat anchors on his eyelids, Jonah forced himself to open his eyes. He couldn't see much. The dappled light passing down through the jungle canopy made it difficult to see clearly even in the best condition. At least he knew he was being carried deeper into the jungle. That was something.

Jonah craned his head, trying to get a good look at his captors. Flashes of orange, yellow, and gray passed through shafts of sunlight that sifted down from above. What he saw send a surge of panic through his body that challenged the drug-induced stupor.

He was being hauled through the jungle on the shoulders of two massive feline beasts, just like the one that had decimated Tionne's pirate forces on the beach. Their wide heads were alert, triangular ears twitching from side to side as they made their way through the underbrush. He tried to wriggle free, but found his bonds far too tight and too well tied for him to be able to escape. Jonah almost wished the poison would take him now so he wouldn't have to face whatever horrors these creatures had in store for him.

As that thought crossed his mind, he realized that he no longer felt the terrible, cold lethargy that had spread down his limbs and into his chest. Though he was still seeing and hearing things, he didn't feel the sense of dread that he could only assume was his own impending death.

Well, due to poison, anyway. Jonah felt that his brain wasn't working as well as it could have, but even so, he knew that being the captive of these two hulking, cat-like beasts probably did not bode well for his continued survival. He wondered what Tiadaria would think when she defeated Tionne and came back down the mountain to find him missing. Would she come looking for him? Or would she just assume that his corpse had been dragged away by one of the many jungle dwelling animals?

His eyes were drawn to the milky white claws that supported the pole. They seemed as long as his hand. Even if Tiadaria came looking for him, there might not be much left for her to find.

There was a burst of hissing, spitting, and low growls from one of his captors. The other one replied in kind. This went back and forth for a while until Jonah realized they were speaking to each other. They paused and the conversation reached a frenzied pitch that sounded like two tomcats fighting in a dark alley. Jonah tried to remain as still as possible, though his ankles, shoulders, and wrists were aflame with agony. He didn't want to call attention to himself.

After what seemed like an eternity, they emerged into bright sunlight. Jonah squeezed his eyes shut against the intensity of the sun while rejoicing in the ecstasy of its warmth. He was lowered into a sand wallow. He could feel it against his exposed skin and he could smell it. He could also smell the beach and the brine. His bonds were cut, allowing him to flop lifelessly into the sand. Jonah wondered if anything had felt so good in his entire life.

He opened one eye, glancing about. Though his vision still hadn't returned to normal, it was getting easier to see. He was back on the beach. There were men milling about. Men in plate armor. Sailors didn't wear plate. It was a one-way ticket to the bottom of the sea.

Jonah's gaze ranged out over the water. There was a dark shape crouched just off shore. He couldn't make out more than an outline, but even with his poor vision and at this distance, the sails were unique.

The ship's sails were emblazoned with the red-and-white chevrons of the Human Imperium, and Jonah had never seen anything that looked so beautiful.

CHAPTER SIXTEEN

When Jonah had told her that the weapon was in the ruins of an ancient Shyraan city, she'd expected a few scattered buildings. The ruins of Am'Corr were enormous. As she rounded the last set of stone steps that led to the top of the mountain, Tiadaria found herself looking out over the ruins of a city nearly the size of Ethergate.

Ornate stonework buildings lay crumbling, moss and jungle vegetation encroaching on structures that would have, at one time, rivaled the most sophisticated buildings in Dragonfell. Why had the Shyraan abandoned this place to live in the jungle below? It didn't make any sense.

That was a mystery that would have to wait. Tionne was up here somewhere and Tiadaria wouldn't put it past the spiteful little wench to be lying in wait. Jonah had already fallen to one of the girl's traps. Tiadaria didn't intend to fall to another.

The sun was beginning to sink toward the western horizon, taking on the bronze quality that the artists so enjoyed. Tiadaria saw no beauty in it, only danger. She didn't know what restless spirits might lurk in these forgotten buildings in the dark of night and she had no desire to find out.

Shadows lengthened and crept out across the ground like grasping umbral hands.

Checking for traps and tripwires made the going even slower still. She moved from doorway to doorway, keeping to the shadows as much as she possibly could. Though her armor didn't draw as much attention as the shiny silver plate the Grand Army wore, she didn't want to risk a chance reflection giving Tionne any advance warning. It was going to be hard enough to figure out where the girl was without having to worry about giving up the element of surprise.

As she stood in a darkened alcove, Tiadaria saw a shadow flit across the wide, cobbled path that bisected the city. At this distance, it was impossible to see what had created the shadow. It could easily have been Tionne, but it could just have easily been a jungle beast or the living memory of something long dead. The hairs on the back of Tiadaria's neck stood on end. Am'Corr was a city of great history and those departed from the physical realm weren't always so ready to be untethered from what they knew in life.

The shadow crossed back, in the opposite direction. That was almost certainly Tionne searching for the shrine where the Horn of Requiem was housed. Tiadaria slipped out of the alcove and made her way down the path. She kept to the left, in the shadow of the tall buildings that hadn't yet, even after all this time, begun to collapse to the predations of the encroaching vegetation.

Tiadaria came to a break in the shadows, an open street that intersected the main path on which she stood. She'd have to cross the well-lit, open area to reach the spot where she thought she'd seen Tionne. That meant she'd be exposed to anyone who happened to be watching. She had one advantage here. There was no one to see her powers who weren't already aware of her unique nature.

The memories she plucked from the Quintessential Sphere were the living embodiment of swiftness. Rabbits and horses, and the long-legged runners that frequented the grassy plains of the Gatzbin Plateau. She channeled those living memories into her body, taking the power that the Ethereal Realm granted her, no matter how temporary.

Tiadaria burst across the road, stopping in the shadow on the other side. She had moved so quickly that she hoped her passage would appear to be nothing more than a trick of the light if Tionne happened to be watching. If she wasn't, then so much the better. Tiadaria stood in the shadow and strained her ears, wishing yet again that the Shyraan hadn't muddled the Ethereal Realm so. Sphere sight would have been a welcome addition to her arsenal. Not just to find Tionne, but to find the Horn as well.

She strained her ears, listening for any indication that Tionne had noted her passing. Tiadaria heard nothing but the low moan of the mournful wind winding its way through the dilapidated buildings. She continued moving forward toward the spot where she thought she'd seen Tionne. She was surprised to find that the main road split in two, each side winding down into a depression in the middle of the city. In the center of that depression was a courtyard with an expansive stairway leading underground, with a towering marble obelisk looming over it.

If Tiadaria was forced to guess, she'd have assumed that the staircase led to the shrine Brait had spoken of. If there was anywhere in this dead city more likely to house a weapon of incredible power, she hadn't seen it. A quick survey of the buildings on either side of the descending road gave Tiadaria no indication that Tionne was waiting to ambush her. In fact, the only indication that Tiadaria wasn't completely alone in Am'Corr was the line of small footprints in the collected dust. The evidence of Tionne's passage was clear in the accumulated debris that shrouded the cobblestones.

Tiadaria followed her trail, down the curving road and into the courtyard at the bottom of the valley. It had seemed large even from above. From down here, the open space was probably large enough to have held the entire population of the city with room to spare. Perhaps that was its purpose, to give the Shyraan a place to assemble near their greatest temple.

The stairs descended into darkness and the failing light of day made the descent seem more foreboding. The steps were smooth and straight, with no evidence of the decay that plagued the rest of the city. As she crossed the threshold, Tiadaria felt a wave of latent power wash over her. It caressed her spine, traveling out to the tips of her fingers and toes like a faint echo of link shock. Whatever the Shyraan had used this place for, the living memory of the temple was dancing with the power of the Ethereal Realm.

Tionne must have lit a torch. A bloom of orange flared below, sending flickering shadows up the wall of the stairwell. The angle of the steps shielded her from Tiadaria's view, but she knew Tionne was down there.

Tiadaria dropped her hand to the hilt of her scimitar. As her fingers wrapped around the grip, she felt the familiar pain lance down her arm and settle under her breastbone. Drawing the blade slowly, so it wouldn't ring against the scabbard, took a special kind of restraint. She wanted nothing more than to charge down the stairs and confront Tionne, to make her pay for the anguish she'd heaped upon Tiadaria and those she loved.

Managing to overcome the urge, Tiadaria readied the weapon and descended the steps with haste, but not recklessly. A torch glowed at the bottom of the steps and another further down a corridor leading deep into the earth. Tionne, however, was nowhere to be seen. Tiadaria could feel Tionne's presence, waiting in the dark. She stepped off the staircase and into the pool of warm orange light cast by the torch. The warmth felt good on her skin and she wasn't sure she wanted to pass out of its gentle embrace.

A loud bang echoed from the end of the corridor, bouncing off the walls and making it seem as if Tiadaria was surrounded by sound. The time for caution had passed. Now was a time for action. Gripping the hilt of her scimitar tight, she ran down the corridor as fast as her legs would carry her. She passed through the globe of light cast by a second torch and rounded the corner beyond.

In the light of yet another torch were the shattered remnants of ornate doors, carved in beautiful relief by the hands of artisans long dead. In her typical callous manner, Tionne had destroyed an object of beauty for no other reason than that it stood in her way.

Tiadaria stepped over the shards of the ruined doors, into a large circular antechamber. The ceiling was enrobed in gold, sending the flickering light of the torches back down to the floor in a warm golden glow. Tionne was nearly to the raised platform in the center of the room where a brilliantly iridescent conch shell was perched on a simple wooden stand.

"It's over, Tionne. There's no way I'm letting you leave here with that weapon," Tiadaria said, her words curiously amplified by the room until it seemed as if her voice was coming from several directions at once.

Tionne turned to face Tiadaria, drawing her obsidian dagger from the sheath on her milky thigh. Her emerald green eyes caught the light and seemed to glow in the semi-dark.

"You say that as if you can stop me."

~ ~ ~

Tionne was quick to release her magic, but Tiadaria was ready for Tionne. When the bolt of darkness streaked across the antechamber, Tiadaria dropped her scimitar's blade and deflected the ethereal bolt with ease. Tionne snarled in frustration and threw another bolt toward Tiadaria, sidling closer to the pedestal where the Horn of Requiem was resting. Tiadaria knew that if her nemesis got her hands on the weapon, she wouldn't hesitate to use it.

Tiadaria called on the Quintessential Sphere, summoning thoughts of swiftness and speed. She lunged across the space between their bodies and lowered her shoulder, striking Tionne in the midriff before she could reach the Horn. The air burst out of Tionne as their momentum carried them across the chamber, away from the Horn and the danger it held.

Raising her scimitar, Tiadaria prepared to separate Tionne's head from her neck, but the girl wormed out from underneath Tiadaria's body and rolled away. Tiadaria swore under her breath. Tionne might have been smaller and younger, but she was more of a pain in the ass than anyone Tiadaria had ever known. Even Zarfensis, the High Priest of the Xarundi and her former nemesis, had been easier to dispatch than this oily little minx who always seemed to wiggle out of Tiadaria's grasp.

As soon as she was free, Tionne made another rush for the Horn. She was single-minded in her determination. Tiadaria had to give her that. She lowered her shoulder again, preparing to ram Tionne for the second time. This time, Tionne was ready for her. She spun on her heel and threw a bolt of black light toward the Swordmage. Tiadaria had to throw herself to the side to keep from being struck by the dark magic. The bolt streaked past her and Tiadaria breathed a sigh of relief. She'd had enough firsthand experience with Tionne's spellcraft to know that she didn't want any part of the evils that came from the depths of the girl's twisted mind.

Looking up, Tiadaria saw that Tionne was standing on the tips of her toes, reaching up onto the platform to lift the Horn from its wooden cradle. There was too much distance between them for Tiadaria to stop her from getting her hands on the Horn. She'd have to settle for killing the girl before she was able to use it. This time, it wasn't her shoulder that she lowered in anticipation of the charge, it was the tip of her blade.

The point of the scimitar gleamed in the subdued light, as if it longed to spill the blood of the one who had thwarted its owner so many times. As if it, too, thirsted for the vengeance that Tiadaria felt was hers by right. With a cry of unfettered rage, Tiadaria ran forward, the blade aimed for the center of Tionne's chest.

Whether Tionne was surprised by the speed or ferocity of the attack, Tiadaria couldn't know, but the girl dropped the Horn back into the wooden stand and spun away a bare fraction of a second before she'd have been run through. Although she tried to check her momentum, Tiadaria careened off the pedestal, which set the Horn to wobbling on its stand. Tionne started toward it, as if she intended to save it from being dashed to the floor, and then thought better of her action when Tiadaria spun and again trained the sword on her.

"Give it up, Tionne. It's done. You've lost. If you give up now, I'll let you live. Maybe Faxon can help you."

"Faxon," Tionne spat the word as if it was venom on her tongue. "The only person he ever helps is himself. Surely you've figured that out by now. That's why you're here, isn't it? Can't be bothered to fix the problem HE created."

Tionne's accusation sent a chill up Tiadaria's spine. It wasn't as if Tionne was wrong. Faxon had sent Tiadaria out to dispatch her. There was a good reason for him to have stayed behind in Dragonfell, but even so, there was a ring of truth to Tionne's insult. Tiadaria knew that the girl blamed the elder Quintessentialist for many of the problems she faced in the Academy of Arcane Arts and Sciences, but the fact of the matter remained. Faxon had saved her. If Tionne had been taken to Dragonfell after her family and her entire village was slaughtered, she'd have been censured...or worse.

"He protected you, Tionne. He tried to give you everything you needed to survive. You should be thanking him, not damning him."

"Thank him?" Tionne crowed, her voice incredulous. "Thank him for what? For his heavy hand? For being an abusive sot? I don't think so. It'll be my pleasure to watch him die with the rest of you. I only hope I'm able to see the fire in his eyes go out when I bury my dagger in his heart."

"He did what he had to do to try to get through to you, Tionne. There's something broken inside you. It's not your fault. If anyone went through what you went through, they'd be broken too."

"Stop saying I'm broken!" Tionne screeched. She flung herself at Tiadaria, the obsidian dagger aimed for her throat. Tiadaria brought the sword up to defend against the slashing blade and knocked it away. A wave of cold ran down the scimitar into her hand, threatening to numb her arm. She quickly withdrew the sword and stepped back out of the range of the dagger.

"Why? Just because you don't like the truth doesn't make it any less true, Tionne. I was there. I saw what the Xarundi did to your family. I saw the claw marks and the gnawed flesh." Tiadaria saw the girl flinch. She was getting inside the girl's head. Good. "Tell me, Tionne, what did it sound like when the Xarundi started eating your family? Could you hear them being torn limb from limb? Did their flesh rending sound like wet burlap tearing?"

"Stop it!" Tionne roared, tossing her head like an angry animal. "Stop it! I swear I'll kill you just to shut you up."

"Then stop talking and do it," Tiadaria goaded her. "I don't think you can. You've tried so many times and yet you continue to fail."

Tionne looked as if she might take the bait, and then a strange calm passed over her features and she brushed her hair back with her free hand. A slow smile crept across her face, making her seem somehow even more predatory than she usually appeared. Another shiver went up Tiadaria's spine.

"Maybe I'll let you live, Swordmage. After all, everyone you've ever loved is dead. Your mentor? Dead. Your pet mage? Dead. Maybe I'll just keep killing off those who are most important to you. You'll be alone, again. It'll only get worse, you know, once I have the Horn. Imagine, won't you? You'll have to watch as I take control of the people most important to you and make them do such horrible things to each other. Maybe I'll force Faxon to kill himself in front of you. Slowly. Wouldn't that just be perfect?"

In that moment, Tiadaria realized how twisted Tionne really was. There was no hope of redemption for her. Her life, as short and brutal as it had been, had destroyed her in ways that could never be repaired. Tiadaria understood why Faxon needed to think she could be saved, but it was better for him to mourn the girl's loss than continue with the misguided notion that she could ever be made whole again.

The Swordmage planted her feet, drew her weapon up, and prepared to attack.

"If that's how it has to be, Tionne, so be it. I promised to try and save you, but if I have to put you down, I will."

Tionne barked laughter.

"That's the problem with you, Swordmage. Always hiding behind your blade."

Words of ancient power rolled off Tionne's tongue, words of languages spoken only in the lightless expanse of evil that was the Deep Void. Tionne extended her hand and whip-like black tendrils shot from the fingers. They struck the ceiling above Tiadaria's head, spreading cracks and fissures that went racing across the gold-gilded dome. The entire structure groaned, as if it were giving voice to the horror of its destruction. Tiadaria tried to leap out of the way, but even with the aid of the Quintessential Sphere, the damage was just too great. She was pelted with huge chunks of stone and dirt. She went to her knees, throwing her arms over her head to try to protect herself from the worst of the assault.

Through the dust and debris of the collapse, Tiadaria saw Tionne snatch the Horn of Requiem from the pedestal and run toward the ruined doors. The girl paused on the threshold, looking back through the tumbling detritus of the antechamber. Her eyes met Tiadaria's, lingering there cold with malice, for a moment before she turned and disappeared into the corridor beyond.

Tiadaria was knocked to the floor as the weakened ceiling finally failed.

The world went dark.

CHAPTER SEVENTEEN

Tiadaria opened her eyes and was greeted only with darkness and the sound of her own breath roaring in her ears. It was hot and she hurt all over. Dust tickled her throat and made her cough, sending spasms and pain through her chest. There was a different kind of pain in her chest as well, a throbbing ache that stemmed from the contact of her flesh on steel. She flexed her fingers. Somewhere in the dark, she was still holding the hilt of her scimitar. She hadn't lost it in the collapse. That was something.

Broken fragments of memory came flooding back in a torrent. Tionne's final spell. The rumbled warning of the temple before the ceiling gave way. *Tionne had the Horn!* The thought came pounding into her head with the rhythm of her heart. Tiadaria tried to flex her shoulders and cried out as the pistol wound in her arm flared from a muted ache into full-fledged agony. The rubble shifted around her, grinding sharp edges into her back and arms. It didn't move much, but it moved. If she could shift enough of the weight off her, she could dig her way out. She collapsed, spent from the exertion. Her breath came in ragged gasps, the dust in the air making her choke and sputter.

Something warm and wet dripped in her eye. It stung. She couldn't see, but she was sure it was blood. The unforgiving dark smelled of copper and sweat. A shard of rock was digging into her scalp from overhead. It felt as if it would pierce her skull if she moved too much. That was likely where the blood was coming from. No time to worry about that now. Catching up with Tionne was her primary concern. There was no way for Tiadaria to know how long she'd been unconscious. Her nemesis could be halfway down the mountain by now.

Flexing her shoulders again, Tiadaria tried to heft some of the weight off her. She was rewarded with a shower of pebbles cascading down onto her from above. She blinked. The dark seemed less, well, dark. Instead of the pitch black she'd become accustomed to, it was now a deep shade of gray. There was light coming from somewhere. If there was light, there was still hope that she could free herself and catch Tionne before she managed to slip away again.

With a roar of rage and frustration, Tiadaria put as much strength into her back and shoulder muscles as she could muster. She called on the Quintessential Sphere for assistance, summoning the living memory of strong plains oxen and the stalwart ice pigs of her homeland, tenacious and stubborn. She coaxed those living memories into her body, forcing them into the muscles that strained at the obstacles around her.

Sharp edges dug into her from every corner and she had to grit her teeth against the new assault. Fresh blood ran down her arms and back where the stone had broken through the links of her armor, tearing both silk and flesh. She forced herself to push through the pain. It was another obstacle, like the stone and earth pressing in around her. With a mighty heave, she burst upright, sending a shower of rocks and debris out in a cloud from the pocket she occupied. She brushed the blood and dirt from her eyes and glanced around.

The light came from the torches in the temple's antechamber. A few were still in their recessed sconces on the wall, but more than not had fallen to the ground, smoldering themselves into oblivion in a yellow-orange glow. The ceiling of the temple had completely given way, opening to the late afternoon sky beyond. The position of the sun hadn't changed much, so whatever head start Tionne had earned wouldn't be enough to stop Tiadaria from tracking her down.

Inch by inch, the Swordmage pulled herself from the rubble. It seemed to take forever, but at last she managed to free herself. Her armor was in sad shape, the silk in tatters in more than one place. The gunmetal rings had parted in some spots, leaving her exposed and vulnerable to attack. What saddened her the most, though, was the state of her scimitars. One was gone. Her sword belt had come loose and was lost in the rubble. The scimitar she had managed to hold on to was mangled almost beyond recognition. The decorative guard had been rendered unrecognizable. The sweeping wings of the Pegasus were broken, twisted by the weight of the rocks that had fallen upon it. The tip of the blade had been cocked askew and the edge of the enchanted metal was notched and grooved by the abuse it had taken.

With a heavy sigh, Tiadaria began to pull herself up through the ruined walls of the temple. It would be faster to just climb out of the wreckage than to backtrack through the long hall that led to the courtyard. That was even if the hall was unaffected by the collapse, a risky assumption in any case, and one she wasn't ready to make.

Beaten and bloody, bruised and battered, Tiadaria rolled into the sweet-smelling grass that covered the gentle hill that led down toward the underground temple. She rewarded her effort with a very brief respite; just enough for her to catch her breath and for the worst of the wounds to stop seeping blood into her already stained tunic and breeches. As she lay there, her wounds throbbing in time to her heart, she realized that she'd lost a boot in the fray. It was probably buried somewhere in the debris. There wasn't time to go back for it. She'd just have to do without.

Tiadaria reached down and slipped the other boot off, giving it a forlorn look as she set it aside. When she'd lived in the Frozen Frontier, boots were a luxury, and she'd been accustomed to walking in nothing more than thin linen slippers. She'd built up callouses that protected her both from sharp rock and the cold of snow and ice underfoot. Living in Dragonfell for so many years had robbed her of these minor protections. Boots were easy to come by in one of the largest trade centers in the Imperium and the thick skin she'd developed had given way to comfort. She'd pay for that now, she expected.

A glint of sun and a shadow on the far edge of the ruined city gave away Tionne's position. She was heading for the cliff stairs and making good time. Tiadaria would have to hurry to catch up, otherwise she might lose Tionne for good in the denseness of the jungle. The path had been simple enough to follow on the way up the mountain, but that had been in daylight. At night, it would be an entirely different story, and without Jonah's sense of direction and tracking, it would be more difficult still.

Ignoring the lump in her throat, Tiadaria ran down the cobbled path toward the cliff. Pebbles dug into the soft flesh of her feet with every step and she did her best to block out the pain. Instead, she focused her thoughts on stopping Tionne and getting the Horn of Requiem back. It needed to be kept safe. If Tionne returned it to the Sirens, there was no telling what horrors would befall the Imperium and her people.

Tiadaria rounded a fall of rubble in the street, remnants from the top of a tall building crouched beside the road. As she did, she caught a glimpse of Tionne's slender form worming her way between the broken buildings. She was nearly to the steps that would lead her back down the mountain. Only a fool would rush down those steps. It was just as likely you'd fall to your death on the rocks below as make it to the bottom.

She was exhausted and wanted nothing more than to rest, but Tiadaria knew that rest wasn't in the cards. Even after she stopped Tionne, there was the fact that they were stranded on this faraway island to contend with. Rest was something that wouldn't come for a long time. There was no benefit in that line of thought, so she forced it out of her head and focused on the task at hand. She made herself run faster still.

The breath burned in her lungs and her body was a mass of pain from the bottoms of her feet to the top of her head. Finally, she was beyond the buildings, on the small parcel of grass atop the cliff stairs. Tionne was there, looking down at the steps cut into the rock face. She whirled at the noise of Tiadaria's approach, the glint in her eyes going from surprise to fear before settling on anger.

"Why won't you just die?" the girl demanded of Tiadaria, bringing her hand up to cast a spell, the other still clutching the Horn.

This time, Tiadaria was ready. Though much abused, her sword still held enough enchantment to counter the spells that Tionne hurled at her. Tiadaria knocked them aside with ease, closing the distance between them. With nowhere else to go, Tionne dove to the side.

They sparred this way for some time, trading magical blows that did little to advance their confrontation. With each countered spell, Tiadaria had to push back the fatigue and nausea that threatened to overwhelm her. The hole in her arm had started bleeding again and there was blood running down her arm. Still, she managed to thwart Tionne at every turn.

Tionne's face twisted with rage, distorting the once attractive features into a mask that more resembled the evil inside.

"This time, I'm going to make sure you're dead, Swordmage."

"Good luck, Tionne. You're going to need it."

~ ~ ~

As if Solendrea herself had realized the import of the battle taking place high above the rocky beach, the wind had picked up and dark clouds were rolling in from the horizon. Distant thunder rumbled a muted warning of the storm to come and flashes of lightning danced in the darkness far out to sea. Tiadaria and Tionne circled each other, neither willing to get too close to the edge of the precipice. Tionne cast a few spells at Tiadaria, but the Swordmage knocked them away with the flat of her blade. The girl looked as exhausted Tiadaria felt. It would be a mercy for both of them to end this quickly.

"Just give me the Horn, Tionne," Tiadaria implored, her voice flat and tired. "You can still come back with me. This doesn't have to be the end for you."

Tionne's bark of laughter bounced off the ruined buildings beyond the clearing and echoed back, a shrill imitation of the sound.

"The end? This isn't my end, Swordmage. This is just the beginning. When I return the Horn of Requiem to its rightful owners, I'll take my place beside Lord Yargen and his people. Between the Sirens below and Stryne above, the Imperium *will* fall."

"You have to know we won't let that happen," Tiadaria said with more confidence than she felt. Tionne seemed so sure of herself, as if wiping out all of humanity in a single fell swoop was no more of a consideration than what to wear in the morning. Her brazenness unsettled Tiadaria in a way that she couldn't quite put her finger on.

"You can't stop it, Tiadaria. It's already in motion. If you haven't heard the rumblings caused by our agents inside the Imperium yet, you will. The plan is already in motion. It has been since before I began my journey. This," Tionne lifted the Horn of Requiem and brandished it at Tiadaria, "this is just the icing on the cake. The weapon that will assure us of complete and uncontested victory. Those who don't surrender will be subjugated and made to serve our will."

Tiadaria shuddered. She had a mental image of what Tionne's will would look like imposed on the helpless masses turned to simple automatons by the power of the Horn, and it wasn't pretty. The girl had a sadistic streak a furlong wide.

No matter how much Faxon wanted to try to save Tionne, it didn't change the reality. His former apprentice was beyond redemption. She was a willing participant in her own destruction. She was a true believer. Between the damage that had already been done and whatever promises the dragon and the Siren King had made, there was no hope left of coaxing what was left of Tionne's soul back to the light. Better to end her life and put a stop to the madness that was running roughshod over Faxon's memory of the little girl he had rescued from that village so long ago.

Her fingers tightened around the hilt of her battered scimitar. Bent and broken as it was, it would still serve to put Tionne down. It would be the last noble act of a faithful tool.

Tiadaria darted forward and she saw Tionne's eyes widen. She'd taken the girl by surprise, but Tionne recovered well. She took a step to the side and brought the Horn up to her lips. Tiadaria saw the girl's cheeks puff out as she blew into the conch.

A haunting, ethereal note sounded across the clearing and all of a sudden, Tionne's transgressions didn't seem to matter. The beautiful noise coming from the Horn pushed all other considerations out of Tiadaria's mind. Warmth and peace flooded through her body. It would be so easy to forget everything else and let herself be carried away on the sweetness of the sound. Even so, something deep inside her raged against the desire to just let go and be carried away. Something primal clawed at her consciousness, keeping her within herself. The Horn's hold on her snapped and Tiadaria shook her head, clearing the last of the song's fog from her mind.

"Impossible!" Tionne spat, looking from the Horn to Tiadaria and back again. "You can't resist the Siren's Song!"

"I can, and I have, and now I'm going to take that vile thing from you before you use it on someone who isn't as stubborn as I am."

Tiadaria put her words into action. Drawing the power of the Quintessential Sphere, she launched herself at Tionne. Thunder roared as her feet left the ground. Tionne, for all her big words and grand allies, was a coward when it came right down to it. As soon as she realized Tiadaria would be atop her in seconds, she turned tail and ran.

The only problem with retreat, as Tiadaria saw it, was that there wasn't anywhere to run to. The small clearing was bounded by a sheer drop on one side, a tall cliff on another, the steps leading down to the jungle below, and the cobbled path leading back into the ruined city of Am'Corr, which Tiadaria was blocking. There was nowhere for Tionne to run, so it took Tiadaria by surprise when the girl bolted for the cliff face.

She landed in the soft grass where Tionne had been a moment before and took most of the impact in her knees. Tiadaria whirled around just in time to see Tionne reach the edge of the cliff and look down. Her black dress whipped around her in the buffeting wind. When the girl turned back toward Tiadaria, she could see the panic in Tionne's huge green eyes.

Tiadaria took a step forward, and Tionne took a step back. She was dangerously near the drop. If she took more than another step or so back, Tionne would go off the edge. Tiadaria knew she had to be stopped, but not like this. She lowered the scimitar, its bent tip pointing at the earth.

"It doesn't have to be like this, Tionne! I can help you. Faxon can help you. Don't do this. I'm offering you a choice between life and death. Choose life."

Tionne shook her head, her eyes blazing. Lightning split the sky behind Tiadaria and the spark of that violent rending danced in Tionne's wild eyes.

"I see no such choice, Swordmage," Tionne said, taking a half step back toward the cliff. Tiadaria's stomach clenched. "I see only the choice between two possible deaths. One chosen for me by you, in which I waste away in some Imperium prison, or worse…and another in which I choose the time and manner of my passing. You will never take that choice from me, Swordmage. Not now. Not ever."

Before Tiadaria could even raise her blade, Tionne had leapt back. Time seemed to slow as Tiadaria watched the girl's feet leave the edge of the cliff. Tionne seemed to hang there, suspended in space and time, the whipping wind wrapping her ebony dress around her pale skin. Then she was gone, disappearing backward over the edge.

Tionne didn't scream. The only sound in the clearing was the roaring of the wind, the crashing of the waves, and distant thunder. Tiadaria's scimitar slipped from fingers deadened by shock. What had just happened? How had it happened? Was Tionne really so broken that she could just step off into oblivion without as much as a second thought?

Tiadaria rushed to the edge and looked down, half expecting to see an outcropping or ledge, something that Tionne could have used to save herself. Instead, there was only open air. Down, down, down the cliff face stretched, all the way to the surging sea. Jagged rocks poked up out of the surf like broken teeth. She scanned the surf and the rocks for any sign of Tionne's body and saw nothing. No broken, pale corpse floating in the violent sea. No smear of blood on the blade-sharp rocks. Nothing. It was as if the girl had never existed.

Vertigo began to overwhelm her and Tiadaria backed away from the edge with haste. A fine mist had begun to fall, making the grass slippery underfoot. Though she was curious about Tionne's fate, Tiadaria had no intention of following in the girl's footsteps. Tiadaria sat in the damp grass for a long time. No matter how hard she tried, she couldn't make her mind accept what she'd just seen. How was she going to tell Faxon? What was she going to tell him?

Everything seemed numb. Tiadaria got slowly to her feet and wandered back to the spot where she'd dropped the scimitar. She picked it up, ignoring the familiar pain that lanced through her at a touch. With great care, she made her way down the treacherous steps and stopped just outside the jungle where she'd left Jonah's body.

He was gone.

In the back of her head, the rational part of her knew that his body, the shell, had probably been claimed by some jungle beast. Tiadaria was in no mood for rational. She hadn't felt so utterly alone since Wynn had died.

She sank to ground, pressing her back to the rock where his body had been. Tiadaria tilted her face toward the sky and waited for her tears to come.

They never did.

Instead, the sky opened up and cried for her. Tiadaria let Solendrea's tears stream down her face for a moment before she struggled to her feet. Head bowed, she entered the darkness of the jungle and began the long trek back to the beach.

CHAPTER EIGHTEEN

The storm was fierce but short, and blew itself out before she reached the head of the trail. Tiadaria made her way to the spot where Tionne would have ended up, and spent the last remaining hour of daylight climbing over, under, and through the jagged rock outcroppings at the base of the cliff. With every second that passed, the sun slipped lower toward the western horizon. She knew that if she didn't start back to the beach soon, she'd be stranded out here. Though there seemed to be no immediate threat from Tionne or the Sirens, Tiadaria didn't want to be alone in the dark. Too much had happened and she didn't feel as if she could handle being alone with her thoughts.

As it was, Jonah popped into her mind at inopportune times. Though she did her best to shove the pain away, it was still there, festering under the surface. Like an infected splinter, eventually it would erupt and she'd have to deal with it. Until then, she'd do her best to avoid it. There would be plenty to do at the beach to keep her mind occupied.

Leaving the ragged jaws of the rocks behind, she made her way down the beach as the sun slipped away. Oranges and pinks stained the far sky and Tiadaria stopped for a moment. She looked over her shoulder at the sunset and suffered a strong pang of loss. Jonah still felt very close. It seemed like a lifetime ago that they had watched the sunset from the deck of the Nightingale. Now everything was gone. Jonah was gone. The ship was gone. The joy of having someone in her life that understood her was gone.

Tiadaria was tired. Tired with more than just the physical exhaustion of the battles she'd been forced to fight for the people of the Imperium. She was tired of losing. She'd lost the Captain. Lost Wynn and Jonah. How many more people had to die before she'd be able to have a real relationship? Would she ever be allowed to have one at all? Or would she die as the Captain had, cut down on the field of battle, alone?

It seemed as though every step she took required twice the effort. The sand seemed to grasp at her feet, trying to pull her down. Her head was similarly mired, moving glacially forward like cold molasses. Maybe she should just deal with the pain before it pushed its way to the surface. This constant tug-of-war hounded her as she made the long, painful journey across the beach toward the dim, flickering lights in the distance.

No matter how tired she was, there was one thing that Tiadaria couldn't ignore. Not being able to find Tionne's body bothered her. Not because she thought the girl was a threat any longer, no one would have been able to survive a fall from that height, but because she had nothing to show for her mission. She'd failed. For the first time in her service to the Imperium, she was going to return to Dragonfell empty-handed. The Horn was lost beneath the waves, and Tiadaria was certain that it would only be a matter of time before the Sirens recovered it. The sea was, after all, their domain.

Good natured shouts and the lyrics of a throaty sailing song drifted to her on the cool night air. Tiadaria didn't know how the men could be in such good spirits. The knowledge that they were stranded on this tiny island off the coast of a foreign land should have spread through the ranks by now. Bad news didn't often keep to itself.

There was a shadow up ahead, backlit by the roaring bonfire. As Tiadaria got near, it fell into step beside her.

"Are you all right?" Captain Odeon asked, his voice quiet. His tone was the most subdued that Tiadaria had heard it since they'd met.

"No," she replied. Candidness had never been a problem for her. "I'm not. I'm beaten, Odeon. Physically, mentally, emotionally. I'm just done."

"I wanted to speak to you before you reached camp," Odeon said, turning his shadowed face to her. "Much has changed since you left, but I wanted to speak with you, particularly, about Jonah."

Tiadaria sighed. She'd be a fool twice over to think that she'd be able to ignore what had happened for long. Her moments on the beach were likely to be the last time she was to be alone with her thoughts. She should have known better. Not only did she have to face his shipmates, but she'd have to report his sacrifice to Princess Felyn as well. Tiadaria had no idea how the Princess would react to that bit of news.

"I did what I could, Odeon. I had to leave him. I think some jungle beast must have taken off with the body. I'll go and look for him at first light, but you have to know that I don't hold out much hope of finding him."

"There's no need for that, Lady Tiadaria. We have him. He was recovered for us by some unexpected allies. I trust the other part of your mission was a success?"

"No. Tionne jumped off the cliff rather than be returned to the Imperium. The only silver lining is that the Horn is gone as well. What allies? And where did you bury Jonah, Captain? I want to pay my respects."

"We haven't buried him just yet, Lady Tiadaria. I—"

"He should have been interred as soon as you recovered him, Captain. It's the only decent thing to do. Who knows how long we'll be out here. I expected better—"

Captain Odeon reached out and grasped her by the shoulders, giving her a little shake to stop her tirade. He released her as soon as she stiffened under his touch. He turned toward the fire, tugging on his waistcoat to straighten it.

"Lady Tiadaria," he said, his voice grave. "I am not in the habit of burying those who are not yet dead."

"He's...?" Tiadaria could scarce believe her ears. A flood of thoughts tumbled through her head, each pushing the others out of the way for a split second consideration before vanishing into the ether.

"Jonah lives, Lady Tiadaria, but only just. That's why I wanted to talk to you before you entered the camp. We've made him as comfortable as possible, but it will be weeks or months before he has recovered fully. Adderberry poisoning is not something that one generally walks away from."

"Weeks or months? How is he going to survive on this backwater rock for days, much less weeks?"

"As I said, the situation has changed a bit since you left us, Lady Tiadaria. We were joined by some unexpected allies. A ship from the Imperium Navy appeared in the bay just after you left in pursuit of Tionne. We were then joined by a Shyraan search party called on by the behest of the commander of the Imperium forces. They were the ones who tracked down Jonah. I suspect by sense of smell. Regardless, we'll be returning to Dragonfell at dawn."

Tiadaria sank onto a large rock. Jonah was alive? There was an Imperium ship in the bay? A Shryaan search party? They were going home? How could she have been gone only a few short hours and things have changed so drastically?

"How did a rescue ship reach us so quickly?"

Odeon shifted on his feet and was silent for a long moment before he spoke. When he did, his voice was low.

"I'm afraid it isn't a rescue vessel, Lady Tiadaria. The ship was sent on the order of King Greymalkin to return us to Dragonfell."

There was a finality in Odeon's voice that Tiadaria didn't like at all.

"What aren't you telling me, Captain?"

"The King, apparently, was not pleased with what he views as Princess Felyn's interpretation of the dangers facing the Imperium. From what I understand, he has imprisoned her in the dungeon and sent his lapdog to return us for trial. The charge is high treason. We're going back to Dragonfell, Tiadaria, but we're going back in irons."

"He doesn't understand," she snarled, waving her uninjured arm at the beach surrounding them. "He doesn't know how close he came to losing everything. We did what we had to do to protect the Imperium. He has to see that."

"It would appear that sending us to trial is easier for him. The trial isn't the worst for you, I'm afraid."

Tiadaria's blood ran cold. There was a weight to Odeon's words that seemed to settle in the pit of her stomach.

"Why is it worse for me?" she whispered, afraid of what Odeon's answer would be.

Odeon shook his head and Tiadaria was glad that it was dark enough that she couldn't see the look in his eye.

"The King has revealed your secret, I'm afraid. When you return to Dragonfell, you return as a rogue mage. Greymalkin has called for your public censure."

All the joy she'd felt at learning that Jonah was alive was sucked out of her in an instant. The world seemed to go gray around her and she wavered on the rock until Odeon put his hand on her shoulder to steady her. Temperate thought the night was, she was cold with a chill that started at the base of her spine and spread out until she felt as if her fingers and toes were encased in ice.

"That's why you met me coming," she said, her voice leaden. "You wanted to warn me. Thank you."

"I'm sorry I couldn't do more, Lady Tiadaria. I'd tell you to run, but his men are already stationed up and down the beach. You wouldn't get far, I'm afraid."

"And it wouldn't do her any good in the long run," a familiar bass voice rumbled from behind her. "She knows how tenacious I can be."

Tiadaria rose and turned toward a barrel-chested figure she recognized well.

"So, Torus, you're to take me back to Dragonfell in chains?"

The commander of the Grand Army of the Imperium ran a huge hand through close-cropped hair. Tiadaria had known him long enough to read his mannerisms. He wasn't happy about his duty, but happy about it or not, he would see it through.

"Those are my orders, Tiadaria. Please don't make me take them literally."

There was a part of her that wanted to test him. Torus was a brilliant solider and tactician, but there was no way he would be able to match the power she could call from the Quintessential Sphere. He knew it. She knew it. They stood three feet, and entire worlds, apart for a few moments before Tiadaria moved.

Tiadaria's eyes went to the sword she'd carried with her from the top of the mountain. She didn't even recognize it anymore. It wasn't her weapon. It was a remnant of a time long forgotten. A time when her friends could be relied upon. A time when she wasn't at war. Tiadaria tossed the blade in the sand at Torus's feet.

"Keep it," she said, her voice low and rough. "I don't need it anymore."

Without another word, she shoved past Torus and headed toward the roaring fire and the warship anchored beyond. Her only concern right now was seeing Jonah.

~ ~ ~

Tiadaria found Jonah in the largest cabin of the Dauntless. Landon, the ship doctor aboard the Nightingale, was sitting with him in the dim light of a single candle. When Tiadaria appeared in the door, he eased himself up out of the chair and made his way with light steps toward the door.

"He's resting as comfortably as we can make him," the doctor said by way of greeting. "Adderberry poisoning is nasty business, but I think we've managed to see him through the worst of it. The best thing for him now is rest and time."

"I'm not sure how much of either of those we have left, but thank you for saving him. I was sure he was going to die."

"Aye, Lady Tiadaria, and he would have if those…creatures…hadn't found him when they did. I suppose all this treason business had to have a silver lining of sorts." Landon grimaced. "Did you put that witch in the ground?"

Tiadaria tried to hide her grimace. "In a manner of speaking. Can I see him?"

She craned her neck over the doctor's shoulder, peering into the cabin. He nodded and stepped out of the doorway.

"Of course. I'll just skip down to the galley for a wee nip. If you need me, you know where to find me."

Discharged of his duty, the doctor disappeared down the corridor. Tiadaria stood in the doorway. She didn't know why she was so reticent to enter the cabin where Jonah lay, but it felt as if he was safer if she was on this side of the door. It seemed to her that if she kept her distance, maybe she'd be able to protect him from the awful luck that seemed to follow her around.

"Tia?"

She closed her eyes against the weariness in his voice, but it was Jonah for sure. He was in there. Still whole, somehow, against all odds. Tiadaria crossed the threshold and went to his bedside, taking up occupancy in the chair the doctor had abandoned not long before.

"I'm here," she said, finding his hand atop the blanket and folding it in both of hers. "How are you feeling?"

"Pretty good, for a dead man," he quipped, opening one eye to look at her.

Tiadaria's breath caught in her throat and she tried to disguise it with a little cough. Jonah gave her a weak smile, the corners of his mouth twitching up a little as he, with effort, opened the other eye.

"I was…" she began, but then faltered. Tiadaria tried a couple variations on that theme, stopping each one as the lump in her throat rendered her speech almost unintelligible.

"I was sure I'd lost you," she finally said, her voice soft.

"I was, too," Jonah admitted with raw candor. "Seems like we were both wrong about that."

Tiadaria gave him a weak smile. "You might soon wish we hadn't been."

"You mean Torus and his orders to bring us back?" Jonah gave a snort, and then a pained look crossed his face. "Why didn't you tell me, Tia? About your powers? I thought we were close?"

By all appearances, her omission had hurt him more than the poison that had almost robbed him of his life and that drove a sliver of ice into her heart. She dropped his hand. She wasn't worthy to hold him. Even that small part of him.

"We are. It's just…I was told not to tell anyone. It was made very clear to me what would happen if anyone in the Imperium found out about my magic. I'm a rogue mage, Jonah. They're going to censure me."

Jonah offered her his hand and she reluctantly took it. His fingers were warm and full of life again. Not the cold things she'd held so briefly in their time upon the cliff.

"I don't think the Princess is going to allow that to happen," Jonah said, his voice distant.

"I'm not sure how she can stop it. She's a Princess, but Greymalkin is the King. His word is the law."

"Yes, and no."

"What do you mean?"

"There's still the King's Council to consider."

"Greymalkin doesn't answer to the Council. They answer to the King."

Jonah laughed. "You don't know much about politics, do you Tia?"

"Most of my diplomacy is conducted at the tip of a blade," she said without apology. She'd known for a long time that she was a tool to be employed at the need or whim of the King. It had become even clearer to her when she'd been neglected for the last few months with nothing to do.

"The Council may answer to the King, but the King is just as accountable to the Council. The men who sit around that table are some of the most powerful and influential men in the realm. Some of the Southern Baronies are larger than Dragonfell. What do you think would happen if the Baronies threatened to secede from the Imperium?"

"Over my censure?" Tiadaria raised her eyebrows, incredulous. "I've only met the Council on a handful of occasions."

"No," Jonah shook his head. "The Council doesn't much care what happens to you."

"Gee, thanks. You know how to make a girl feel special."

Jonah grinned and squeezed her hand in apology.

"Not what I meant, Tia. What I'm saying is that not all of the Council would automatically side with Greymalkin if it came down to a political challenge. Princess Felyn has been very adept at holding the attention of more than a few powerful people in the Imperium. I expect the King is in for a rude awakening."

"Even so, how does it benefit Princess Felyn to be on my side in this? Isn't she just opening herself up to more problems?"

"She chose you, Tiadaria. I know you don't know her well, but if Felyn chose you for something, it's because she believes in you. She isn't going to let you hang for something she recruited you to do. That's not her way."

Tiadaria was quiet for a long time. She hoped Jonah was right. He knew the Princess far better than she did. If nothing else, his words had given her a faint glimmer of hope. A spark that settled into the pit of her stomach and helped push away the awful cold that had been growing there.

"I want to believe you," she said at last. Tiadaria sighed. "I guess we'll find out soon enough."

"Have I ever given you a reason not to trust me?" Jonah asked, pulling away from her. His eyes had taken on a hard glint and Tiadaria raised her hands in surrender at that regard.

"No, Jonah, you haven't." Tiadaria sighed. "It's not you. I trust you. I just don't trust anyone else in this. Things have gone sideways and I'm not sure where everyone is going to end up when all is said and done."

She paused, gnawing at her lower lip for a moment before continuing.

"Torus is one of my best friends, and yet here he is, taking me back to Dragonfell on orders. How could he betray me like that?"

Jonah lifted a shoulder and shook his head.

"Cut him some slack, Tia. He's in a bad position. He answers directly to the King, but he has to know that you'd whip him soundly in a straight fight. Hell, they sent a warship with a full company of soldiers to bring you back. You should take that as a compliment of sorts."

Tiadaria didn't want to cut him any slack. She wanted him to be there for her, the way a friend would. In the end, her sense of the ridiculous got the best of her and she dissolved into a fit of laughter. Jonah eyed her curiously, as if concerned that she was losing her mind. Then he smiled.

"Let me in on the joke?" he asked.

"It's nothing. Just wondering what Greymalkin thinks I'm capable of, to send Torus and all his men to bring me back."

Jonah's smile evaporated and he shook his head, his face sad.

"I don't know. Greymalkin was a great man, but whatever madness has infested him has taken his greatness from him. As funny as you find it, don't underestimate the man, Tiadaria. Your safety is my primary concern."

"I won't, I promise."

Jonah attempted to say something else but was wracked with a coughing fit that left him gasping for breath. The doctor stepped out of the shadows near the doorway. He gave Tiadaria an appraising look as he passed.

"I think it's best if you cut your visit short now, Lady Tiadaria. Jonah still needs his rest. I'll see to it that he's well cared for."

Jonah's eyes met hers in mute apology and she gave him a little nod and a smile.

"Of course. He needs his rest. Please take good care of him, Landon."

"Aye, Lady. You have my word."

Tiadaria wasted no time in making her way back to the deck of the great warship. She went as far forward as the deck would allow, climbing up atop the great winches that would hoist the anchors from the bottom of the sea.

She drew her knees up to her chest, wincing at the protest of her sore muscles. Tiadaria was torn between anxiety and elation. That Jonah had survived was a blessing ten times over, but Tionne's disappearance weighed heavily on her heart.

Tiadaria was so consumed by her thoughts that she didn't hear the approach of boots on the deck planking. When Torus spoke, she whirled on him, furious with him for taking her by surprise. For his part, he took a step back, putting up his hands in entreaty.

"Easy, Tiadaria. I think we need to talk."

CHAPTER NINETEEN

Down, down, down Tionne fell, the wind roaring in her ears as the white-tipped waves rushed up to meet her. It seemed as if she'd been falling for an eternity when suddenly she smashed into the unforgiving sea. The air exploded out of her lungs as she hit the water, hard as stone. Somehow, she managed to keep her fingers wrapped around the Horn of Requiem.

Then she was sinking, the black waves reclaiming their treasure and her along with it. Cold brine flooded into her mouth and Tionne struggled to vomit it out. She could feel icy death invading her lungs, warring with the pain in her body. For a fleeting moment, Tionne felt fear. Felt it in her heart for the first time since that dark night when the Xarundi had ripped her family apart. That fear was mercifully replaced by blackness as her injuries and the sea tore her consciousness from her.

Tionne didn't understand why she wasn't dead. Nor was she in the silver-white tinged fringes of the Ethereal Realm where the newly dead crossed from the face of Solendrea to become one with the Quintessential Sphere. Where she was, there was no light. Only darkness and an odd, reassuring pressure that seemed to weigh down every inch of her body. She hurt. Oh, merciless Eternals, how she hurt. It felt as if all the bones in her body had been shattered. She tried to open her eyes, but the effort was just too much.

Distant whispers echoed in her ears. A thousand different voices calling out to her, coaxing her back to consciousness, keeping her from slipping beyond the physical realm. Part of her wanted to ignore them, to evade their tenuous grasp and lose herself to the shifting void of the Ethereal Realm.

"Tionne, Daughter of Darkness, return to me."

Forceful, commanding, a clarion call that cut through the din of all the other voices. Lord Yargen's summons came from inside her head. It grounded her and made any thought of shuffling off the mortal coil impossible. It was as if that simple command had anchored her soul to her body.

She found that she was able to open her eyes now. When she did, she found Lord Yargen bent over her, his gills adrift in an unseen current. Tionne's hand went to her throat and she felt the fine chain there, the amulet that the Siren King had given her. Colors danced along the ceiling, purples and greens, oranges and blues. Tiny iridescent shapes that danced in the subdued light.

"The Horn," she gasped, feeling the water move over the gills that the amulet provided her.

Yargen's webbed hand clasped her shoulder and his mouth full of teeth quivered.

"Returned to its rightful owners, Tionne. By your hand. You did well."

Tionne closed her eyes, feeling as if it was finally safe for her to relax. She had done her duty. The Horn was safe. The Swordmage and her ilk would pay for their transgressions. Her body unwound as the tension evaporated like fog under the morning sun. A sudden tightness crept into her chest almost as soon as she relaxed.

Having returned the Horn to the Siren King, her duty to Lord Yargen was now complete. Tionne would be expected to return to Stryne, the great white dragon that had tasked her with finding the siren weapon in the first place. She felt the gentle caress of the siren's mind within her own. She didn't bother to try and block out the pain she felt when she thought about leaving the abyssal deep. It was the only place that she had ever felt as if she belonged.

"You may stay with us as long as you like, Tionne. You will be welcomed by my people as the hero you are. Your body may be human, but your soul belongs to the Great Abyss."

"Lord Stryne would never allow me to stay."

The Siren King barked an approximation of laughter.

"How can he stop you, Daughter of Darkness? Not even such a great and powerful foe as a dragon would dare attempt a siege on Selethrion. I will, of course, speak to him on your behalf if that is your desire."

Tionne closed her eyes. Relief flowed through her like a soothing balm. If Lord Yargen hadn't been a powerful ally, Stryne wouldn't have sought him out in the first place. That the Siren King was willing to intervene on her behalf made her believe even more fervently that the aquatic city was her one true home. She opened her eyes and looked at Yargen.

"I don't wish to make an enemy of the great dragon, but my place is here. I feel it. It's unlike anything I've ever felt before or may ever feel again."

"Then here you shall remain. You will be an integral part of the machinations that return my people to their former glory and eradicate this plague once and for all."

"My life is yours, Lord Yargen. Command me and I will do your bidding."

Tionne, who had spent her entire life running from submission, chaffing at the uncomfortable yoke of life as a Quintessentialist, was now placing her wellbeing in the webbed hands of the most sinister race on all of Solendrea. In a distant corner of her mind, she wondered if she ought to be scared of the implications of that surrender. Tionne ground that thought into dust as she would an insect under her boot heel. There was no other place on Solendrea where she felt accepted for who she was and what she desired.

Even Stryne, for all his hatred of humanity, hated them only for what they had done. Tionne's hatred ran deeper. She hated all of them, not for what they had done, but instead for what they stood for. They had a spirit that seemed unbreakable, but she would see it broken. Soon they would see all of their resilience and honored self-sufficiency wouldn't save them. Instead, it would make them outstanding thralls in the service of their true masters.

Lord Yargen's hand squeezed her shoulder again and Tionne snapped back into the present, drawn out of her fantasies by the contact.

"You must rest, Tionne." Lord Yargen's tone offered no latitude for bargaining. It was a command and she recognized it as such. "There is much to do, but with the return of the Horn, we have the luxury of time where there was none before. My people will see to your every need."

The Siren King left her then, and Tionne couldn't help but feel a little deflated by his sudden departure. She had, after all, been instrumental in the return of their weapon. The artifact that would deliver them into a new age of prosperity.

Foolish girl, she chided herself, *he has the wellbeing of his people to see to. A war to plan. He can't sit here holding your hand.*

It was several days before she was healed sufficiently to leave her room. True to the King's word, his people had cared for her every need during her recovery. With each passing day, she felt more ill at ease. She needed to be doing something, to know that her status among the Sirens had truly changed. She wondered if his subjects knew of her return to the city and what they would think of her desire to stay. Their rejection, their fear and loathing, was still very fresh in her mind from her first visit.

As she left the room where she'd been kept to recovery, Tionne was surprised to find that she'd been brought back not to some type of infirmary, but to Lord Yargen's palace. Tionne approached the main entrance doors to the palace and the guards there opened the doors for her to exit. They gave no other indication of what they thought of her presence. Telepathy was a handy adaptation that came all too easily to the sirens. Tionne would have been especially pleased to have her own form of that particular talent.

Still, she'd wanted to stay. Now she had to make the best of the good and the bad. Webbed feet propelled her out into the courtyard surrounding the palace and she was amazed to find it packed with sirens. Siren spawn swirled around her, mobbing her in their excitement, which they broadcast with such enthusiasm that she felt it crawling along the skin of her arms.

Where there had been fear and distrust before, there was now welcoming and acceptance. Strange land-walker though she was, Tionne had delivered them the instrument of their salvation and she could feel their gratitude and excitement radiating off of them in waves.

Tionne swam toward them, and they embraced her, pressing in on all sides to touch her. Wherever they made contact, a new thought bloomed in her mind.

Savior. Hero. Chosen.

Their admiration was almost overwhelming and it went on for what seemed like hours. At long last, the teeming crowd of well-wishers dissipated, going their separate ways to attend to tasks delayed to welcome their prodigal daughter back into the fold.

A great weight settled onto Tionne's shoulders, but she would bear it with gratitude. Lord Yargen's people saw her as their salvation. The tool that would deliver the souls of humanity to the starving sirens who needed that sustenance to survive. It was a daunting challenge, but one she would rise to with every fiber of her being.

Tionne had finally found her home and she would do everything in her power to protect it.

~ ~ ~

Kicking her webbed feet, Tionne drove herself through the black water toward their destination. There was no need to look behind her. She knew that a host of siren soldiers followed her, their tridents and spears at the ready.

A pouch crafted from woven fronds of sea grass hung across her chest. In it, the Horn of Requiem thrummed with muted power. It was almost as if the artifact knew that it was about to be put to use once more.

Black faded to dark gray as the sea became shallower near shore. Somewhere high above them, the moon was full in the night sky. Tionne wondered if she even remembered what the sky looked like anymore. Days had blended into weeks, and the longer she spent among Lord Yargen and the others, the more her memories of life on dry land began to feel like distant dreams.

Waves began to roll over them, racing to meet the shore. Tionne slowed her advance and flashed a series of hand signals to the nearest sirens. She focused her thoughts on the plan she and Lord Yargen had agreed upon. The sirens indicated their understanding. They were to wait in the shallows. Tionne would bring their quarry to the water.

Shooting forward, Tionne crested a large wave and rode it in until she stepped with halting steps onto the wet sand. As soon as her feet touched the packed grains, air flowed into lungs that had magically emptied of water at the behest of the amulet around her neck.

Her hands flew to her neck, feeling for the gills that now seemed more natural than her human lungs. Breathing air felt wrong. She had to force her chest to rise and fall, keeping her alive. Tionne felt as if she were suffocating. She forced herself not to panic and instead turned her thoughts to the process of breathing. At length, she was able to overcome her body's rejection of the air around her.

Tionne checked the fall of the sea grass pouch, ensuring that the Horn of Requiem hadn't shifted during her approach to the beach or her moment of weakness. It was there, where it was supposed to be. Standing outside the tiny fishing village on the coast, Tionne smiled.

With more confidence in her steps, Tionne moved across the beach toward the flickering lights at the end of the wharf. There was a man there, leaning against a piling. A night watchman by his garb, and asleep on the job.

Tionne hoisted herself up onto the wharf and approached the sleeping man. With a voice hoarse from disuse, she uttered words of command and coaxed memories of death and disease from the darkest corners of the Quintessential Sphere. The watchmen jerked upright as inky black tendrils slipped into his mouth and nose. He clawed at his face, gasping for air that wouldn't come. Blood oozed from his ears as his face turned a ruddy purple, and a moment later, he was still. The body fell over sideways, and Tionne released her hold on the Quintessential Sphere.

Not a single living soul did she encounter on her short walk from the pier to the small courtyard that graced the center of the little village. A few lanterns hung from high iron hooks, casting dim circles of pale yellow light onto the cobbles below. That light would soon bear witness to a growing darkness.

Reverent fingers dipped into the bag she'd carried on their long journey from the siren homeland. She plucked the Horn of Requiem from its safety net, holding it in trembling hands. Excitement made her vibrate like a plucked harp string and it was only with difficulty she managed to remain still. Tionne wanted to rejoice in this moment, to dance and revel at the destruction that would soon befall mankind, and to surrender to the elation of knowing that she would be an integral part of its destruction.

Tionne brought the Horn to her lips, the cool shell pressing against her flesh in an intimate embrace. She drew breath into her lungs and felt her chest swell, growing until it seemed as if she would burst. At long last, she blew the horn, pushing the air she'd taken in through the instrument.

A long, mournful note issued from the end of the curved shell. Even protected as she was by the amulet given to her by the Siren King, Tionne could feel the incessant call of the Horn caressing her mind, trying to find the tiniest cracks to seep in and take up residence. She held the note for as long as she could. The length of the note was key, Lord Yargen had told her. The more powerful the initial blast of the Horn, the less likely the people of the small sea-side village would be able to resist its clarion call.

Tionne lowered the Horn and waited. One by one, doors began to open along the main road that led through the village. Bleary-eyed residents stumbled into the streets still in their nightclothes. They lurched toward her with shambling steps, unhindered by sharp stones in their path. Tionne had seen the newly reanimated dead walk the same way. Perhaps, on some level, their bodies had already given up on life.

Raising the Horn again, she issued a second call. Any who had managed to resist the first summons would surely fall to the second. As she expected, another handful of doors opened. Men, women, and children filed into the street, silent under the watchful gaze of the full moon. They gathered around her, blank eyes turned toward her but seeing nothing.

Tionne placed the Horn back in her bag and surveyed her handiwork. An entire village full of bodies stood clustered around her, swaying on their feet like wheat in a gentle breeze. None moved, none blinked, and none made a single, solitary sound. Throwing back her head, Tionne laughed. It was a full-throated cackle, a sound that would have made skin crawl if anyone had been aware of it. The empty buildings caught her voice and threw it back at her, adding a chorus to her outburst. Tionne smiled.

"Come," she said simply, and turned toward the pier.

Bidden by the power of the Horn's magic, the villagers followed her. Their plodding made their progress slow, but even so, it didn't take very long for them to reach the small dock that supported the fishermen of the village. The watchman was still slumped where she had left him, and a few intrepid blue crabs had climbed up out of the small bay to pick with sharp pincers at his already decaying flesh.

They raised their claws as she passed, warning Tionne away from their prize. She paid them no heed. Instead, she walked to the end of the dock and stopped. Her followers stopped as well. Tionne looked over the edge of the dock. In the water there, she could see the faint luminescence of a hundred pairs of eyes, lurking just under the surface. Tionne's hand went to the locket at her throat, a smile twisting the corner of her mouth.

Then she turned to the mindless automatons behind her.

"Into the water, all of you."

A command was given and they had to obey. By ones and twos, they walked off the end of the pier and vanished below the churning waves. There was no jumping, or diving, or even any indication that they realized that they were stepping into nothingness. They just walked off the end and into the waiting clutches of the sirens beyond.

Crimson foam sprung up on the surface of the bay as some of the villagers were consumed by the waiting sirens. Others would be taken back to Selethrion where their life force would be used to nourish those sirens who were too sickly to make the long journey to the Imperium's shores. They would tend to those most in need first. That was Lord Yargen's command.

After a few minutes, the last of the villagers had disappeared into the black water, leaving Tionne alone on the dock with a single corpse and the crabs. Her eyes ranged over the buildings now emptied of their precious supplies. The assault on the Human Imperium had begun, not with a shot or a shout, but with a simple, complete, and elegant act of subterfuge. It could be days or weeks before someone alerted Dragonfell that this little out of the way village had fallen. By then, the sirens would have moved on to their next target.

They'd always be at least one step ahead of the humans.

A blue head broke the surface, its fang-filled mouth stained crimson around the edges.

"Coming, Daughter of Darkness?"

"I'll be along shortly. Send Lord Yargen my regards."

The siren warrior cocked his head at her, as if he was loathe to leave the Horn of Requiem with a land-walker. Then he leapt from the water, flashed his tail, and disappeared. If today hadn't proven her loyalty to the siren cause, nothing would. Though Tionne couldn't blame them for being cautious.

Surveying the village one last time, Tionne turned and launched herself into the water. Ice cold, it drove the breath from her lungs, but that didn't matter. She felt water pass over the newly formed gills, taking the air she needed. Thick webbing grew between her fingers and toes and she kicked forward.

By morning she had returned to Lord Yargen's palace and informed him of their great success. She offered him the Horn, but he demurred.

"You are one of us now. It is your weapon to wield, Daughter of Darkness. You will extinguish the human light, once and for all."

An almost erotic sense of joy flooded through her at the thought. The final darkness was

descending on Solendrea, a void that would
consume all humanity, and she was its harbinger.

CHAPTER TWENTY

If the ship hadn't been full up to the deck with refugee sailors from the Nightingale, Tiadaria wasn't sure that Torus would have permitted her to stay in the cabin with Jonah. He hadn't been expecting to be bringing so many people back to Dragonfell on the single warship they'd brought in pursuit of Princess Felyn's ill-fated expedition, so there were bodies crammed into every available berth. Some of them men were sleeping in shifts just so everyone had a place to lay their head for a few hours.

Though the cabin was roomy by seafaring standards, Tiadaria recognized it for what it was. A cage. Two of Torus's lieutenants were stationed outside the cabin door at all times. They even went so far as to follow her to the head when the need arose, something that made Tiadaria's skin crawl. She wondered if Torus had told either of them that she could snap their necks like twigs if the desire roused her sufficiently to do so.

Threats wouldn't make this any better, she knew, so she resigned herself to just sucking it up and dealing with it. They were making good time toward Dragonfell and she had the fervent hope that Faxon would be waiting on the dock to sort all of this out. Though he wasn't a member of the King's Council, Faxon was the second highest ranking Quintessentialist under Head Master Maera. As the Head Master's envoy to the capital, he enjoyed some of the perks normally reserved for diplomats.

Jonah stirred in the bed behind her and Tiadaria was by his side in an instant. His color had gotten better over the few days they'd been out at sea and he was even able to sit up for a few minutes here and there throughout the day. Those brief moments of activity always ended with him pale and shaking, sinking back into the bed sweating as if he'd just outrun a dragon.

She hated seeing him this way. The extremity of his illness only underscored that being laid low could happen to anyone, no matter how strong or vibrant. All it took was the right weapon. In this case, a few drops of poison that had worked into his blood and robbed him of his vitality, and almost his life.

"How are you feeling?" Tiadaria plopped in the chair by his bed and took his hand in hers.

"Same as yesterday," he groused, snatching his hand from hers. "And the day before that, and the day before that. The doctor told you it could be weeks or months before I recover. Why keep asking?"

She didn't flinch from the angry glint in his eye. Tiadaria made a point of reaching out and taking his hand again before she spoke.

"Because if you need anything, I want to see that you get it. I know you're frustrated, but don't take it out on me."

For a moment she thought he was going offer a heated retort. He surprised her when he blew out a long sigh and settled back into the pillow behind his head.

"I'm sorry." Jonah looked over her shoulder, through the thick porthole, and out to sea. "Why do you put up with me?"

"Because I love you," Tiadaria said with a smile. She leaned over and kissed him on the forehead. "And because I've been injured before and I know how awful I am to be around when I'm hurt or angry. Just wait…you'll see."

Jonah pantomimed an exaggerated shudder.

"Maybe I'll take the doctor's advice after all. A long stay at the infirmary in Blackbeach might do me good."

Tiadaria laughed. Jonah had been adamant about not needing a stay in the infirmary. He could heal just as well at home as he could in a strange place, he'd said. The doctor had spent two hours trying to convince Jonah of the myriad benefits such a stay would offer before he finally gave up and stormed out of the cabin in a fit of pique. He hadn't been back since, instead relying on Torus's men to inform him of any changes in Jonah's condition.

In a way, the doctor's attitude made Tiadaria feel better about Jonah's recovery. Though prone to dramatic fits, Landon was both skilled and competent. If he had thought that Jonah wasn't in good condition, his sense of ethics wouldn't have allowed him to stay away. That he didn't feel the need to check up on them at every hour of the day was a tacit admission that Jonah was getting better.

"I still think you should consider it," she said, ignoring his grimace. "I know why you don't want to, but the healers and clerics in Blackbeach make all others pale in comparison. They saved Faxon when he had nearly crossed over to the Ethereal Realm."

"Faxon nearly died? I didn't know that."

"Probably more than once, if I know Faxon." Tiadaria chuckled. "This was before the second Battle of Dragonfell. Took a crossbow bolt to the chest that nearly hit his heart. If Lacrymosa hadn't gotten him to the infirmary in time…"

Tiadaria trailed off as a sudden lump formed in her throat. She hadn't realized she was still so emotional over the day that Faxon had come so close to dying. Funny what still got to her in unexpected places after all these years.

"But she did," she finished briskly. "And he lived to annoy, harass, and bother the highborn citizens of the Imperium."

"Felyn certainly holds him in high regard," Jonah said, deep in thought. "That was one of the reasons she wanted you for this disaster. She had heard that the two of you were...close."

Jonah's tone had shifted in an odd way and Tiadaria's spine stiffened. Was he jealous? If he was, he had nothing to worry about. Because *eww*. It was Faxon...and just...eww.

"Exactly how close do you think we are?" she demanded, giving his hand a harder squeeze than she had intended.

"Ow! Hey! I don't know. You hear things, you know? I don't know. He's powerful and you're--"

"I'm what?" Tiadaria's eyes flashed. "You better be very careful how you finish that sentence, Jonah."

"You're beautiful, is what I was going to say. Faxon, or anyone else for that matter, would be lucky to have you."

It wasn't so much what Jonah said that struck her, but what he didn't say. For all his strength and knowledge, for having the instincts of a trained killer, there were still things in which he lacked confidence. He looked down at the bed sheet draped over his legs. Tiadaria dropped his hand.

"Jonah."

"Yes?"

"Jonah, look at me." She waited until he raised his face to hers and she reached across the bed and took his cheeks in her palms. "There's no one else.

Faxon is a very dear friend, and a mentor, but that's all he is. I love you and you alone."

Tiadaria paused, shook her head, and gave a little laugh. "Though I understand if you'd rather not love me back. The life expectancy of my lovers isn't the best."

Jonah reached up and took her wrist.

"I'll take my chances."

He hadn't regained his strength yet, but he was still strong enough to draw her toward him. She sat on the edge of the bed and lowered her face to his. As their lips touched, a spark ran through her that had nothing to do with the power of the Quintessential Sphere.

After they finished, she melted into him, laying her head on his shoulder.

"I'm scared, Jonah."

"I'm harmless and it was just a kiss."

"Not of you, you idiot. Of what's coming next. I have a bad feeling about our return to Dragonfell. I'd feel a lot better about it if you'd be able to stand by my side."

"I won't be doing any standing for a good long while," he said with a grimace. He tapped above her heart with his forefinger. "But no matter what happens, I'll be in here. That'll have to do for now."

"I guess so."

"Try not to be too happy about it, my love."

"I'll see what I can do."

As the Dauntless moved inexorably toward Dragonfell, the sun slipped low in the western sky, bathing the cabin in its warm orange glow. By the time twilight had fallen, Tiadaria was over the worst of her melancholy.

What would happen, would happen. She'd face it as she had faced every other challenge in her life: head on and with the ferocity of an angry bear. Though she hated almost everything to do with her heritage, she had to admit that the clan predilection for not knowing when to quit had come in handy more times than she cared to admit.

In time, the gentle rocking of the ship lulled them both to sleep.

~ ~ ~

The morning the Dauntless sailed into the harbor was leaden gray. Dark storm clouds hung low over the water, meeting the dense fog that shrouded the port and seemed to deaden every sound. Tiadaria didn't mind. The weather fit her mood.

Jonah had tried, for the umpteenth time, to try to convince her that things wouldn't be as bad as she was expecting. Tiadaria didn't have the heart to tell him that she knew that was a false hope. Torus hadn't been down to the cabin once since they'd set sail. That he was avoiding Tiadaria told her everything she needed to know. *Funny,* she thought as she stared out at houses and buildings that lined Crystal Bay, *for as much courage as he has on the battlefield, I wouldn't have pegged him for such a coward.*

Realizing he was getting nowhere fast, Jonah just stopped talking. They'd spent the last two hours of the voyage in silence. The small cabin had all the atmosphere of a prison awaiting an execution. For all Tiadaria knew, that was exactly what they were sailing into. The knock at the door startled them both.

Tiadaria was expecting either the doctor or one of Torus's lieutenants to poke their heads inside. She wasn't expecting Torus himself to come through the door, ducking to miss banging his head on what, to him, was a low doorframe.

"Look who finally decided to grace us with his presence, Jonah."

"Tiadaria, I—" Torus's already ruddy face darkened at her outburst.

"Save it, Torus. I don't want to hear it."

"We don't have to talk, Tiadaria. In fact, I'd prefer if we didn't. I just came to put these on you."

From a pouch on his belt, he produced a pair of small manacles. They were crafted from a dull gray-blue metal that Tiadaria recognized with a shudder. Witchmetal. The same thing her collar had been made of. Her tongue suddenly felt very big in her mouth and she had to work at it to get a sound out.

"No," she managed to croak. Somehow, she found the strength to form more words. "No. You're not putting me in those. Torus, how could you?"

"It's either these," Torus produced a second set of manacles, almost identical to the first. Instead of Witchmetal, these were steel. "Or these. You have a choice of which you go in, but not a choice about going in them. I'm sorry."

"Are you?" She spat. "You don't seem very sorry."

"He's the King, Tiadaria. YOUR king. His edicts are law and I am bound by that law to follow them. Don't make this any harder than it has to be. Are you going to submit? Or do I have to subdue you?"

"Do you have any idea what you're asking, Torus? Do you really understand?"

Torus brushed the back of one hand, still clutching the manacles, over his face.

"I do." He sighed. "I do, but that doesn't change anything. Whether you believe me or not, I really *am* sorry. I'm just following my orders."

"Is that what the Captain would do?"

Torus's features twisted as if she'd slapped him across the face. Tiadaria took some comfort in that. At least he wasn't the stone-hearted automaton he appeared to be. The pained look left

Torus's face and he gave a little shake of his head. Tiadaria wondered if he was rejecting the idea of the Captain, or his own part in the unpleasantness that was unfolding between them.

"No," he said, his voice soft and measured. "No, it isn't. But that doesn't matter. Royce is dead, and I'm the Captain now."

He jerked his thumb toward his chest as if he was trying to convince himself of the words that were coming out of his mouth. Tiadaria shook her head. The anger was dying fast, replaced by a terrible, lethargic sadness that seemed to spread over her like a blanket.

"Oh, Torus," she said, her voice quavering. "What are you doing?"

"What has to be done," he said. His voice had gone cold and hard. "Now let me do my duty."

Tiadaria offered her arms, wrists out and upward, but she didn't drop her eyes from his. If he was going to go through with this farce of justice, he was going to have to look her in the eye while he did it.

"There will come a day, Torus," she said as the Witchmetal cuffs closed around her wrists. Pain blossomed through her, streaking up her arms and settling into the space under her breastbone. She had to stop and take a deep breath before she could continue speaking. "There will come a day when you have to decide between doing your duty and doing what is right. I hope, by the will of the

Eternals, that you make the right choice on that day. If you don't, you risk not just losing a friend, but losing yourself."

Torus stared at her for a long moment, his jaw working behind lips closed in a thin white line. Without another word, he whirled away from her and ducked back out the door, slamming it behind him with such force that she felt the deck boards rattle under her feet.

The cabin was quiet except for the gentle rasp of Jonah's breathing. Tiadaria closed her eyes. As much from the pain that radiated up from her restraints as from the pain that stemmed from a much deeper and much more private source. Torus had always been a friend. A man of honor and integrity that she looked up to. Far he had fallen in her eyes, and his fall was almost the most painful thing she had to bear.

"Well, that went well," Jonah said after the silence had filled the cabin to bursting. Tiadaria wasn't in any mood for his jokes and Jonah seemed to recognize that. A moment later he asked, "Are you all right? I mean, as all right as you can be?"

Tiadaria looked down at the Witchmetal cuffs that encircled her wrists. She felt tears prickle at the back of her eyes and for the first time in a long time, she didn't shove them away. She wasn't a silly little girl anymore, crying over the imagined slights and pains of her adolescence.

She was a young woman now, grown and standing on her own. Tiadaria knew that no matter what happened, her relationship with Torus would never be the same. That was what she cried for. That was what she mourned and it was right and proper for her to do so. Silent tears slipped from her eyes and rolled down her cheeks. They quivered for a moment along the curve of her jaw, before breaking free, perfect jewels in time and space for the briefest moment before being destroyed by the impact with the boards below her feet.

"No," she whispered, her voice tired and distant. "I'm not."

In that moment, Tiadaria wondered if things would ever be all right again. Torus was her oldest friend. Besides the Captain, he was the first person she had met after being brought to the Imperium from the Frozen Frontier. It seemed like a lifetime ago. She guessed it had been. Tiadaria certainly wasn't the girl who had been sold into slavery. Yet here she was, in chains once more.

Once King Greymalkin had been a father figure to her, the man she could respect in a way that she would never respect her blood father. Now, as she looked at the restraints that bound her in the same Witchmetal her father had sold her into, she hated Greymalkin in much the same way that she hated her father.

"This madness needs to stop, Jonah. It needs to stop before it tears apart the Imperium and everything the people have built for the last three thousand years."

"Why is it your fight, Tia? They just put you in chains, and you're going to fight for them?"

"The people didn't do this, Jonah. One person did."

"That person happens to be the King, Tia. I'm all for thinking big, but—"

"I'm not asking you to help me, Jonah. I'm just saying that it needs to stop, and if I'm the one that has to put an end to it, I will."

"Whoa, slow down girl." Jonah put up his hands. "What you're saying sounds an awful lot like treason and I think we're in enough trouble as it is."

"Know what?"

Jonah looked her up and down for a long time before he answered. When he did, his voice was slow and cautious, as if he was facing off against a dangerous animal. "What?"

The ship gave a little lurch as they were brought up against the dock. She could hear Torus's men in the hall outside, probably preparing to move them from the cabin up onto the dock and on to wherever they would be held. Tiadaria turned to face Jonah, giving him a good look at the grave look on her face.

"If you think we're in trouble now, you haven't seen anything yet. If Greymalkin wants to go to war against me, I'll give him his war."

CHAPTER TWENTY-ONE

Tiadaria half expected Adamon to be waiting on the docks, ready to censure her at the King's bequest, so she was disappointed in a perverse kind of way when she was marched down the gangplank of the ship to find that the dock was conspicuous in its emptiness.

The dock should have been a bustle of activity at this time of day, with fishermen out tending to their nets or mending lines, and what had always seemed to her like an endless stream of merchant vessels moving on their lazy way in and out of the harbor.

It was clear that something was wrong. It seemed empty, dead, and that bothered Tiadaria more than the restraints around her wrists. Had Greymalkin sealed the harbor? Had he cut Dragonfell off from the rest of Solendrea? Or had he just cleared the docks so that there would be no witnesses to the betrayal he was committing against her?

The latter seemed more likely, but with as aberrant as the King had been acting of late, it was impossible to tell. Torus had debarked before Tiadaria and Jonah had been removed from their cabin. Running off to give his report to the King, no doubt. Tiadaria spat and one of her escorts gave her a sidelong glance.

"What?" she demanded. "Not ladylike?"

Her escort paled under his helmet. He was just a kid, and so green that he could put down roots at any second. Torus really needed to find better lieutenants. Of course, if this is what they spent their time doing, she couldn't blame anyone for not wanting to join the once illustrious ranks of the Grand Army. The kid shrugged as if he couldn't come up with a suitable answer. Tiadaria spat again.

"Just wait, kid. You haven't seen anything yet."

There wasn't much she could do with the Witchmetal cuffs around her wrists. If she escaped now, she'd still have to figure out a way to get them off. Hitting them with a hammer and anvil wouldn't do. Witchmetal was strong stuff, and any impact with a metal object caused the enchanted metal to contract. If she hit the cuffs with a hammer, all she'd succeed in doing was breaking her wrists.

When Faxon had created the stuff, he'd also created the enchanted tools to forge and manipulate it. Unfortunately, she didn't have access to either the tools or to Faxon, so she'd have to wait until Torus's men removed them. That meant waiting until she was put into storage.

An unseasonably cold wind blew across the back of her neck as they wound their way through the tight streets of the dock district. It was empty here, too. The word must have been spread far and wide that anyone found on the street during her transfer would not be spared the dire consequences. Greymalkin was shrewd, she'd give him that.

They stopped in front of a battered oak door banded with rusted iron. Tiadaria knew the door well. Torus's offices were just above, on the second floor. Below was the prison colloquially known as 'the pit.' Only the worst offenders in the Human Imperium went into the pit. Very few came out again. If you were rotten enough to be thrown in the pit, your execution wasn't far off.

The lieutenants knocked on the door and waited. The window slid back and they were given a challenge phrase, which they answered. Blackness loomed as the maw of the door stretched wide and allowed them to enter. Tiadaria had only ever heard the building referred to as the 'army building.' If it had a name, she didn't know it. She suspected that it didn't really need one. If you said you had to go to the army building, people assumed you meant the squat stone building just off the dock district with its paired guard towers at each end.

Though not large enough to be considered a fortress in its own right, the army building was certainly imposing enough to earn the respect it was given. Tiadaria had been in the pit on several occasions, but she had always been dropping off captured criminals or fugitives. She had never been the one in chains.

They led her down the long, curved ramp that spiraled into the depths of the earth under Dragonfell. Torches lined the walls at predictable intervals, but did little to drive back the crushing darkness or the penetrating chill. Tiadaria almost expected to see her breath puff out before her as she walked.

Before long, they arrived at a chiseled hole in the wall, barred by a steel grate. One of the lieutenants unlocked the cell and opened the door, and the other gave her a little shove toward the opening. It was a good thing that she was still bound, because if she'd been free, Torus's lieutenant probably wouldn't have lived to see morning.

Still, she had to pick her battles. If she killed him now, it was much less likely that they'd remove the cuffs once she was inside. Tiadaria stepped past the steel bars, feeling a hint of pain in her chest as she neared her magic's nemesis. Then she was inside. The bars slammed shut and there was a click as the lieutenant turned his key in the lock.

"Hey!" she called, brandishing her wrists. "Aren't you going to take these off?"

The younger lieutenant shook his head. It was hard to read him in the dim light, but Tiadaria saw something behind his eyes. Was it fear? Or sadness? Either way, there was a weakness there to exploit…if she could buy herself time to exploit it.

"Captain's orders, Lady Tiadaria." The other lieutenant had already begun the climb up the long spiral ramp, but the younger man lingered, his hands on the bars. "I'm sorry."

He pushed off and followed his comrade. Tiadaria looked around her new quarters. Saying they were bleak would have been a massive understatement. The cell itself was chiseled out of solid rock, the original cut lines faded and smoothed by countless hands over the thousands of years Dragonfell had stood. There was a cot with a tattered blanket, a foul-smelling pit in one corner that Tiadaria assumed was for biological necessities, and an algae infested wooden bucket.

Hardly any light filtered into the cell from outside the barred door. Perhaps the dimness was a blessing. Without much light to see by, she couldn't be properly appalled by the squalor Tiadaria found herself reduced to. Her thoughts went to Jonah and she hoped that he was faring better than she was.

The ship's doctor had insisted he be taken to the infirmary for treatment. That was the only reason he hadn't been thrown in the pit at the same time as Tiadaria. From the conversation between

Torus's men as they'd brought her through Dragonfell, anyone who survived from the Nightingale now found themselves brought up on charges.

It wasn't fair for anyone, but least of all for the sailors who had done nothing more than their duty, following the orders of their Captain. Odeon had been taken from the ship in cuffs as well, but Tiadaria hadn't seen or heard from him since. She hoped that the stolid old sea dog would be able to navigate these troubled waters as easily as he did the sea.

A soft, grating sound caught Tiadaria's attention and she turned her eyes toward the wall of the cell. A chunk of rock, about the size of her fist, worked its way free and bounced off the cot, almost rolling into the privy pit.

"Stop that before it gets away," a voice said from the hole. "Need to put it back if we're to keep the guards from finding out our little secrets."

Tiadaria leapt forward, kicking the stone away from the malodorous hole. She retrieved it from under the cot where it landed, and went to the opening in the cell wall.

"Who are you?" She peered into the darkness, but could see nothing more than a silhouette on the other side.

"Tia?" the voice asked incredulously, "Is that you?"

Now that it wasn't bouncing off all the walls in her cell, Tiadaria thought the voice had a familiar quality. In fact, she was sure she knew who was incarcerated in the cell beside her, and her heart sank.

"Faxon?"

"In the flesh," the voice answered without even a hint of Faxon's customary good humor. "I was hoping the rumors were wrong. I was hoping you escaped before Torus and his men got to you."

"Obviously not," Tiadaria said, trying to keep the bitterness from her voice, but failing. "How did they grab you?"

"At the point of a spear. Half a dozen of them, actually. Charged me with treason when I went to speak before the King's Council."

"That's awful."

"Indeed," Faxon agreed. "At least I don't have to worry about it for much longer."

"Why is that? Is Maera coming to have you released?"

"Oh, no," Faxon said with a mirthless chuckle. "Nothing like that. My execution is scheduled for tomorrow morning."

~ ~ ~

"Your WHAT?" Tiadaria shouted, her voice echoing off the walls of her cell and passing out into the pit, which seemed to amplify it until it was a wall of noise washing over them.

"Please don't yell," Faxon hissed at her through the opening in the wall. "It gets the guards all riled up and makes it much harder for the inmates to talk."

"I'm sorry," she said, keeping her voice low. "Your execution? You can't be serious!"

"I'm very serious. In fact, you might say I'm *dead* serious," Faxon said with a hint of his normal personality. "In any event, Greymalkin was my judge and jury. Sentenced me on the spot, right there in front of the Council. I don't think they were too pleased about it, but no one wanted to stand up for me. So here I am."

"He can't do this, Faxon."

"Sure he can. He's the King. He can do whatever he wants. He imprisoned his own daughter. Do you really think he's going to think twice about killing me? He's never really liked me, you know."

Greymalkin's distrust of magic, and the Quintessentialists who practiced it, was legendary. When he had been in full command of his faculties, he had tempered that distrust with the knowledge that those who channeled the forces of the Ethereal Realm were doing so in the best interests of the people of the Imperium. He seemed to have forgotten that at some point. Now his paranoia was running rampant.

"How is Felyn? Do you know where she's being kept?"

"Oh, yes. She's very close."

Tiadaria didn't like the tone of Faxon's voice. It made the hair on the back of her neck stand on edge.

"How close, Faxon?"

"Two cells over on my right. She's not in very good shape, I'm afraid." Faxon's voice was both soft and full of hatred. Tiadaria could feel the heat of his anger radiating out from him as if he were a desert. "Greymalkin ordered her scourged for sending out the Nightingale."

Tiadaria gasped. She was something of an expert on a father's betrayal, but such an act never failed to catch her breath in her throat.

"He's her father, Faxon!"

"I know that. You should know better than most that blood isn't always a tie that binds."

Tiadaria sank to the rickety cot. Waves of emotion were crashing over her, relentless in their assault. Not only did she remember, with vivid clarity, the day her own father had betrayed her, but she could also imagine Felyn's slight frame ravaged by the bite of the whip. She understood Faxon's anger. She felt it herself, and nurtured it.

That spark of anger would become a fuel of rage. She'd have to tend to it and keep it burning. Stoke it with the injustices perpetrated by the King and his allies. Then coax it into a roaring fury that would strike down any who dare oppose them. As quickly as her rage was born, it shrank away from her.

How was she supposed to strike down anyone when her wrists were still bound together by Witchmetal? Would she be forced to sit idly by as Torus's men came for Faxon to lead him to his death?

"What's the plan, Faxon?" she asked, her voice as even as she could make it.

"I'm open to suggestions. I haven't quite worked this out yet. There's too much steel in the pit for me to work my magic…in the most literal sense."

"And I'm in Witchmetal cuffs," she griped. "So I won't be of much help. Thanks for that."

"I created it for a legitimate purpose, Tiadaria."

"I'm sure. One day you'll have to explain to me what legitimate purpose extends to slavers and power-mad Kings."

Faxon, making the only wise choice available to him, remained silent. Tiadaria laid back against the wall, resting her head on the smooth stone. It was several minutes before Faxon spoke again.

"Tia, how are you feeling?"

"Angry. Betrayed. Bloodthirsty."

"No, I mean, how are you feeling physically? Any burning in your chest? Headache? Pain?"

"No, not really. Why? What are you getting at?"

"Thinking out loud," Faxon mumbled. "So you're not affected by the steel bars?"

Tiadaria shook her head, though she knew he couldn't see her. "No, not really. I mean, I can feel it…but it isn't bad."

Faxon went quiet again. Tiadaria wanted to reach through the hole and throttle him. The elder Quintessentialist had an unnerving penchant for keeping his own council. Sure, one could drag what one wanted to know out of him eventually, with some effort, but giving a straight answer was something Faxon seemed utterly incapable of. She left him alone for a few minutes before finally she couldn't take it anymore.

"Why, Faxon?"

"Why what?"

She rolled her eyes so hard she felt as if they might fall out of her sockets. For someone as brilliant as Faxon was, he could be so incredibly obtuse.

"Why did you ask about the steel bars?"

"Oh, that. I'm wondering if you can channel the Quintessential Sphere."

"Then why didn't you ask?"

"I thought I did."

Tiadaria sighed. She closed her eyes and slipped into sphere sight. The silver-white wash of color that accompanied the entrance into the

Ethereal Realm passed over her. She cast out along the curved ramp of the pit, seeking out Felyn's cell.

The young woman was laying on the floor, the back of her white robe streaked with crimson stains. Tiadaria's hold on the Quintessential Sphere wavered as a surge of hatred went through her. Faxon was right. Felyn was in bad shape. Though her spiritual form was intact in the Quintessential Sphere, the living memory of her soul was dangerously frayed around the edges. It wouldn't take much for it to unravel altogether. Even so, the soul was bright and had a curious, sparkling quality that Tiadaria hadn't before seen in the Ethereal Realm. She'd ask Faxon about it, but she didn't have time for another of his non-answers.

Tiadaria released her spirit form and snapped out of the Quintessential Sphere, swallowing back the nausea that always seemed to accompany the transition.

"Yes, I can," she said, her voice flat. "Whatever we're going to do, we need to hurry, Faxon. Felyn is in worse shape than you thought. What are we doing?"

"I'm still working that out, Tia."

"Well work faster!"

Faxon remained silent as Tiadaria fumed. It wasn't as if she had anything worthwhile to add to the situation. She might be able to slip into sphere sight, but her powers wouldn't do them much good otherwise. She could move supernaturally fast, leap higher than a human, and swing a sword, but none of those were talents that helped them at all when they were locked in cages.

"Okay, I think I have an idea," Faxon said. "But you're not going to like it."

A chill went up Tiadaria's spine. They'd been through enough together for her to know that if Faxon was already putting caveats on his plan, it wasn't going to be fun.

"What?"

"I need you to Etherwalk from your cell to mine."

Tiadaria groaned and shook her head.

"I can't! And you know I can't! Royce taught me that my powers are only physical."

"He taught you that because it was convenient for you to believe it. Knowing that you were capable of full command of the Quintessential Sphere could have been dangerous. It would have opened you up to reprisal."

Tiadaria went quiet. Her thoughts were going a million miles an hour, crashing into each other and careening off on tangents. If she could control the full power of the Quintessential Sphere, she was even more powerful than the King imagined. Or did he know? Had Adamon or someone figured out the secret that not even she had known? She forced those thoughts out of her head. There would be time for that later. She forced herself to slow her breathing and speak.

"All right," Tiadaria said. "Let's say I'm capable of it. Even so, I haven't had the training. Aren't you the one who's always telling me that trying to Etherwalk if you're uninitiated is suicidal?"

"Well, yes, but I was hoping that wouldn't be an issue."

She put her face in her hands and screamed into them. It didn't muffle the sound entirely, but it was enough to keep it from echoing up through the pit. When the worst of the tension had left her shoulders, she stopped and took her hands away from her face.

"Feel better?" Faxon asked.

"Not really, no. Okay, so this Etherwalk...how do I do it?"

"It's easy, you just go into the Quintessential Sphere, will your spirit form where you want to go, and then pull your physical body through behind you."

"Oh, is that all? Why haven't I been doing it all along?"

"I wouldn't ask you do it if there were any other way," Faxon snapped, reaching his breaking point. "Do you think I like putting you in danger? Do you think I like being trapped in here, instead of out there, able to help you? I can't take care of you in here."

There was a loud crash from Faxon's cell. Tiadaria thought it sounded as if he'd kicked his water bucket into the cot.

"Hey," she called, keeping her voice calm and soft. "Hey, Faxon. It's all right."

"No, it isn't. Tia, I promised Royce that I'd look after you…that I would make sure you were safe, and I've failed in that spectacularly. I'm sorry. I'm so sorry."

Faxon's voice cracked and Tiadaria put her hand against the wall to his cell, as if he could feel it. She put her cheek beside the hole.

"You've done as good a job as anyone could, Faxon, and I'll always love you for that. You were there for me when no one else was, or could have been. You haven't failed me. Not yet."

She paused and wiped a stray tear from the corner of her eye. "Now tell me how I pull this off."

What followed was years of magical theory crammed into a series of terse instructions. Tiadaria tried to commit as much as she could to memory, but it was so much information in such a small amount of time that she was sure she was going to end up lost forever in the timeless expanse of the Ethereal Realm.

The incantation to open the Quintessential Sphere and bring her body through was complicated, with variations of pitch and inflection that she should have practiced for months with a teacher as a guide before trying on her own, but they didn't have that kind of time. She'd just have to try it and hope for the best.

"Are you ready?" Faxon asked, a thin veneer of confidence only just masking the fear in his voice.

"No," Tiadaria said, feeling that honesty was the best policy before her impending death. "But that's never stopped me before. Let's get this over with."

Tiadaria slipped into the Quintessential Sphere and glided through the living memory of the wall between their cells. Faxon was sitting on the cot. As she suspected, the water bucket laid upended under it. The incantation tumbled from her lips as each syllable flashed into being, a burning sigil in her mind. Tiadaria channeled everything she was into the spell, becoming one with the forces of magic that were flowing through her and around her.

As she spoke the final word of power, the world seemed to tear itself apart. Fragments of visions, both delightful and demonic, flashed through her head. It was as if she was the whole of Solendrea for an instant that lasted an eternity.

Then there was blackness, pressing in on her from all sides. Tiadaria began to retch.

"Easy," Faxon said, retrieving the bucket from under the cot and sliding it under her until she'd finished heaving. "Easy. You'll be okay."

It took Tiadaria a moment to realize that she was sprawled on the floor in Faxon's cell. She was still restrained, but at least they were together.

That was the only thought Tiadaria had time for before she plunged headlong into unconsciousness.

CHAPTER TWENTY-TWO

When Tiadaria woke, she was laying on Faxon's cot, covered by a blanket that smelled of mold and mildew. She shrugged it off, rolling toward the edge of the bed and putting her feet on the floor. Her stomach was still roiling as a result of her physical translocation, and it felt as if a man inside her head was beating gleefully on a huge bass drum.

Faxon was pacing the width of the small cell, halfway between the cot and the steel bars. He seemed to be so consumed with his thoughts that he hadn't even noticed her sit up.

"How long was I out?" Her voice was rough, her throat sore. Tiadaria didn't feel well at all, but she supposed that was the price of defying the natural order.

"Fifteen minutes, maybe? Half an hour? I don't know," Faxon said, coming to the cot. "Time is weird down here. How are you feeling?"

"Awful. What's the next part of our daring escape? I want to get out of here."

"You and me both. Give me your hands."

Tiadaria slid her palms across Faxon's outstretched hands. Link-shock danced between them, sending pins and needles up her arms and down into her spine.

Faxon closed his eyes and began chanting words of power, calling to ancient memories and spirits of the Ethereal Realm. With every passing word, a feeling of warmth began to spread through Tiadaria's body. It started in her belly, growing, as if it were coiling around her spine. It crept into her chest, dispelling the chill she'd had there since traversing the Quintessential Sphere. She gasped as it reached her most private places, bathing her in an almost sensual pleasure.

"Faxon! What are you doing?"

"Using your body as a conduit to the Quintessential Sphere. Now hush."

He continued to speak, weaving together languages Tiadaria had never heard before. The pleasure the feeling produced quickly subsided as the feeling went from warmth, to burning. She tried to pull away, but Faxon caught her hands and held them tight.

Tiadaria gritted her teeth against the pain. Her body seemed ablaze now, burning with ethereal fire. Ghostly flames erupted from her arms, racing down her skin toward the metal cuffs on her wrists. She could feel the blaze as plainly as if a brand had been laid against her bare skin. At last, she could take no more, she screamed.

The sound seemed to echo off the walls and inside her head. At her cry, the intensity of the flames increased until they were blinding. Tiadaria was sure that her flesh was melting from her bones and still she screamed. She screamed until her throat refused to make any more sound, issuing only a hoarse rasping sound.

Somewhere in the distance, there was the clank of metal against stone. Faxon released her hands and the pain vanished. Though the pain was gone, Tiadaria teetered on the verge of consciousness. She felt as if giant hands had lifted her up and wrung her out, emptying her of all the strength and vitality she possessed.

She sank to her knees, putting her arms across her chest to try to ease some of the insidious cold that seemed to be flooding into her body. As she gave herself a little hug, she stiffened.

"Oh!" Tiadaria exclaimed as she looked at her wrists, now free of the Witchmetal cuffs. They were on the floor, warped beyond recognition by the ethereal flames. She ran tentative fingers over the skin of her arm. No blackening or char, not even so much as a tender burn.

"How—" she began, but Faxon shook his head.

"There will be time for explanations later, Tiadaria. We're still not free yet."

"I've got an idea. Think you can get the guard down here?"

"I'm sure I can…what's the plan?"

"Explanations later."

Faxon looked as if he wanted to argue but then shrugged. He got as near the bars as he could and started shouting. The pain of his proximity to the steel showed in the lines etched on his face. Tiadaria tucked herself into the shadows beside the cell door.

It took several minutes of Faxon's manic ramblings before Tiadaria caught a glimpse of a guard coming down the ramp. It was the older of Torus's lieutenants.

"Stop that racket, prisoner."

"I can't take anymore! Please, just let me out," Faxon blubbered.

"You're not going anywhere, magician. I hear there's quite the buzz about your execution." The guard laughed, his tone sinister. "You know what they do to traitors, don't you? They'll hoist your remains in a gibbet on the Trade Road. You'll be naught more than bones by harvest time."

The lieutenant put his hands on the bars, leaning in to leer at Faxon's rather theatrical mask of horror. That was what Tiadaria was waiting for. She grabbed him by the wrist, yanking his arm through the bar. The man gave a startled shout.

"Shut up," Tiadaria hissed. "Keys, now, or I break your arm."

"Rot in hell," the guard grunted.

Tiadaria pinned his wrist to the bars with one hand and took his finger in her other. With a quick motion, snapped the finger backward. A crack like pistol fire echoed in the cell and Faxon winced. The guard screamed.

"I don't have time for this and you don't have many fingers left. Give me your keys."

Face sheened with sweat, the man reached into a pouch on his belt and produced a set of keys. He fumbled with them for a moment before they slipped through his fingers and hit the floor.

"That's okay," Tiadaria said. "Kick them under the cell door."

It was difficult for the man to move with his arm still pinned on the other side of the bars, but he managed to nudge the keys until they ended up on the floor by Tiadaria's feet.

"Very good," she said. "Sorry about this."

Before the man could respond, she reversed her hold on his arm, pushing him away from the bars, and then she yanked him back as hard as she could. His forehead slammed into the steel with a sickening crack. The guard's body went limp and he collapsed in on himself.

"Tia—"

"War is war, Faxon. Anyone standing in our way is an enemy until we're safe."

She left him standing there, his mouth working as he tried to think of something to say. Tiadaria took the ring of keys, ignoring the pain that lanced up her already sore arms. In short order, she'd reached around the bars and opened the cell. She pushed the door up against the wall and stepped outside.

Crouching beside the guard, Tiadaria put her fingers to the guard's neck and felt for a lifebeat. It was there. Faint, but steady. He'd have a hell of a headache when he woke, but at least he'd be alive. With deft hands she searched the body. There wasn't much she thought she could use, but she took the long dagger from his belt and after a bit of thought, cut his purse free. They might need the coin later.

Now that she was armed, she felt better. She took the keys and went to Felyn's cell. She opened the door and motioned to Faxon who rushed in to check on the Princess.

"Help her out, Faxon. I'm going buy us some time. Meet me topside."

Before he could reply, she was gone, loping up the ramp in long strides. She opened every occupied cell she came to. There was no way of knowing what these people had done to end up in the pit. No doubt, some of them deserved to be there, but Tiadaria didn't have time for such details.

Right now, all she cared about was that they would create a welcome distraction for the guards in the army building. As she reached the top of the ramp from the pit, chaos had already descended. Some of the inmates had made a run for the door, but others had stopped for a bit of revenge before going on their way. They were attacking the guards with whatever they could get their hands on, from chair legs to abandoned swords.

"By all the Eternals," Faxon swore as he reached the top of the ramp. Felyn was draped over his shoulders. "What did you do, Tia?"

"I gave us a fighting chance. Stick to your bailiwick, Faxon. Don't judge me in mine."

"Remind me not to get on your bad side."

"Later," she grunted. The door to the army building was standing wide open. Tiadaria spied a merchant's cart not far beyond. It had been swarmed by the men she'd released, and the merchant was trying, unsuccessfully, to make his way through the bedlam.

"Come on, our ride is here."

Tiadaria made a path through the flailing bodies in the ready room. A kick here, a deft punch there, and they were past the worst of the combat and out into the street.

Almost as an afterthought, Tiadaria shoved men aside, away from the merchant's cart. Faxon laid Felyn in the back and climbed in behind her. Tiadaria leapt to the driver's bench in a single fluid movement.

"I can kill you and take the reins, or you can give them to me," she said to the driver, her voice calm, almost serene. "Your choice."

The merchant dropped the reins and scrambled down from the cart. Tiadaria gave them a flick, spurring the workhorse forward. They'd almost reached the main road that ran through Dragonfell when she dared cast a look over her shoulder.

A familiar form towered in the door of the army building. Torus shouting orders to his men, his face drawn in a black rage. Their eyes locked for a moment and Tiadaria thought she saw his narrow. Then they were around the corner and onto the wide street.

~ ~ ~

"I'm pretty sure Torus knows we're gone," Tiadaria called back to Faxon as she navigated the cart through the streets of Dragonfell.

They'd had the misfortune of staging their jailbreak in the late afternoon, when the people of Dragonfell were either returning from work or out getting a bit of last minute shopping in before the shops closed for the night. That meant there were far more bodies on the road than Tiadaria cared for. Not that she could push the workhorse to its limit. Doing so would give Princess Felyn a rougher ride than she deserved.

Faxon, for his part, had emptied some of the merchant's sacks and spread the burlap over the Princess to keep her safe from the dying light of day. It also helped disguise her, which is what Tiadaria was more concerned with. Right now, all they had to contend with was Torus's men and the city guard. If the people of Dragonfell thought that Tiadaria and Faxon were kidnapping the Princess, things would go sideways in a hurry.

"Not much we can do about that now, except try to outrun him." Faxon glanced around, checking as Tiadaria had been doing, for any sign of pursuit or patrol. "It occurs to me that we never discussed your mission."

"We were a little busy, Faxon."

"Don't I know it...Is she dead?"

"I think so," Tiadaria said, flicking her eyes sideways to catch the grimace that crossed his face. "Not by my hand, if that makes it any better. She jumped off a cliff rather than return with me."

Tiadaria turned her full attention back on the road, flicked the reins, and drove the cart down an alley only just wide enough for them to fit down. She knew this alley well. It would bring them out just beyond the Market Square. At the end of this alley, she'd seen her first Xarundi. The intervening years seemed like a lifetime.

"Thank you for trying," Faxon said, his voice so soft the noise of their passage almost drowned it out.

Tiadaria didn't answer. Her attention was on a knot of men who were crouched in the shadows up ahead. They wore dark cloaks over their day clothes, the hoods pulled up over their heads. It was warm in Dragonfell. Whoever was under those cloaks must have been sweltering.

She clucked at the horse and pulled back on the reins, slowing the wagon.

"Trouble?" Faxon popped his head over the driver's bench for a better look.

"Maybe. Be ready."

Wrapping the reins around her left hand, Tiadaria clutched the dagger she'd liberated from the guard with her right. As they drew up alongside the group of men, one of them lunged out and grabbed the horse's bridle.

Tiadaria wound into a crouch, aided by speed granted from the Quintessential Sphere.

"Hold, Tiadaria!"

Whomever Tiadaria thought they were, she wasn't expecting them to know her name. The surprise was enough to make her hesitate. That gave the man enough time to drop his hood. Stringy, dishwater brown hair hung down over the man's eyes, which were narrow and hard.

"Adamon!"

"Adamon?" Faxon peered over the driver's bench again.

"Of course. Who else would have been summoned to perform your Rite of Censure?" Adamon made a face, as if he'd stepped in something unpleasant. "The King all but commanded I made haste to Dragonfell at once."

"Is that why you're lurking about in alleyways? In case I happened by?"

"Don't be absurd, Tiadaria. We don't have time for bickering. You left a sizable imprint in the Quintessential Sphere with your, ah, newfound abilities. It wasn't difficult for us to track you down."

"Who else is with you?"

The man who had grabbed the horse reached up with his free hand and pushed back his cloak, revealing graying hair and a long beard. Tiadaria recognized Olin Oldwell, but she didn't much care for the addition of the beard.

"Good to see you, Tiadaria."

"And you, Olin."

The others dropped their hoods, but Tiadaria didn't recognize the girl with the long blond hair or the young man with the unmistakable air of a farmhand. Primrose was also there, her dark hair pulled back in a rather severe braid. Her staff was slung over one shoulder, and after a quick nod to Tiadaria, she leapt into the back of the cart.

She gave a strangled exclamation when she saw Felyn's crumpled form under the makeshift disguise. Faxon did his best to comfort her.

"Enough with the pleasantries. We don't have much time," Adamon snapped, his eyes flashing. He climbed atop the cart, casting an eye at the dagger she was still holding. "Where are your weapons?"

"Lost in battle," Tiadaria replied through gritted teeth.

Adamon winced. For whatever reason, that seemed to strike a nerve. She'd never understood the Grand Inquisitor of the Orders. She doubted she ever would. The strangest things seemed to resonate with him.

He reached down and pushed his cloak aside, his fingers dancing across the belt hung low across his hips.

"I trust you're going to want to retrieve your friend?" he asked as he removed the belt and offered it to her.

"How did—"

"Princess Felyn isn't the only one with spies in her employ, Tiadaria. Take this. I expect it back."

Tiadaria had never seen Adamon without the hand cannon hanging at his side. That he was offering her his prized weapon bothered her more than anything else that had so far happened on awful adventure. He shook the belt at her when she hesitated.

"Take it and go, Tiadaria. It won't be long before the city becomes impassable."

She took the belt with numb fingers and looped it around her waist. It felt strange. Much lighter than the weight of the swords she was used to. She knew the pistol had a power all its own, but she much preferred the heft of a blade on her hip and in her hand.

"There is a hunter's cabin two hours west of the South Pass. We'll take the Princess there. We'll wait as long as we can. If you have trouble finding it, use your sphere sight. With so many Quintessentialists in one place, we'll light up the Ethereal Realm like a beacon."

Adamon sounded less than thrilled at the prospect and Tiadaria could understand why. So many of them in the same place made them vulnerable to attack. Still, the Princess wouldn't be strong enough to Etherwalk for a few days, at least.

Tiadaria jumped down from the cart and went around to the back. Faxon was waiting by the tailboard.

"Take care of them, Faxon."

"I will," Faxon said, and Adamon snorted from the front of the cart. Faxon shot a glance over his shoulder and then turned back to Tiadaria. "Take care of yourself. We'll be waiting at the cabin."

"We're out of time," Adamon said.

Olin and the others boarded the cart and he gave a flick of the reigns. Tiadaria stood in the empty alley and watched the cart until it disappeared around the corner. They'd cross the Market Square, then head down the main Trade Road and out of the city. They might encounter some resistance at the city gate, especially if Torus had sent out a warning with runners, but she had no doubt that three fully trained Quintessentialists and the others could manage against an entire phalanx of soldiers.

Staying on the street would be asking for trouble. She needed to be out of the way of Torus's patrols. She slipped into the Quintessential Sphere, easier than she ever had with her swords by her side, and called forth the living memory of wind and leaping things, of frogs and the long legged runners from the plains. With the assistance of the Ethereal Realm, she leapt atop the wall running the length of the alley.

Nimble as a cat, she ran down the wall, vaulting up onto the roof of the building beyond. Rooftop to rooftop, she made her way toward the squat, greenish building that housed Dragonfell's infirmary. The King's attitude toward magic discouraged many true clerics from making their residence in the capital, but there were enough healers to go around. If Torus was true to his word, Jonah would be there.

Almost as if someone was reading her thoughts, the great bell atop the army building began to peal. The alarm was picked up by smaller bells atop guard towers across the city. Tiadaria wasn't sure what had taken Torus so long to send out the call to arms. Maybe there was a part of him that was still loyal to the memory of what their friendship had been.

Tiadaria slowed her pace across the rooftops. The last light of the sun was setting in the west and the last thing she needed to do was slip and fall thirty feet to her death. She was almost there anyway. No need to announce her arrival.

Fortunately, there was a tavern near the infirmary. The roof would give her a perfect vantage point from which to make a proper assessment and the noise would mask her movements. She crept up to the edge of the roof and peered down at the courtyard in front of the healer's building.

"Damn," she swore to herself. She'd been expecting a few guards. Maybe even a company of soldiers from the Grand Army. She wasn't prepared for what she saw below.

Torus, his massive frame enshrouded from head to heel in plate armor emblazoned with the crest of the Grand Army of the Imperium, was standing in the middle of the courtyard speaking to a couple of his lieutenants.

"Damn," Tiadaria swore again, shaking her head. This wasn't going to be easy.

CHAPTER TWENTY-THREE

Torus finished speaking with his men and they moved off, leaving their commander standing alone in the courtyard. Tiadaria shrank back from the edge of the roof when he lifted his head to scan the tops of the nearby buildings. Torus was too good of a tactician to make getting the drop on him easy. Although Tiadaria preferred a direct approach, in this instance, subterfuge was a better option.

She scanned the alleyways around the healer's complex, finally finding one with a sturdy-looking rainspout that ran down the side of the building. From there, it would only be a few steps to vault the low wall that surrounded the courtyard. Then she'd be in reach of the steps that led down into the mortuary. Tiadaria was painfully familiar with that part of the infirmary. She'd spent a number of long hours with Wynn's body after he'd died to save her.

Tiadaria swallowed against the sudden lump in her throat. When she thought of Wynn, there was an ache in her chest that never quite went away. Even now, years later, the sting of his loss was still sharp. He'd come to her once, when his memory was still strong, as a spirit. He'd saved her then, too, but he was gone far too quickly and had never returned.

She'd heard that, over time, the living memories that resided in the Quintessential Sphere grew disinterested in the activities of the mortal plane. Some spirits could cross over for a time— those particularly powerful in life or who had some sort of unfinished business from their days in the flesh. For the most part, however, the denizens of the Ethereal Realm kept their distance from the living.

With light steps, Tiadaria made her way across the slate rooftops toward the spout she'd seen. Passing between the buildings required her to make a longer leap than she had been, and she misjudged the distance as she lifted off. She slammed into the far wall, the edge of the roof biting into her chest just below her breasts.

She made an involuntary grunt as the breath went out of her. She was in a dangerous position and she knew it. She threw one leg up onto the roof and swung the other over, rolling up onto the gentle incline. Tiadaria lay there for a moment, trying to catch her breath. She felt her ribs. They were tender, but not broken. Being sore for a few days was a certainty.

Voices below told her that her passage hadn't gone unnoticed. Tiadaria wondered if the voices belonged to the residents of the building or Torus's men. She couldn't very well pop her head over the edge to see. If she was spotted now, there'd be no chance of getting inside the infirmary. She wished she'd been able to drop down near the tavern. At least there, the noise would add some protection. Here, there was a real risk of being heard as well as seen.

Being very careful not to scrape against the stone roof, Tiadaria rolled over onto her hands and knees and made slow progress toward the edge of the roof where the downspout dropped into the alley. She slipped into sphere sight and drifted down from the rooftop, into the narrow space behind the building. Whoever had come to investigate the noise was gone. As far as she could tell, she was alone.

Snapping back into her body, Tiadaria swung over the edge of the roof and embraced the spout. Slowly, she walked her way down the side of the building. About ten feet from the ground, the rusted rivets that attached the drain to the side of the building gave way, squealing their protest at such neglect and abuse. There was no time for her to react. She landed on the cobblestones in a sprawled pile and the spout clattered to the ground beside her.

At least it hadn't fallen on her, which was something. It hadn't been subtle. Tiadaria knew she had only moments before Torus or some of his men rounded the corner from the courtyard to the alley. She got to her feet, clumsy and awkward, and stumbled toward the low wall. Vaulting it was a simple matter, and rather than run for the steps, she launched herself toward them, curling herself into a ball as she fell.

Her hands and arms protected her neck and head, and Tiadaria had been through worse on the battlefield, but this she had done to herself. She bounced from step to agonizing step, stopping at last in the shadow at the foot of the stairs. Getting to her feet, she brushed as much of the dirt from her clothes as she could and stepped back into full shadow.

The lanterns surrounding the infirmary were a double blessing. They'd illuminate anyone at the top of the stairs, but keep her hidden in darkness from the light-dazzled eyes searching from above. As if on cue, one of Torus's men, a sergeant by his scale armor and the stripes on his armband, stopped at the head of the stairs. He peered down into the dark, and Tiadaria held her breath.

The sergeant descended onto the first step and craned his neck toward the spot where she was standing. Her hand fell to the hand-cannon in its holster. She didn't want to use it if she didn't have to. Especially since its roar would alert everyone in the immediate area. It was a last line of defense.

Tiadaria crouched down as quiet as she could and slipped the dagger from where she'd tucked it inside her boot. She stayed coiled in the crouch, waiting for the man with the sergeant's stripes to press further into the darkness. A moment later, a muted voice called from beyond the stairwell, and the man's head swiveled toward the sound.

"No," he called to the unseen voice. "Nothing here. All clear."

The man gave one last look around, shrugged, and left the stairwell. Tiadaria let loose the breath she'd been holding with a sigh. Finally, something had gone right. Her right hand still wrapped around the hilt of the dagger, she reached out with her left and felt along the roughness of the door for the latch.

The cold metal burned at her touch and with nimble fingers, she depressed the release and opened the door a fraction of an inch. A lone lantern burned inside, casting a dim yellow light into the darkness at the foot of the stairs. Tiadaria saw nothing and heard nothing. She slipped inside and closed the door.

"I'm appalled that you think me such an idiot, Tiadaria. I thought we knew each other better than that," Torus said from behind her. She whirled to face him.

His sword was drawn, but the point rested on the floor. His eyes flicked to the holster hanging at her hip.

"A hand-cannon?" He made a face. "I wouldn't have expected you to resort to a weapon with such little finesse."

Tiadaria shrugged, her eyes hard. "I wouldn't have expected you to betray your friends. I guess we're both in for some surprises."

"I betrayed no one," Torus snapped, his gauntleted hand tightening on the hilt of his blade. "I did my duty to King and country. I'm doing what honor and loyalty demand be done. I'm returning you to your cell, where you'll await a proper trial and punishment."

She laughed. It was a hard, thin sound, and she didn't care for it one bit. Still, she laughed and saw his eyes narrow.

"Torus, you can't possibly believe you can stop me. You just said it yourself. You're not an idiot."

Royce had trained her well. He'd taught her to anticipate the enemy's moves and plan for them, acting before reacting. She saw the subtle shift in stance, saw the minute tightening of the muscles. In that split second, she called on memories of hares and horses and took from the Quintessential Sphere the essence of their speed.

By the time Torus had raised his sword and taken a single step, Tiadaria had drawn the hand-cannon from its holster and pointed it toward his eye. He was a giant of a man, so the weapon wasn't exactly at eye-level, but it sent a powerful message nonetheless.

"Don't," she said, her voice quiet. "I don't want to kill you, but don't think for a moment that

I won't. If you make me choose between you and Jonah, you'll lose. Every time."

Torus took another step forward and she thumbed back the hammer on the pistol. It was a fine weapon, smooth and sleek. Tiadaria understood why Adamon favored it. What it lacked in elegance, it made up for in raw power. She and it were similar in that way.

"I don't think you will, Tiadaria. We've been through too much. We are friends. You won't kill me."

"We *were* friends, Torus. I'm not sure what we are now. Don't test me."

Somewhere at the edge of her perception, she felt his movement. She felt the tightening of his calves, the intent to take another, fateful step forward. She slipped into sphere sight and let the power of the Ethereal Realm guide her hand.

An instant later, the morgue's antechamber was filled with fire and thunder. The hand-cannon bucked in her hand like a wild animal, but she forced it to submit. A piercing whine split her ears and she cringed away from it. Through her own strength and the assistance of the Quintessential Sphere, she brought the weapon to bear and fired again. She expected the whine this time, but it was no more pleasant. Her ears rang and felt as if they were stuffed with cotton.

When the smoke began to clear, she saw Torus slouched against the far wall. His eyes were closed and there was an almost serene look on his face. Tiadaria went to him and put her fingers on his neck. The life-beat was there, strong and steady. She looked at his breastplate, dented in two places, but punctured in neither. She'd bought some time, nothing more. He'd be in pain when he awoke, but like a wounded animal, nothing would deter him.

She had to find Jonah and get out.

~ ~ ~

Tiadaria met two of Torus's soldiers, short swords in hand, on their way down to investigate. To their credit, they took stock of the look on her face and the weapon she carried before they turned around and went the other way.

As she reached the top of the stairs, she came face to face with a knot of healers having a hushed conversation. Their sea-foam green tunics betrayed their profession as readily as their conspiratorial manner, Tiadaria thought. She didn't brandish the hand-cannon, but neither did she try to hide it.

"A man was brought in for Adderberry poisoning today. I need to know where he is. Now."

Most of them seemed stunned into immobility, but a diminutive woman with chestnut brown hair and bright eyes seemed unfazed.

"Are you going to hurt him?"

Tiadaria shook her head. "I'm here to save him."

The healer's eyes searched Tiadaria's face. After a moment, she seemed satisfied with what she saw there.

"Very well, this way." She set off down the hall, ignoring the startled protests of the colleagues she'd been speaking to. She glanced over her shoulder at Tiadaria as they walked at a brisk pace. "I recognize you. You fought at the Battle of Dragonfell. I was there, tending the wounded."

"I'm sorry. There were many."

"There usually are," the healer said leaving Tiadaria to wonder what she meant by the cryptic response. She pulled up short near a curtained room. "Through there."

The healer motioned toward the curtain and without waiting, turned and retreated back the way they had come. Tiadaria spared her a curious look then pushed through the curtain into the small room beyond.

It was appointed as most such rooms were, with a single bed, a chair, a basin stand and water pitcher, and a lantern hung from a hook in the wall. Tiadaria half expected the room to be empty, but Jonah was there, laying atop the bed.

"Tia?" He asked with a start. "What are you doing here?"

"Getting you someplace safe. We need to go. If your life depended on it, could you walk?"

"Probably, but—"

"Good, because your life likely depends on it."

"What happened?"

"They had Faxon. They were going to execute him. We broke out of the pit."

"I heard they took Princess Felyn."

"We have her. Faxon is seeing to her injuries."

"She's hurt?"

Tiadaria poked her head out through the curtain and scanned the hall. It was still empty. She withdrew and looked at Jonah.

"Yes. Badly. I know you have questions, but we're out of time. We can talk later. Right now we need to run."

Jonah swung his legs over the edge of the bed and got up onto his feet. Tiadaria was glad to see that while he wobbled a bit, he was pretty steady. It would have to do. They didn't have much of a choice. He jammed his feet into the soft shoes on the floor next to the bed. They weren't as good as boots, but at least he wouldn't be barefoot. Tiadaria hoped they wouldn't be doing much walking outside the city anyway. Her first order of business would be to borrow a horse. Or liberate one if a legitimate bargain couldn't be reached.

They exited through the curtain and no sooner were they in the hall than Jonah tapped her on the shoulder.

"On your left," he said, in an almost conversational tone.

Two soldiers were coming down the hall toward them. Tiadaria raised the hand-cannon and fired. The shot slammed into the wall beside the advancing men, showering them with bits of plaster and wood. Their steps faltered, and Tiadaria and Jonah took advantage of their pause to put distance between them.

Jonah, to his credit, had paid attention to the details when he was brought into the infirmary. At several junctions, Tiadaria was torn about which direction to go until he chimed in with his advice. With his guidance, it wasn't long before they'd passed through the rear door of the infirmary and into the small courtyard at the back of the building.

Tiadaria leapt the wall and turned to help Jonah over. By the time his feet were on the cobblestones beyond the courtyard, the rear door had burst open, disgorging more soldiers. She aimed at the wall above them and pulled the trigger. Twice, the cannon roared to life, sending the soldiers scattering from the falling debris, then it just uttered a dry, lifeless click.

There were more shells in the belt, but she didn't have time to fumble with the mechanism. She'd bought them some time, but not much.

"Come on," she said, grabbing Jonah by the hand.

Dragging him down the alley behind her, Tiadaria navigated toward the south side of the city as best she could. All around them, bells in the guard towers rang their incessant warning. Whatever had delayed the initial alarm certainly wasn't an issue now. Shouting seemed to surround them on all sides.

At some point, Tiadaria took a wrong turn and led them down a blind alley that came to an abrupt end. Faced with a blank wall, panic welled up inside her. Jonah must have seen it in her eyes, because he grabbed her by the shoulder and spun her so her face was near his.

"Tia, relax. Calm down and think. You're going to get us both killed if you panic."

"Oh, but no pressure, right?" she asked, only just managing to keep her voice from cracking. But he was right. Panic wasn't going to help them. She could hear the city guards calling to each other nearby. They were only a street or so over. It wouldn't be long before they were discovered.

Tiadaria's eyes went back to the wall. It wasn't very high. She could reach the top and go over with ease, aided by her powers. Getting Jonah across was a different story. He was too weak to climb on his own. He was gray with just the effort they'd exerted to this point. There just wasn't enough time to get him over the wall.

Flickering light drew their attention. Torches, near the far end of the alley. They were almost found. Tiadaria looked at the wall again. Jonah glanced at it, then at her.

"Go, Tia. It's fine. I'll find you if...when I can."

"I'm not leaving you," her voice was hard, defiant. There was no trace of panic or fear in it now. "We both get out of this, or neither of us does."

"We don't have time for this. The Princess is going to need you. Go!"

He gave her a little shove toward the wall. Tiadaria planted her feet. It wasn't going to end like this. There had to be another way. There was. She just hadn't seen it before.

She grabbed Jonah by the hand and dragged him toward their salvation.

A few moments later, they were huddled together, ankle deep in fetid sewage. The stench was enough to make them gag, but the flickering light of the searching torches passed over them without incident.

Tiadaria slipped into sphere sight, fighting to maintain enough control over her protesting stomach to remain in commune with the Ethereal Realm. She managed to hold herself together long enough to plot a way out.

Though it took several hours of slogging through the rank waste, they eventually dropped from the sewage pipe into a bog outside the city. It still stank, but it wasn't as confined, and for that, they were both thankful.

They had just climbed up on the bank when Jonah collapsed, rolling over onto his back with a groan. Tiadaria was beside him in an instant, grimy fingers roaming over him, searching for unseen injuries.

"I'm fine," he groused, batting her hands away. "Just tired. I'm not hurt. Don't touch me until you've cleaned up."

"Because you're in such pristine shape?"

"No, because I don't want any of that near my face. Trust me, the first thing I want is a good scrubbing."

"Hmpf," Tiadaria grunted, crossing her arms. "I take you out someplace nice and this is the thanks I get?"

Jonah stared at her for a moment and then burst out laughing. Tiadaria joined him. It was the first time in weeks that she felt almost normal. Things were going to get worse before they got better, but right now, covered in stinking filth on the shore of a smelly bog outside the capital of the Imperium, things were okay.

She laid back in the cool grass and laughed until it hurt too much to do so. Tiadaria was sore from head to toe, but she was alive. Jonah was alive. They were both free. She'd call that a win. Jonah peered at her, eyebrows raised.

"Are you all right?"

"I'm better than I've been in a long time, Jonah."

Tiadaria sat up and glanced back in the direction of Dragonfell. They'd come a long way, but they had farther yet to go. There was a long road ahead of them to get to the cabin.

"Rest up, love. We've got another adventure before us."

CHAPTER TWENTY-FOUR

Getting Jonah to the hunter's cabin wasn't the hardest thing Tiadaria had ever had to do, but it wasn't going down in the books as the easiest, either. Through a system of bursts of walking followed by longer periods of rest, she got him to the cabin in one piece, exhausted, but no more the worse for wear. It was almost dawn when they stumbled up the crushed gravel path toward the cabin, their footsteps crunching at an obscene volume in the pre-morning light.

Tiadaria heard someone step out onto the path behind them. Tiadaria whirled, her hand dropping to Adamon's cannon. Faxon showed her his palms.

"Easy, Tiadaria. It's just me. I'm glad you made it out and I'm glad you were able to find your friend."

"So am I. Though I'd preferred it if I'd had time to find Odeon as well. He didn't deserve to be left behind."

Faxon nodded, his dark eyes troubled. "I know, but if this is to be a war, there will be losses. On both sides."

The Quintessentialist said nothing more, but his eyes asked an unspoken question. Tiadaria knew he couldn't have possibly known that she'd ended up facing off against Torus, but he wasn't stupid. He'd probably made some guesses and assumptions that weren't far from the truth.

"Torus almost had me at the infirmary. I had to shoot him twice to put him down."

The elder mage stiffened, then relaxed and passed a hand over his face.

"I'm sorry. I wish it hadn't come to that."

"He's alive, Faxon." Tiadaria was somewhat comforted by Faxon's discomfiture. They weren't so far gone that they were considering old friends complete enemies just yet. Torus was, without question, on the wrong side of the conflict, but Faxon wasn't going to give up on him and that alone made her think they might be all right after all.

"He is?"

"That breastplate of his is thick. Like shooting an iron stove. I'm surprised I didn't end up hitting myself the way the shells bounced off." She laughed quietly. "But I reckon I gave him something to think about this morning."

Faxon smiled. "Yes, I imagine so."

The Quintessentialist stepped up to Jonah but stopped short of offering his hand. "I don't think we've met. I'm Faxon Indra. Princess Felyn has told me a lot about you."

"All good, I hope?" Jonah asked with something approaching his normal affability.

"Not exactly," Faxon said with a grin and a wink. "But nothing that surprised me very much."

"What would?" Tiadaria interjected and Faxon's grin widened.

"Very little, actually. Let's get you up to the cabin and wet you down before you go inside. You smell as if you crawled out of the sewer."

"Through it," Tiadaria and Jonah replied in unison, and laughed at the comically disgusted face Faxon made.

"The things we do for the ones we love," he said, and preceded them up the path.

Jonah watched him go with a curious look on his face. Tiadaria sighed.

"You're not still jealous, are you?"

Jonah gave a quiet chuckle.

"No." He reached down and took her hand. She was eager for him to have it, even caked in filth as they both were. "I was just thinking that I understand your relationship now. I was stupid to have worried."

"See?" Tiadaria asked with a flippant cock of her head. "You should listen to me. I'm right. A lot."

"I have no doubt."

Hand in hand, they walked up the gravel path toward the buckets Faxon was drawing up from the well.

The water was brisk and made them shiver in the morning's chill, but the young woman who had been with Faxon in Dragonfell, Janessa, brought them blankets from the cabin to wrap themselves in. The young man, Baris, made an offering of black, bitter coffee that was just as welcome, if not more so. Primrose was inside, tending to Felyn who still hadn't woken up.

Tiadaria studied the pair of them while Faxon prodded flames to life in the fire pit. Faxon had made terse introductions as she and Jonah huddled near the fire. They were journeymen from the Academy of Arcane Arts and Sciences. In fact, of the people at the cabin, she and Jonah were the only two who hadn't been trained in the Academy.

It was a strange feeling that, for the first time, Tiadaria didn't have to hide who and what she was. Greymalkin had taken the secrecy out of her life and whether he realized it or not, he'd done her a favor. She hadn't realized the weight of the burden she'd been carrying around until she no longer felt it upon her shoulders.

What happened next was her only worry. She'd been branded a fugitive and they'd escaped from the pit. Those were things that wouldn't just go away on their own. Greymalkin, and Torus to a lesser extent, had an affinity for the laws of the realm that bordered on reverence. Things would need to change before Tiadaria was welcome in Dragonfell again.

If she ever was.

A curious sadness overtook her. For all the pain and resentment the city and some of its people had caused her, Tiadaria would miss it if she was never able to return. She thought of her apartment over the tavern. Trinkets, mementos of dozens of battles and skirmishes, lined the shelves. The books she'd taken from Wynn's collection. The chest the Captain had given her. All her things had been taken from her.

As bad as that felt, she had her life. She had Faxon and Jonah. They'd saved the Princess and lived to fight another day. Things could be replaced. Their friends, the people they loved, could not. Tiadaria reached down, found Jonah's hand beside hers, and gave it a squeeze.

He'd been listening to Faxon talking to the young Quintessentialists, but he looked at her now.

"All right, Tia?"

"I'm fine. Just thinking about what we've lost and what we were lucky enough to save."

"I'm glad I made the list," Jonah said with a smile.

"Me too. I guess I'll keep you."

When Tiadaria leaned in to kiss him, he responded with something like his normal strength and a passion so intense that Janessa and Baris turned away from them. That made Tiadaria start laughing and the moment was broken. Jonah saw their discomfort and shared in Tiadaria's laughter, which set Faxon off.

The three of them were still laughing when Adamon and Olin appeared at the foot of the path with a large wagon and a pair of aurochs.

"I'm sorry we missed the levity," the Grand Inquisitor said in a terse tone as they approached. He handed the beasts off to Olin, who walked them behind the cabin. "You made it out, Tiadaria. I trust you'll be returning my weapon?"

The belt, still somewhat fragrant from their misadventure, was hanging on a stubby branch nearby. She motioned to it.

"Perhaps a little worse for the adventure, but it saved our lives. Thank you, Adamon."

"You're wel—faugh! What did you do?"

"You're probably better off not knowing. There was a sewer involved."

The Inquisitor sputtered for a moment, his narrowed eyes going from Tiadaria, to Faxon, and back again. He stomped off, calling for Olin to bring him a brush and a bucket.

"You might want to give him a wide berth for a few days, Tiadaria." Faxon's tone lacked his customary good nature. "I'm not sure he'll get over that so easily."

"We'll be fine." Tiadaria was confident they would be. She and Adamon had a strange relationship. He enjoyed pointing out her flaws and imperfections, but he'd never let her down before. He'd had plenty of opportunity. "I think we understand each other."

"As if one can really understand Adamon," Baris quipped, which set them to laughing again.

Though they laughed and talked for much of the afternoon, Tiadaria couldn't quite shake the feeling that they were sitting in the shadow of an unseen specter. Dragonfell wasn't far off, and she found herself checking the path leading out to the Trade Road with alarming frequency.

As the sun dipped toward the western horizon, Faxon tapped her on the shoulder, link-shock dancing between them. He motioned down the path.

"Tia, a word?"

"Sure."

Jonah gave her a questioning look. They had hardly been out of each other's sight all day long. She gave him a reassuring pat on the shoulder and stood up. He shrugged and turned back toward the fire.

When she reached him, Faxon was looking back toward the group, his hands tucked into the voluminous sleeves of his much-stained and tattered ivory robe.

They stood in silence for a long time. Tiadaria had found with Faxon that the times they weren't talking were the ones that spoke the loudest.

"You don't need to worry about Torus or his men finding us here," he said at last, when the silence had crossed from familiar to uncomfortable territory.

"Who said I was worried?"

"Tia."

"All right," she laughed. "Is it that obvious?"

"A bit. But as I said, you needn't worry. Adamon, Olin, and I enchanted the trail and the forest around the cabin. Anyone who tries to sneak up on us is going to be lost for a good long while."

"That's evil," Tiadaria said and then giggled.

"Desperate times."

They lapsed back into silence and Tiadaria waited for his next comment. They weren't done yet, she knew. There was still something that he needed to ask her. Something that would take all his considerable willpower to put out in the open.

Faxon had felt Wynn's death very deeply. Deeper than Wynn's own parents probably had. He felt that he'd failed his apprentice and that sense of failure and the ache of loss had never left him. Faxon blamed himself for Tiadaria losing the first man she'd ever loved.

"Is he good for you?" Faxon asked, his voice rough.

Tiadaria stole a sidelong glance at Faxon and saw the glimmer of tears reflecting back the firelight.

"Yes. He's very good for me. Between the two of you, I'm well taken care of."

She reached down and took the elder Quintessentialist's hand.

They stood there in the dark, Faxon pretending not to cry, and Tiadaria pretending not to notice. After a while, they returned to the others at the fireside. Neither of them spoke further. There were no other words that needed to be said.

Night fell, wrapping the forest in a blanket of darkness. Cots had been made up inside the cabin for them. Someone had pushed two together for Tiadaria and Jonah. They took the hint.

Jonah was asleep almost as soon as his head hit the bag of sweet rushes they were using as a pillow. His soft, discordant snoring was more of a comfort to Tiadaria than anything else she could imagine.

Tiadaria lay awake deep into the night. Listening to life go on outside the cabin. A wolf's howl here, the cry of an owl there. The animals carried on, unconcerned with what diabolical schemes humanity was putting into place. Closing her eyes, Tiadaria willed herself to sleep.

Morning would come all too soon.

# # #

FROM THE AUTHOR

Thanks for reading this Magic of Solendrea adventure. If you enjoyed Pirates of the Siren's Sea, here's what you can do next:

Please consider leaving a review on Amazon. Positive reader reviews are critically important for the success of this book. Your help in spreading the word about the Magic of Solendrea series is greatly appreciated.

The next Magic of Solendrea adventure will be available in coming months. To be notified of new releases, as well as promotions and events, you can sign up for my newsletter here:

http://martinfhengst.com/newsletter-sign-up/

ACKNOWLEDGEMENTS

First and foremost, I want to thank the backers of the Kickstarter project that funded the development and marketing of Pirates of the Siren's Sea. Without your support, this book would not have been possible. Thank you.

Kickstarter Hall of Fame
Jim Frazier
Danielle Campbell Lyle
Maisha Elonai
Amy Ambrose Corr
John Shaffer
Chris Mulvihill
Robert Anderson
Ann Marie Miller
Phil M.
Justin McHugh
Athena Franks
Rob Steinberger
Laura Natcher

Thank you to every single reader and fan who has made the Solendrea stories a success. Your interest and support means more to me than you will ever know. From the bottom of my heart, thank you.

Thanks to those who volunteered their time to beta read: J.R.H, Monty L., Barbara H.

Thanks to my editor, Amber Bungo, for all her hard work.